The Stolen Treasure

ISBN-13: 978-1535409452

ISBN-10: 1535409452

Publisher: CreateSpace, 2020

Cover design by Andrea Pedro

© E. David Hopkins

To Angela who has always been a fan of Star Trek
To Cathy, who read this book three times, and gave me editorial
feedback
To all my friends who have brightened my childhood:
Ginger
Catherine and Laura
Melissa
Andrew
Dallas
Charline
Meghan
Mike
Sarah
Jesse

Other books by E. David Hopkins:
The Sheltered Life of Betsy Parker

Table of Contents

1 Jame Arden   1
2 Melissa Maguire   5
3 Jame's Journey   11
4 A New Kind of Friend   14
5 Crazy Max and the Robot   29
6 Tonya   34
7 Jame's Punishment   41
8 Letters   45
9 The Broken Friendship   52
10 The Fire   60
11 A New Beginning   65
12 The House of the Maguires   72
13 The Inter-Family Meeting   81
14 Aboard The Horizon   91
15 A Threat Brought Back   96
16 The Mind Deck   104
17 A Monster in the Night   113
18 Tonya's Story   118
19 The Latimus Prospectors   125
20 Family Conflicts   134
21 The Costume Party   151
22 Captain Ing's Companions   169
23 A New Crew Member   177
24 Chased Again   187
25 The Secret is Revealed   193
26 Alcarsh's Plan   204
27 An Acceptance and a Promotion   224
28 A Friend's Return   234
29 Tonya's Last Message   237
Afterword   245

1 Jame Arden

Jame Caroline Arden dreamed of travelling in space. Since early childhood, she gazed out the window at night looking at the sky, imagining what was beyond this old and rickety house, which smelled like a bat cave. She knew she was never wanted; not by her parents, not by her classmates, not by her teachers, not by anyone.

Jame had dark skin. Her hair was black, and her face somewhat narrow. She had brown eyes. Before her birth, her parents had planned on having a son whom they had intended to name James. When they saw it was a girl, they dropped the 's' off the end.

"It almost sounds like 'Jane' or 'Jade' without the 's'," her father had commented.

Jame had always disagreed. To her, her name did, indeed, sound like "James" with the 's' cut off. It did not sound remotely feminine, and it was a constant reminder that her parents did not want her.

Every day of Jame's life had been the same as the last: get up, get dressed, do chores, get denied any conversation with her mother or father; be told she could not have any friends in the house; have breakfast, head to school, come home, have supper, go to bed.

"You weren't the boy we had hoped for," Jame's father often grumbled. "Boys have no interest in parties, and they're not interested in giggling, frolicking or fooling around."

"What nonsense," Jame remarked. "In fact, Fred from school invited me to his birthday party."

"Oh, get out of here," grumbled her father. "We have no interest in parties."

"If you want a boy so bad, why don't you have another child?" Jame suggested. "Your second child might be the boy you want."

"Because it might be another brat like you!" snapped her father.

Not only were Jame's parents no fun, they were mean. Jame had one particular memory she could neither forgive nor forget.

Once, at only seven years old, Jame had woken up in the middle of the night screaming from a terrifying nightmare. An army of human-sized spiders were chasing her, clicking their fangs, wanting to sting her and eat her alive.

On her sudden horror-struck awakening, there was her father marching into her room, bending down to his daughter's bed and roaring "Stop that!" straight into Jame's face.

Jame could not go back to bed. She stayed awake the rest of the night, crying, shaking, terrified. In fact, for three days thereafter, she had refused to leave her room at all. She read her favourite books and was terrified to go to bed the following night, the night after that, then the next. Her parents slipped her food under the door, and she only left her room to use the bathroom.

School was the only place where Jame felt some happiness. Mostly, she was an outcast, but she found one other girl, a year younger than her, who had become Jame's friend.

Tiffany was sympathetic, sweet and kind, but not quite Jame's ideal companion. Tiffany was an enthusiastic, extroverted, party-type girl. The wildness was too much for Jame. Jame told Tiffany that life at home was rough, but could never muster the courage to tell Tiffany, or anyone for that matter, that what she was facing was nothing short of child abuse.

Jame grew to an impressive height of 5 feet, 11 inches and became a strong player on her basketball team, The Passenger Pigeons, at her high school.

Finally, well into her teen years, she was just starting to find life tolerable: Basketball player, decent grades (mostly B's), a fairly decent friend or two, teen stubbornness, that even her parents found

The Stolen Treasure

hard to control.

Jame could not see anything worthwhile in her future. She had never had a job, and she had barely had any opportunities to relate to other people. Many kids at school called Jame an unsociable bore. Other kids were happy, confident, cherished, in relationships, each one like some different flavour of ice cream, some even made up like a sundae. Jame saw herself as one single, small scoop of vanilla, nothing more.

Fortunately, the year was 2100 and it was the age of space adventure. Sometimes, people took off from Earth to learn about what was beyond the planet and solar system.

Jame was still a minor and she would not be allowed to embark on a space trip without her parents' permission. She wasn't even going to ask. There was no way her parents would allow Jame beyond her school, let alone beyond her planet. If she even asked, she would certainly get grounded.

A person viewing Earth would see the usual wide stretch of houses, with people travelling in electric cars. Nobody owned these cars or parked them in driveways. A person wanting or needing to travel would request one electronically, and it would take them to their destination. These cars looked like miniature rockets. They would glide a short distance in the air, but travel slowly enough for the driver and the passengers to admire the scenery.

People communicated with holoputers in this day and age. When one typed a set of numbers into a holoputer, the holoputer projected a hologram of the person contacted, enabling the caller to virtually talk to the recipient of the call in person. Holoputers could even be used to communicate over interstellar distances, using tachyon (faster-than-light) particles.

As for food, people ate mostly a plant-based diet, and whatever meat they did eat was either plant-based or was created from stem cells. People sometimes ate eggs created from stem cells too. All the milk that people drank and used for making ice cream, cheese, butter, and yoghurt was made from rice, nuts, or coconut.

Jame had done her research. She had read, in Space News, that to celebrate the turn of Earth's century, Captain Ing was going to lead a three-month space trip aboard his spaceship, The Horizon. This trip would include journeys to the clean, beautiful planet Atwydolyn where intelligent creatures called the "Grachas" lived, planet Uberdan, where beings called the Latimus Prospectors mined, and the Captain's home planet, Arshga. Captain Ing would take up to four Earth passengers on board on a first-come-first serve basis.

Jame felt prepared to give or do anything if it meant going on that trip. Even if it was for only three months, it would be worth more than anything Jame could ask for. It would be a break from this dingy house, from her dull, prison-like life, with her parents as guards.

Also, on this evening, Captain Ing had accepted a new Commander, Mandy Finks, to his crew aboard The Horizon. Only Percia Gordon was surprised, but since she had been dissatisfied all her life, any news felt surprising to her.

Jame gazed out the window at the stars. It was 9:00, her bedtime. Yes, even at seventeen years old, Jame's parents insisted on putting her to bed at nine every night like a little kid.

She showered, brushed her teeth, put on her purple pyjamas (purple was her favourite colour) and slid into bed, another typical ending to another typical day.

2 Melissa Maguire

Melissa Emily Maguire was a sweet, happy girl in grade five. Her hair was light brown, reached down to the middle of her neck, and was done up in many small braids tied with glass beads of rainbow colours. She had freckles and angelic, innocent blue eyes. For an eleven-year-old, she was amazingly small, with a height of three feet, ten inches.

Her grades were a fairly even mix of A's and B's. She had a large circle of friends and playmates, boys and girls alike, many of whom thought Melissa was the nicest girl in the school.

Melissa's parents, George and Katrina Maguire, loved their daughter, who was also an only child, with all their hearts, and did what they could to please Melissa and provide for her wellbeing. But Melissa was not a spoiled child. She didn't ask for much and most of what she did ask for was not for herself, but for a friend, family member, animal, or anyone important to Melissa. She was known for every good deed, from comforting a friend who was upset or injured, to helping a drowning insect out of water. Melissa loved the world with an enormous, open heart, and all she wanted in return was a little respect.

Occasionally, some nastier kids mocked or teased Melissa because of her stature, calling her "pinky finger" or "girl dwarf" or tried to take advantage of her kind, mellow demeanour by acting mean or harassing towards her, but Melissa told them off when necessary, ("My name is not 'pinky finger;' it's Melissa, and I'm a human being"), ignored them when necessary, and told her teacher when it was clearly out of hand.

She had a favourite stuffed animal, which was a dog her parents had given to her for her fifth birthday. Melissa had named him

Rover. Rover had blue eyes and white fur with a black patch on his back. When Melissa had seen this present, it had been love at first sight. Rover was still very dear to Melissa, but his white fur had turned grey and he now smelled somewhat of old sweat from Melissa hugging him so much.

Melissa played floor hockey at her school. Her team was The Foxes and, today, she was playing against The Bulldogs.

"How can we win?" asked her friend, Rick, as they were preparing for the game. "The Bulldogs slaughter us every time."

"Not slaughter us," replied Melissa. "We get closer to winning every time. Last time, we only lost by a hair. I'm sure if we all try our hardest, this will be the time we finally win."

Everyone gathered in the gym. The referee called out, "After I count down from three and blow my whistle, the game will begin."

Everybody waited anxiously as the referee counted.

"Three, two, one." There was a loud blast on the whistle and the game began.

First, Rick hit the puck. It slid to Melissa's friend, Amy, who hit it towards the Bulldogs' net. The puck was sliding straight for the net, but at the last second, the Bulldogs' goalie hit the puck back. A few passes between various Bulldogs took place. Matt, from the Foxes, got hold of the puck for a second, but a Bulldog stole it back. It slid past the Foxes' goalie and into their net. The Bulldogs had scored a goal.

Then, Graham Walker, from the Foxes, shot the puck back, but a Bulldog picked it up and hit it back. It slid into the Foxes' net again. It was two to nothing and time was running out.

Luckily, there were not many Bulldogs in front of the net at the moment, so the Foxes' goalie took his opportunity and shot the puck back. It skidded across the floor towards the Bulldogs' net. The Bulldogs' goalie got ready to shoot the puck to prevent a goal, but

The Stolen Treasure

was too slow, and the puck slid in. The Foxes cheered. They had scored a goal at last.

Rick was the next person to receive the puck. He shot, but Bulldog, Frank Morgan, stole it from him. He shot it towards the Foxes' net, but Alice Black, a Fox, stole it back. She shot the puck quickly, for time was almost up, and it slid straight into the Bulldogs' net. Another goal for the Foxes. It was a tie and there was only one minute left in the game.

The puck skidded to a halt in front of Melissa's hockey stick. By now, all the Foxes were frantic. They were so close to winning. Who would break the tie? Melissa, too, was excited. She shot the puck and watched it carefully as it slid across the floor. One Bulldog attempted to hit it toward the Foxes, but missed. The puck came to the Bulldogs' net; the goalie did manage to hit the puck, but in an awkward manner, and it slid in anyway.

The Foxes cheered. Melissa stood exhilarated and amazed. They were finally winning. A couple seconds after Melissa's goal, the referee blew his whistle, and announced "Time's up!"

Everybody, Foxes and Bulldogs alike, cheered. Even the Bulldogs were in admiration of the Foxes' victory.

Later, as the teams were heading back to class, Graham Walker smiled to Melissa. "Well done! You were amazing, scoring that winning goal!"

"Thank you," Melissa beamed. "It was nothing. Of course, I would have been happy with a tie. But it feels good to win for a change."

"You did a very good job," commented Rick. "You were right. With a little skill and just the right attitude we were able to pull it off."

"It was nothing," Melissa smiled.

"Did you hear about the space trip, Rick?" Melissa asked. "It was our news hologram this morning."

"Yes," Rick replied. "I've already signed up. After you sign up, you get these: a list of the crew. It says that Captain Ing is using Arshgan ranking system." He showed Melissa a piece of Microfoil (Microfoil was the equivalent of paper that people in this time used. It was paper-thin, foldable, but electronic, with an electronic pen, and could be used and reused any number of times). It read:

Captain: Ing

Commander: Mandy Finks

Engineer: Len Hamilton

Doctor: Eric Fact

Lieutenant: Linda Bishop

Ensign: Lucy Walkman

"This Captain also has a really cool way of getting around in space called Space Swoop," said Rick after Melissa had finished reading. "He uses a capsule called a Space Swoop converter that converts the whole ship, along with everyone and everything on board into tachyon energy, sort of how phones from many years ago converted speech into radio signals. At the destination, the tachyon energy is re-transferred into whatever it was at the beginning, in this case, Captain Ing's ship."

"Amazing!" cried Melissa. "I can't wait!"

"Captain Ing told us that people who haven't signed up who come onto the ship will be considered stowaways and will be sent back without hesitation," he continued.

In the last few minutes of class, Melissa's teacher, Mrs. Kent, was telling the class about the upcoming space trip.

"We will be spending the next three months studying exotic space planets and their inhabitants and how we have made ships travel faster than light and even conquer the problem of time dilation," she explained to the class. "We will start out with learning all the different jobs of working on the space ship, tests you must pass to be accepted as a member of a ship's crew and how to judge what sort of rank a member of the crew should be sorted into.

"After that, we will look at different planets where Space Explorers have walked, along with their revolution and rotation length, their climates and, of course, who and what inhabit them.

"We will take a look at some space adventure history, such as the event that took place here on Earth, only five years ago, when the evil monster Alcarsh devoured the space hero Mr. Noin. We will also take a peek at the story of when Samantha and Joseph John first set foot on Arshga, where the renowned space captain, Captain Ing lives.

"Of course, we will also be studying the stars we see in the sky and their constellations, as well as what time of year we can see these constellations. We will also study the revolution of the other planets in our own solar system.

"Now, during our studies, Captain Ing himself will be leading a trip on his spaceship, The Horizon. If we are lucky, we will be able to watch some scenes and events from the trip in hologram.

Mrs. Kent looked around the classroom again, at all of her students seated in their desks, as though waiting for them to speak.

"Does anybody have any questions?" she asked.

Ben Alberts raised his hand.

"Yes?" asked the teacher.

"Is this starting tomorrow?" he asked.

"Yes, it is starting tomorrow," said the teacher.

At that moment, the bell rang.

"Class is dismissed!" called Mrs. Kent.

Melissa was excited to head home.

"We won at hockey today," Melissa told her parents. "I scored the winning goal!"

"Congratulations," beamed her mother, pulling Melissa into a tight hug, "Well done!   And to celebrate, you may go on the upcoming space trip with Captain Ing!"

"Thank you very much. I would love that," the child beamed.

3 Jame's Journey

It was the eve of the space trip. Jame did not return home from school that day. Instead, she packed all her supplies (micro-notes, toothbrush, clothes, pyjamas) in her back pack when she left for school in the morning. Then, when school ended, Jame departed by foot, planning to walk from the school to the Grand Lodge Spaceport, where the ship would be departing. The school day ended at 3:00, and departure was at 9:00, but Jame felt that, if she left school immediately and walked constantly, she would just make it.

As Jame walked along for the first hour, she felt invigorated and rebellious, like she was proud she was taking a deliberate step in disobeying the parents who had made her life a living hell. Surely, they wouldn't worry when she didn't come home. What had they ever done to show they cared about her anyway?

Eventually, Jame did start to feel guilty. The air was cold and biting, and Jame was starting to feel like a bad person, running away from home, not telling her parents where she was going. What if they did worry? What if they thought Jame had been kidnapped? Then, a more sinister possibility occurred to Jame. What if, on her long walk, she really did get kidnapped? Her parents wouldn't know where she was, where to look, or where to tell the police to look.

Jame brushed that worry out of her head. Yes, it was possible, but the odds of it happening were remote, astronomical, almost certain not to happen. She decided she would keep walking.

As the hours wore on, Jame grew tired and hungry. The sun was setting, and the February air was biting. Despite her determination and rebelliousness, her guilt was constantly growing. Surely her parents were worried sick. Maybe, the police were even out now, looking for her.

While, at first, Jame felt convinced her parents wouldn't care if Jame left and never came home, maybe even rejoiced at never having to bother with her again, Jame was now praying with all her might that her parents didn't care.

By 7:00, night had fallen. The sky was alight with stars, and Jame sighed and sat down on a nearby rock. She could not go on. She had to go home. She was running away from home. Besides, what would the Captain do if Jame appeared on his ship, unannounced, unexpected, a stowaway? She couldn't imagine he would be happy. He might even want to know where she had come from. Jame thought, maybe she should turn back now, but she was hours from home. It had taken four hours to walk this far. It would take four hours to walk back. She was now closer to Captain Ing's ship than she was to home. She might as well proceed to The Horizon.

Jame looked up into the sky and gazed at the stars. They were so beautiful. Jame wanted to see them for real, see their planets, see what was there. Jame felt so small. Jame yearned to see more, to be more, and the only way to see this was to embark on Captain Ing's space trip.

"Come on," she thought, as she lifted herself back up onto her feet. "I will get myself on that space trip if it's the last thing I do."

And she proceeded. Jame was getting blisters on her feet, but she didn't care. Her legs hurt, but she didn't care. She was hungry, but she didn't care. Her parents and maybe even the police might be looking for her, but ... well she did care, but Jame was determined, Jame had made up her mind and it was too late for Jame to back out now.

As she was nearing the ship's port, Jame began to feel a new sense of happiness she had never felt in all her life. She could feel something light up in her heart. What could this mean? She didn't know how to describe this feeling. There was a glow of light in her heart, as though, somehow, she knew life was going to get better, but she didn't know how or why, and it was all so irrational. Why should life get better now? She used to pray for rescue, but rescue never came. She used to pray for her life to improve, but it never did. Was this feeling even real, or was it nothing more than wishful thinking? Jame had given up on prayer years ago and even started to doubt the existence of God. She was beginning to think, "How could there be a good God if he allows all this bad to happen to me?"

Jame froze in her path. She heard it, the sound she had been dreading for hours. It was a siren. Could it be the police? Could they be looking for her?

Out of the blue, Tiffany ran up. "Jame! There you are! I have been looking all over for you! Your parents are ballistic. You have been confirmed missing in the news. The police are looking for you."

"Tiffany!" Jame cried. "How? Uh, what are you doing here?"

"You are coming right home this instant!"

"I can't," panted Jame. "I have to escape."

"Jame! No!"

"I am getting on that spaceship whether you like it or not, and so help me if you get in my way!"

"Jame! You can't! You won't be allowed! You're a stowaway! It's not dignified!"

"I can't miss this opportunity," Jame breathed and she ran.

The ship was about to leave too. The engine was roaring. Jame made a run for it before it was too late. Would she make it? It looked like it would lift off any second. It was very noisy now, partly from the police cars, and partly from the spaceship. Tiffany was chasing Jame. At the last second, Jame jumped onto the ramp and ran into the ship. Immediately after, the ramp closed and the ship took off, with Tiffany left behind on Earth.

4 A New Kind of Friend

When Jame woke up, she looked at her watch. It was 9:45 AM. Lights from around the ship were illuminating Jame's hiding place. She was in the cargo room and she could hear voices.

"That indeed was a pleasant rest," came one voice.

"Where should we go first?" came another.

Footsteps came closer and closer to the room where Jame was hiding and then the door burst open. An alien man with grey skin appeared. He was wearing a green uniform.

"Who are you?! What do you think you're doing, you stowaway? Trespassing on our ship without signing up? Why do I find someone has stowed away on my ship? You must get off at once. I am Captain Ing!"

"You are the Captain and you want me to leave?"

"Yes!" he insisted, "and it's up to me to make decisions like these!"

"Well," Jame stuttered, "I'm a-a. My name is Jame, Jame Arden and I have stowed away, because I heard about the space trip and I wanted to see how incredible it really is."

"You could have signed up," replied the Captain sternly.

"Well, by the time I heard, it was already too late. Please let me join your ship."

"You don't seem like the type who will help us."

"Oh, I will help you. I promise and I'll do anything, if you just let me join your ship."

"Are you under the age of eighteen? If you're a minor, you need a parent or guardian's permission to be a passenger on this trip."

"Well, um," Jame stuttered. Jame didn't know what to answer. She thought of telling the Captain that she was a street person, but figured, that, even with her miserable background, she still didn't look miserable enough to be living on the street with no one looking after her. She thought of telling the Captain her real age, seventeen, which was *almost* eighteen, but figured chances were that would not satisfy him. "I am eighteen," she finally announced.

The Captain sighed. "Oh all right, if you insist, but I'm warning you; at the first sign of disobedience, I will take you back to Earth."

"Got it," stuttered Jame, "but how is it that you can speak English? If you're another life form from a whole other planet, how could you possibly understand or speak any human language?"

"I have a translator in my shirt," the Captain replied. "I speak my home language, Arshgan, and it translates it into English so that everything I say can be understood by your ears. Also, everything you say is translated into Arshgan by the translator so that I can understand everything you say."

The Captain sighed. "Well, I guess it's about time I introduce you to the crew. I'm from planet Arshga. It's quite a rocky planet, but it's also abundant in fertile soil, and rain. We will probably be travelling there one day during this trip."

Jame followed the Captain up the stairs. When she got to the top, she was in the most fascinating room she had ever seen. The floor, walls and ceiling were all made of metal and there were panels of buttons, dials, switches and wires.

"This is the Bridge," explained Captain Ing. "It is the room the room where the Commander and I will pilot the ship. When we want to take you to a certain planet, we will head to the controls in the centre of this room and take you there. This ship has many other rooms, such as The Lounge which is just outside The Bridge (he pointed at another door leading out of this room), the kitchen, Sickbay, two sets of sleeping quarters, one for the crew and one for the passengers and of course we have a Gravity Generator, so we're not all floating about like clouds."

"Like clouds," smiled Jame. "That would sure be interesting, floating around as freely as can be."

Captain Ing just frowned. "You wouldn't say that if you had the experience. Could you ever imagine trying to catch food that was floating around, or try to take a drink? Even more difficult would be brushing your teeth and how would you like to learn how to use the toilet all over again?"

Jame laughed a little at Captain Ing's statement.

Captain Ing's face returned back to a pleasant smile. "You will soon be receiving a tour for finding your way around this ship," he explained. "You should be used to the layout of this ship in only a few days.

"We have five ranks of people on the ship. The top one is the Captain and that's me. Then, there's the Commander, the Lieutenant the Engineer, the Doctor and the Ensign. They are the crew."

A woman, clearly human, who looked sort of beautiful and sort of ridiculous, appeared. Her cheeks were rosy and she had long, rippling brown hair. Covering her body was a bright pink uniform.

It was what she was wearing on her feet, however, that caught Jame's attention the most. She was wearing the highest heeled shoes that anyone had ever seen. Her feet came about a full foot off the floor, making the top of her head almost touch the ceiling.

"Who are you?" asked Jame in a completely baffled voice, after she had regained her words.

"This is..." Captain Ing began, but the stranger interrupted him.

"Could I please introduce myself?" she asked in a soft, high-pitched voice.

"Go ahead," said Captain Ing.

"My name is Commander Mandy Finks," she began, "and I will

be commanding your ship. I suppose that Captain Ing has told you all about me already," she smiled.

"No, I am new here," said Jame in a very puzzled voice, "Why the weird shoes?"

"These? They're part of the culture I come from, the Latimus Prospectors. Latimus is a very rare mineral made out of a great quantity of substances. Many such substances are rarely heard of. The Grachas on planet Atwydolyn use Latimus as their money. Finding enough Latimus to make into money is very difficult. If one Latimus Prospector were to work for a full year in a spot that had it, he would only produce a single coin and there are only ten miners, including me. A coin used to be a thin disk of metal people on Earth used for money a hundred years ago. The Grachas value Latimus so much that you'll often find a gough (she pronounced it as 'gug') of Grachas guarding it."

"Excuse me," said Jame, "but what is a 'gough?'"

"It is the name for a group of Grachas."

"Commander Mandy Finks is my best friend," explained Captain Ing.

Two more men stepped forward. "These are our Doctor and our Engineer."

"Our Doctor, Eric Fact, is a robot," the Engineer informed Jame and the rest of the passengers. "This is to ensure that he never becomes infected with human pathogens. I built him, and it is part of my job as Engineer to maintain the Doctor. You can call me 'Engineer Len.'"

"In addition to being your Doctor," said Dr. Fact, "I will be staying awake every night and watching out the window to keep The Horizon safe while everyone is sleeping. During night hours, and when the controls are not in use, The Horizon will be on autopilot."

"Ensign and Lieutenant," called the Captain and out came two young women. The first one to enter had grey eyes and red hair. She had a fairly short stature.

The other one's hair was blonde and her eyes were grey as well. She had a red uniform.

"This is Lieutenant Linda," stated the Captain, pointing at the crew member with red hair. "This is Ensign Lucy," he stated pointing to a larger crew member with light blonde hair. "They are very good friends.

"Passengers!" the Captain called.

Out came two children: a boy and a girl.

The girl was very small; not an inch more than four feet tall. Yet, she looked like she could be as many as ten years old. Her face looked sunny, playful and warm, with eyes of a light blue, that shone with happy laughter and gentle care.

The boy was fairly average in stature for his age, which looked around eleven or twelve years. He had brown hair and brown eyes and fairly round face. He looked too different from the girl to be her brother, but by the way he was smiling and standing close to her, they seemed to be good friends.

"These are our passengers," continued the Captain. "Melissa Maguire and Rick Harrison. Melissa and Rick, this is Jame. She is a new passenger. She has stowed away, but I have decided to give her one chance."

Jame ran up to greet Melissa, but knocked her down. You can imagine someone who isn't even four feet tall being knocked down by someone six feet minus an inch.

"What was that all about?" the little girl cried. "You don't have to stow away on the ship and knock people down, you know!"

Lieutenant Linda turned to Jame and said, "Watch it. Be more careful next time. I was surprised the Captain even let you on this ship in the first place."

"I just wanted to say 'hello'," Jame stuttered, embarrassed.

Melissa got up and replied, in a definitely surprised voice, "Hello, Jame. It's a pleasure to meet you," and then, Melissa sat down at the table.

Jame, embarrassed that she had, first, made a bad impression with the Captain, then with this "Melissa" girl, stepped back from Melissa. Then, Jame remembered how she had stowed away the night before. "Maybe later we could talk in private," thought Jame.

"I will now show you The Lounge," announced Captain Ing.

He opened the other door, and led everyone into another room the same size as The Bridge. This room had soft chairs with a metal table in the middle. Jame spotted what appeared to be a game board leaning against the wall.

"What is that, Captain Ing?" she asked.

"This? It's Space Chess," he replied.

Jame was intrigued as Captain Ing set the box down on the table and opened it.

It was filled with playing pieces all right, but they were not regular chess pieces. Instead, they were several different types of objects found in space.

There were black pieces, and white piece, as with any usual chess set. However, within each colour, were two asteroids, two comets, two Arshgas, a sun, a moon and eight five-pointed stars.

"Wow," cried Jame. "I never know that chess came in a space version."

"Well, now you do," beamed Captain Ing. "I invented it myself. The stars are the pawns; the asteroids represent the castles; the comets represent the knights; the planets are the bishops; the moon is the queen; and the sun is the king."

"Do you want to play a game with me, Melissa?" asked Jame, sitting down on the far chair from the entrance door. Jame was charmed by this little girl and wanted to do something fun with her to make up for a bad first impression.

"You want to play chess with me?" replied Melissa in a bit of a shy but intrigued manner. "Sure, I will play a game with you."

Jame felt guilty. Melissa still looked and sounded a little intimidated by Jame's over-enthusiastic greeting.

"Hey, I'm sorry I frightened you," explained Jame, as sincerely as she could.

"It's okay," smiled Melissa. "Look, you can be white, so you can start."

It was a simple gesture of thoughtfulness, but a touching one. Jame smiled at the new girl. Could Melissa make a good friend for Jame? Jame's friends were so few and far between and Melissa was so much younger.

Melissa and Jame sat down at the table and they started to play a game.

It was exciting playing chess in this new version. It took a short time for the two to get used to what each space object represented. The game actually helped add excitement to the trip.

Half an hour later, Jame won the game. "You let me win, didn't you?" she grinned at Melissa.

"I don't let people win at games," Melissa explained. "You're supposed to try your hardest to win, not be soft on your opponent. It takes the point out of the win if your opponent gives it to you."

"Are you good at chess?"

"I'm pretty good," Melissa replied thoughtfully. "I win some games, lose others. Having fun is more important and I still have fun when I lose."

"Did you have fun with that game?"

"Of course," Melissa replied with a smile of a loving, enchanting quality Jame had never seen on anyone before. She had to get to know this girl more. Jame lacked proper friendship skills and there was something about Melissa that charmed Jame and tickled her heart.

"Well, thank you for playing with me," said Jame.

"Thank you for asking me," Melissa smiled.

"Melissa," Jame continued. "Do you think you could come with me? I would really love to talk to you."

Jame didn't know where she wanted to take Melissa. The cargo room was too small to fit two people, and it would be useless to close the door and talk in the dark. They couldn't talk just anywhere no one else was around, because someone might enter while they were talking.

"Jame," Melissa called out, after Jame had been leading her around the ship for a good five minutes, "You don't want to hurt me, do you? I don't even know you well, and my parents have always told me to never go anywhere alone with a stranger."

These words pierced Jame's heart. She had never seen a child who looked so innocent, and even the thought of hurting her, especially being two feet shorter than herself, was worse than unthinkable.

Jame opened the next door she found, and found that behind it was the kitchen. Jame led Melissa to the table. The kitchen table seemed to be well out of ear shot of everyone else, and it seemed unlikely anyone would enter within the next few minutes.

"I wanted to talk to you about the real reason I am on this spaceship right now," explained Jame. "I ran away from home. I stowed away to escape my parents."

Melissa's eyes grew wide. "But why?"

"I was angry," Jame stuttered. "I was desperate. All my life, I have wanted to run away from home. I hate my parents. They never wanted me, and if they ever did want a child, it was to be a boy. They yell at me, frighten me, even hit me sometimes. My friend from school tried to stop me last night. She said my parents were frantic that I had never come home from school, and the police were searching for me."

"It's all right," said Melissa soothingly, "none of this is your fault. Your parents have been abusing you."

"What do I do now?" Jame asked. "I don't want to go home. But maybe I should. I never should have left my parents."

Melissa let out a sympathetic sigh and looked thoughtful. "Maybe you should go home if your parents are so worried," she replied. But then Melissa thought, the minute Jame set foot in the door, that Jame would probably face grounding for running away and Melissa couldn't stand it. "But I will leave the decision up to you. And Jame," Melissa continued. "If your parents are really as nasty as you say, I suggest you call the police."

At the mention of the police, Jame sat upright in her chair and remembered the sirens and Tiffany's yelling from the night before. What would the police do to her parents anyway? As much as she couldn't stand her parents, Jame didn't want to imagine them locked in jail, and where would Jame go once her parents were shut away? Jame opened her mouth to say, "I can't," but couldn't get the words out. Instead, Jame asked, "You won't tell the Captain I'm escaping from my parents, and that they and the police are frantically looking for me, will you?"

Melissa searched her soul, for she could feel the dilemma. To not tell the Captain, or anyone aboard the ship, about Jame's story would extend the panic that was happening back on Earth, and those aboard the ship would be effectively kidnapping Jame. Still, when Melissa saw Jame's eyes, Melissa could see a pleasant girl, probably not much different from herself, except lost, stolen, wasted. In those eyes, Melissa could see Jame's empty past, tears welling up, fear. To tell the Captain and have Jame sent back to Earth would be nothing less than cruel. "I won't tell," Melissa said soothingly, but Jame could detect the hint of conflict in Melissa's voice that sounded like it would be a guilty secret for the girl to keep.

"You promise?" asked Jame.

"I promise," Melissa smiled.

"You won't break your promise will you?"

"I have never broken a promise in my life."

Jame decided to change the subject. "Why did you come on this space trip?"

"I wanted to see how beautiful Atwydolyn really is."

"You seem like such a delightful girl. Is Rick your brother?"

"No," Melissa replied. "He's been my best friend since kindergarten. I'm an only child."

"So am I," replied Jame. "My parents didn't bother with having another one. I do feel pretty lonely though."

Melissa looked concerned. "I have always wanted a sibling. It is kind of lonely being an only child. I have many school friends, but I have always felt something missing. My mum's a kindergarten teacher, so she probably just has enough kids in her life."

Jame felt the conversation was turning into another unpleasant direction so she changed the subject again. "I play basketball by the way. I am a strong player for The Passenger Pigeons at my school."

"Good for you. I play hockey at my school. I also volunteer at a shelter for orphaned animals," Melissa replied, "and I'm in Girl Guides, flute lessons and swimming lessons."

"I think you're really kind," Jame grinned.

"That's what lots of people say," Melissa explained, "but of course I'm not perfect. Nobody is perfect."

"I'm in grade eleven," Jame continued. "I am also seventeen years old."

"I'm eleven and in grade five," Melissa explained. "My birthday was six days ago."

"Well, happy belated birthday," Jame beamed.

Melissa smiled. "Thank you very much."

Jame looked at Melissa. "You're so sweet and good, but we can't possibly be friends. I'm six years older than you."

"'I promise to share and to be a friend.' That is my Girl Guide motto," Melissa beamed. "I love everyone who is good to me and to others. You can be my friend if you want to. I wouldn't mind. You actually look like someone who could use some help."

"And you think you can help me?"

"I don't see why not. It's what's inside that counts. I will be willing to overlook our age difference if I can help you be happy. Besides, I'm starting to think I would really like to have you as a friend."

The next question popped out of Jame's mouth uncontrollably. "What do you think of yourself, Melissa?"

Melissa smiled, as though she found the question sort of funny. "A fairly nice kid a lot of people like," she said. "Let's just say, overall, I think I like myself, but it's not something I think of much."

Jame had only been acquainted with Melissa for minutes, but she found Melissa's opinion of herself a gross understatement. "Well, let's just say that if you wanted to hug the nicest girl in the world, all you'd have to do is wrap your arms around yourse-"

"JAME! DON'T!" Melissa yelled, and Jame jumped in her seat startled. Melissa noticeably looked embarrassed and was blushing a little.

"I'm sorry," said Jame. "I guess I was going over the top with my flattery, especially since I've just met you. I didn't mean to tease you."

"Apology accepted," said Melissa. "I suppose I shouldn't have yelled at you either, especially after what you have been through. We should go back to The Lounge. The Captain will be giving us a tour of the ship soon."

Melissa and Jame left the kitchen and made their way back to The Lounge. Then, everybody followed their Captain and Commander out of The Lounge and down a corridor.

At the end of the corridor, they turned left, where about two metres ahead, they arrived before another set of doors.

Captain Ing opened these doors and before everybody's eyes was a fairly home-style kitchen, the very same kitchen where Melissa and Jame had been talking, minutes before.

It had a white tiled floor with pink around the edges of every tile. Directly to the right was a stove and diagonally across was a wooden cupboard, with a series of shelves above it. Along the wall in front of everyone was a long, metal machine with a slot on either end.

"This will be our kitchen," smiled Captain Ing. "We will come here at o'nine-hundred hours every day for breakfast, twelve-hundred hours everyday for lunch and eighteen-hundred hours everyday for supper.

"This," he began, opening a set of doors, "is Meal Preserver. While, and only while, these doors are closed, time passes at one thousandth the speed it passes outside, and so, the food is kept fresh and hot for a long time. Don't any of you shut yourselves into this cupboard though. If you spend just one minute, to your own time perception, in there, sixteen hours, and forty minutes will pass outside.

The Captain took a piece of toast out of the Meal Preserver. "Hold your hand above the toast," directed the Captain.

The people on board the ship took turns holding their hand an inch above the toast. The air above it felt warm.

"You won't believe it, but that toast has been in the pantry since yesterday evening," Captain Ing smiled. "It's perfectly fresh and crunchy too."

He took a knife, cut the toast into small squares and gave each person one piece. It was warm, crispy and satisfying, exactly like it would have been if had just come out of the toaster.

"That," Captain Ing continued, pointing at the long metal machine, "is our dishwasher. All you have to do to wash your dishes is turn it on and place your dirty dishes in that slot." He pointed to the end that was nearest to the door.

"I have even left a dirty dish here for demonstration. Watch closely."

Captain Ing walked up to the machine and clicked a switch on the side of it. It began to make a rumbling noise.

He picked up his plate, which was covered in toast crumbs and smears of jam and placed in into the slot he had indicated.

The plate disappeared inside the machine, while everybody could hear the swishing of water and the sound of scrubbing, through the rumble of the motor.

Finally, after a few minutes, the plate came out through the other end, shining and cleaner than new.

There was a full minute of applause, as Captain Ing slipped the plate back into the cupboard on top of the other plates.

Captain Ing couldn't help it. He actually took a bow.

"Now, now!" cried Commander Finks, snuffing the applause. "Let's have some order here. We have to get on with the rest of the ship's tour."

Captain Ing joined the Commander and the passengers and crew followed their Captain and Commander out of the kitchen.

This time, Captain Ing led everybody across the short hallway that led into the kitchen and up a flight of metallic stairs.

The stairs curved left in a loop and when everyone reached the

The Stolen Treasure

top, they found themselves on a whole new floor.

"This way!" called Captain Ing. "I am going to take you to where our Doctor works."

Near the beginning of this new hallway was a door that said 'Sickbay' on it.

Nobody had realized, before now, that the Doctor was already in Sickbay. They had thought he was with them in the crew. The passengers and crew followed their Captain and Commander into Sickbay.

"Hello everyone," smiled the Doctor with a slight nod. "My name is Doctor Fact, but you can just call me Doctor.

"Just so you know, I can tend to most injuries and ailments. Luckily, most of the patients I get are not too severely injured, but in the grand scheme of events, who knows what sort of patients I may have to take care of? I have had some patients under my care for several days.

"As you can see, I have three beds in this room, but don't worry. I am very capable of looking after more than one patient."

"Thank you, Doctor," beamed the Captain. "Now, Jame. We showed everyone their quarters last night, but you weren't here, so I think it's about time to show you yours."

Jame stood by Captain Ing's side, and followed him out of Sickbay. The Commander led everyone else back to the Bridge.

Captain Ing led Jame down the hallway of the ship's second floor.

To their left, halfway down the hall, were two doors about five metres apart.

"These are the crew's sleeping quarters," Captain Ing explained as he stepped up to the doors. "The door on the left is for men."

When Captain Ing and Jame arrived at the end of the hallway, they turned left, and headed down another shorter hallway. This corridor had two doors along the left side of it.

Captain Ing stepped up to the first door.

"These are the passengers' sleeping quarters," he explained. "Your Commander is going to sleep in this room with you during the ship's night time hours, so you have someone to watch over you."

"But Captain Ing," asked Jame. "There are only two beds in here. The Commander will sleep in one; Melissa will sleep in another, but where will I sleep?"

"No problem!" exclaimed Captain Ing.

He pressed a green button on the side of the wall, and the most amazing happening occurred.

A rectangular portion of the wall fell forward, to show another bed on the other side. It knocked the floor where, which rotated down and up to replace the wall. There were now three beds in the room.

Jame stood with her mouth wide open at what she had just seen. This was so amazing that she was lost for words for a few seconds.

"Your ship sure has a lot of surprises," stated Jame at last.

"I'm delighted you would say that," smiled Captain Ing in approval. "There is also a washroom and shower in the side of this room."

The two headed back to the Bridge.

"We will make a jump to Space Swoop now," explained the Captain. "Space Swoop is our method of moving around space super fast, far faster than the speed of light. The Gravity Generator will generate gravity to counter our acceleration so we won't get crushed."

"That's awesome!" beamed Jame. "I've always wanted to feel the jump to a super fast speed in space."

"To start off our adventure, we will explore the Grachas' planet Atwydolyn," the Captain announced.

5 Crazy Max and the Robot

The ship whizzed through a Space Swoop and a planet that looked a lot like Earth moved its way into their view.

"Everybody out," called the Captain.

A bright, cheerful light met everyone's eyes to reveal the most gorgeous place they had ever seen. There were trees that grew a kind of fruit-like substance and streams of clear, sparkling water. It was pleasantly warm and swimming in a lake was a kind of duck-like bird, only much smaller and there were a couple of creatures, which stood on two legs and had grey hair all over them, including on their faces.

Captain Ing and Commander Finks led the crew and then the passengers out of the ship and onto the surface of this exotic planet. The air was filled with a pure and sweet smell and there were tons of flowers everywhere that were every bright and glorious colour everyone could ever imagine. The sky was a gorgeous turquoise.

"Beautiful place, isn't it?" asked Captain Ing.

"It's far beyond beautiful," cried Melissa. "It's paradise. I wish I could live here."

Near a pair of these grey furry creatures stood a house made of stone, about the size of a one-storey house on Earth. A kind of mossy substance insulated the walls and the floor, with sticks and mud holding the structure together. It had windows of a glassy substance. The door was a moss rectangle that worked as a tent flap. Sticks pinned the flap to the house. Other houses stood around it, forming a row which stretched as far as everyone's eyes could see in both directions, with each house about thirty feet away from the next. Way off in the distance, on both sides of the row, were similar rows of houses.

Then, they heard the shout of a man.

"What are you doing with my Grachas?"

A fat, evil-looking man, with white hair with a bald patch, was approaching them. In his hand was a loaded gun.

"Are you after my prize catch?"

"What do you mean?" cried Captain Ing. "You're not trying to shoot those creatures are you?"

"That's exactly what I'm going to do."

"We're not going to let you shoot them," cried the Captain. "Come on, everyone! Let's stop him!"

Ensign Lucy tried to jerk the hunter, so he wouldn't shoot straight. Lieutenant Linda tried stomping her feet to scare the aliens off. As the hunter was jerked forward, his legs landed on the ground spread apart. Melissa took this opportunity. She darted through his open legs. This caused him to trip and the gun went flying out of his hands. Everyone cheered. The gun caught on a nearby branch and shot the ground. Everyone cheered again, but not for long.

"Curse you!" he shouted. "I'll get you for that!"

Just then, a Gracha came running up to the hunter and bit him on the leg. Then, everyone got a big surprise. There was no blood, nor torn flesh; just lights, wires and switches.

"My goodness," cried the Captain. "He's a robot."

The Engineer looked around. "You see that block?"

"Yes," said the Commander.

"It's a power source," said the Engineer. "If we destroy it, we can destroy the robot!"

"Destroy me?" cried the hunter. "You can't do that. I'll-I'll shoot *you!*"

"It's a very large and complicated power source," continued the Engineer. "It's sealed, and the only way to destroy it would be by a great impact. There's no way we can destroy the hunter, because he would shoot us before we got near. Our best bet is to crash the ship

The Stolen Treasure

into the power source."

"Curse you!" the hunter shouted.

A cover opened on the robot's arm and he punched a code of numbers.

In seconds, a humming noise vibrated in the sky. A space man landed. The space man removed his helmet and glared at them all.

"Let's see what Crazy Max has to say," the robot smirked.

"You?" cried the Captain, gazing at the newly-landed spaceman in astonishment, "but I defeated you. I hunted you down and we duelled. I zapped you with my zapshot. You were so wounded and weak, I didn't think you could do any more harm, and I wasn't going to zap a helpless man to death."

"I know," shouted Crazy Max, "and I didn't like it much either, but I cannot die, and I have my ways of coming back."

"So that's it," cried the Captain. "It was because of you those Grachas almost got shot. You built that robot, didn't you? And that wasn't just any gun; that was a Colodiggan Gun invented by you. You were trying to turn those Grachas evil, just like yourself."

The Captain, crew and passengers darted to The Horizon. Captain Ing pressed some buttons, turned some switches, and the ship flew off Atwydolyn's surface.

A torpedo from Crazy Max zoomed past and struck the bottom of the ship.

"It's burned out the Space Swoop!" cried the Engineer.

"Circle back to Atwydolyn and crash the power source!" called Captain Ing.

"I can do that!" Jame cried.

"But you've never flown a ship before. You don't know what you're doing!" Captain Ing protested.

"Just leave it to me!" she insisted. "When I came on board this ship, you said 'You don't seem the kind who would help us,' so now

I'll show you. I'll *help* you!" Jame insisted and pushed Captain Ing away from the controls.

"What you're doing is mutiny!" yelled the Captain, who pushed himself off the floor and made a dash for the switch.

Before Captain Ing could regain access to the controls, Jame yanked the control switch, and in no time at all, the ship crashed into the power source, which exploded.

Then, there came a horrid crunching noise as The Horizon crushed bushes, hillocks, and house after house, belonging to the Grachas, as countless Grachas came hurrying out.

The Grachas' hunter started winding down. He tried to use the last of his power to rocket himself toward the ship, but it was too late and the robot collapsed! The ship, however, kept gliding along. Objects inside the ship were falling and everybody was holding on so they wouldn't fall. Finally, the ship skidded to a halt.

"Look at the damage the ship did after it destroyed the power source!" cried Melissa.

It was true. A couple dozen Gracha houses had been destroyed by The Horizon.

"At least it didn't kill any Grachas," breathed the Rick.

"No," said Captain Ing, "but it has made a lot of Grachas homeless. It's going to take a lot of time, resources, and a lot of their money for them to repair all of that."

"Can't Grachas share?" asked Jame.

"Share!" stammered Captain Ing. "Share? How would you like it if some stranger came barging into your house, demanding to live there? Grachas are territorial creatures. Their homes are their homes."

Crazy Max's eyes were glowing red, and his face was burning with fury. "You may have destroyed my robot for now!" he yelled, "but just you wait. I will leave you be for the time being, but I will be back and by that time I will have an army you will never be able to defeat!"

Crazy Max strapped a portable rocket to his back and rocketed away.

"That was close," breathed the Ensign.

"Not close," the Captain sighed. "This is just the beginning. Crazy Max will be back, and then, who knows how he's going to strike?"

"But just what is a Colodiggan Gun?"

"It is an evil invention of Crazy Max. Crazy Max is an Arshgan man like I am, but he turned from the path of good long ago. When one of his bullets strikes you in any part of your body, you go into a kind of sleep. Later, you awaken, but you are no longer yourself. You are a Space Wanderer like Crazy Max and have no recollection whatsoever of being good. After you become a Space Wanderer, that's how you will be forever and there is no turning back."

6 Tonya

A tiny black dot appeared in the sky.

"I think a ship is coming in our direction," exclaimed Captain Ing. "It's noticed us!"

The ship landed and a space woman appeared. She had long, rippling brown hair and brown eyes. Her skin was a fair colour and her face was long and thin.

"I know you," the woman grinned, facing the Captain. "You're Captain Ing. I'm Tonya; world famous Space Explorer, or should I say universe famous Space Explorer. Hop into my spaceship."

One by one, the crew and passengers introduced themselves to Tonya. Then, the Captain, crew and passengers made their way into Tonya's spaceship. It was very different from The Horizon. This one was quite a bit smaller and had a pearly-white floor. Along the walls, there were wooden shelves which held many gadgets neither the Captain, crew nor passengers had seen before.

"What are all those gadgets on the shelves?" asked Rick.

"This," began Tonya, holding a tiny pink flashlight with a red switch on it, "is the Enemy Repulsion Light. Wherever you are, you are protected from Crazy Max. There is one catch you must be aware of. It is very easy to break."

She handed the Enemy Repulsion Light to Melissa.

"This," Tonya went on, "is a Mindcoat." She pointed to a folded black coat next to the Enemy Repulsion Light. "It shows you other peoples' experiences or can also make you re-experience your own. Before you put one of these on, you simply say a date and a time. You can also add the name of another person if you want to feel like someone else. Then, you simply put it on and you're drawn into the world of that moment. It keeps going until you close your eyes and take it off. Closing your eyes is essential if you want to remove it."

She handed the Mindcoat to Melissa.

Then, Tonya made her way to a wardrobe, to the right of the shelves. She opened it. It contained a whole bunch of purple suits that appeared really hard.

"These are Dome Clothes," explained Tonya. "Put these on and you will be protected against Colodiggan bullets."

"These could come in handy," remarked Captain Ing. "Can we keep them too?"

"Of course," replied Tonya, handing the Dome Clothes to Melissa, "and the Mindcoat, and the Enemy Repulsion Light."

Captain Ing smiled. "But what about you? If these are yours, you won't have them to protect you if you give them to us."

"Oh, don't worry about me," said Tonya. "I've used them to keep myself safe for years. After all this time, I think it's best that I pass them on."

"How about you come with us onto our ship then. If we are all together with your inventions and you, we will all be safe."

Tonya sighed and shook her head. "I'm afraid it's better if I don't," she said. "My ship, 'The White Sailor' is all I have left of my past, before I had to become a hermit. If I left it, and it got destroyed, my grief would be beyond repair. If Crazy Max ever finds me and destroys me, at least it would be a more fitting death for me if I still had my ship.

"Thanks for stopping to help us," smiled Melissa.

"You're very welcome."

"Would you happen to know how Crazy Max came back?"

"I wish I could," replied Tonya. "Nobody does, except maybe Crazy Max himself. Now that he's back, nobody is safe anymore. You must be careful who you talk to and who you let on your ship, now that Crazy Max has returned. Should I tell you all the story of how he turned against me?"

"Absolutely," said Captain Ing. "Anything you could tell us, we would be more than happy to hear."

"All right. I once belonged to a group of Space Explorers called The Star Masters. I had been interested in life beyond Earth since I was born. The Star Masters was like family and Crazy Max was once like my brother."

"You knew him before he was evil?" asked Captain Ing. "What was he like?"

"Well, he wasn't evil, but he was not exactly good either. He was a show-off and very ambitious. His name was simply Max then. A group of six people, myself and five others, had signed up for a space course under the trainer Gongo from planet Uberdan. Our names were Rogan, Albin, Sordin, Mark, myself and Max. We signed up with Gongo over long range holoputer and he brought the lot of us to learn at Atwydolyn, since we were all from different planets. Max was an Arshgan man, just like your Captain.

"As the years went by, we learned of planets, spaceships, defence against attack and advanced technology. But all this was before the violent times, before the war that changed everything."

"What war was this?" asked Rick.

"The Atwydolyn war between the Byalnlings and the Calps, mostly concerned with territory and superiority. Well, Atwydolyn was no place for us. Gongo left us, to fight in the war, and we were taken to Arshga under the care of Samantha and Joseph John, the first Earth people to set foot on Arshga. However, unbeknown to us, Arshga was under attack by the Space Wanderer Guatmillad. He was out to take over the whole planet and aimed to kill anyone who stood in his way.

"However, we stuck together as the brotherhood we had

promised to become. We all used the skills we had learnt, mustered an army and we ultimately destroyed him.

"All of us, including Max, were heroes in the eyes of the Arshgan people. They made us rulers of the whole planet and were willing to grant us any wish we asked for."

"What happened to Gongo?" asked the Doctor. "Did you keep studying with him?"

"Ultimately, no, we never did. Max was never satisfied. He always wanted to keep learning. In my opinion, he didn't help throw Guatmillad down to free the Arshgans, but to give himself a sense of power, a sense that never left him. We could tell, within a few months, that he was growing apart from us. He trained to pilot a spaceship, to become a shapeshifter and he even sought to become immortal, even indestructible.

"Ultimately, he drew up a large band of allies, a team of his own. Only they could know his secrets, which he so desperately kept from the rest of us.

"I longed for him to come back to us. I pleaded with Max and reminded him of our promise to learn together. He supported and saw us less and less, and, in the end, he was gone.

"I give Crazy Max much credit for my inventions, actually. I once eavesdropped on him and his friends to see if there was any way of convincing him that he was going too far and striving for too much. I heard him talking about a series of weapons he wanted to make. I decided to use those designs out of the will for good. I made those very devices, but instead, the design was against Max and his supporters, as, by now, we were growing quite afraid of him."

"Did Gongo ever come back?" asked the Lieutenant.

"Eventually. We all hoped that Gongo's return would remind Max of how he used to train and fight with us and it would cause Max to abandon his progressing path to wickedness. Gongo returned from the war and proudly announced that Atwydolyn had won and all its inhabitants were safe and free. Then, in a stunning move, Max killed Gongo. We were shocked and outraged beyond words and retaliated without thinking. Max ended up killing everyone in The Star Masters except myself. He noticed the Enemy Repulsion Light, the Dome Clothes and the Mindcoat, and figured out that I must have made them. He tried to kill me, but in the end, all he managed to do was erase the design from my memory so I could not make any more and that is why they are so valuable to myself and us all, now. I feel that, all I ever learned from that space course is, you can't trust anyone you think is your friend.

"In a week, I will be waiting for you at New Gachshire, the name of this nation on Atwydolyn," said Tonya.

The Engineer opened a hatch on The Horizon and removed the burnt Space Swoop capsule. Then, he opened his box, and replaced the capsule with a spare capsule. Then, he closed the hatch.

"Thank you, Len," smiled the Captain.

"No problem," Engineer Len replied.

"By the way," concluded Tonya, "you can call the Enemy Repulsion Light the ERL from now on."

"We will Tonya," acknowledged the Captain. "It think it's time we set a course for Earth. We have to get our child passengers to safety."

***

As the children on board The Horizon were on their way home, they thought about the events that had occurred.

"Wasn't it amazing, when Tonya rescued us and gave us those devices?" Jame exclaimed.

"And how we deactivated that robot," exclaimed the engineer.

"He was Crazy Max's invention!"

"Those devices of Tonya's are the most amazing things I have ever encountered," smiled Captain Ing, "but there won't be another space trip," he added. "So much horrible stuff happened on this trip that it's all cancelled and to think that I brought three children with us."

Ensign Lucy made her way over to the Captain.

"It wasn't your fault," she began, "you had no knowing that Crazy Max would return."

"You're right," the Captain replied, "but I put us all in terrible danger."

The Ensign simply shook her head. "Nobody, anywhere, can rest until we have defeated Crazy Max. It is up to us to find out how he came back, make sure there are no more ways and destroy him once and for all."

At this point, Jame stepped over to Melissa. "Melissa," Jame whispered. "I know I'm going to be in big trouble when I get home. You will come and visit me, won't you?"

"Certainly," replied Melissa.

"My address is 213 Cedar Street," explained Jame. "I don't know when would be a good time for you to come, as I know my parents won't want me to have any friends over after what I have done. It will have to be when they're not at home, so they don't know. Tell your parents about me. Do you think they would understand?"

"Yes," explained Melissa. "My parents are very kind and understanding of others."

Immediately after these words were out of Melissa's mouth, she regretted speaking of her parents as loving and good while Jame's were miserable and cruel, but, apparently, Jame didn't mind.

"You're lucky," Jame replied, finally with a little smile. "I wish I could live at your house."

"You belong in your house," Melissa smiled. "I cannot take away the mistreatment you are suffering, but I can help you. You can holoputer me at 35567544."

"My holoputer number is 56754676," Jame explained.

On the rest of the trip back to Earth, the whole crew remained silent for a long while.

The Stolen Treasure

7 Jame's Punishment

The ship landed at the Grand Lodge Spaceport. The air was cold and brisk. Jame didn't know what to do. Did she dare to go back home? Jame gazed at Captain Ing, longing to stay with him. She didn't care what sort of danger was out there.

Jame had a burst of surprise when she saw Tiffany show up again.

"There you are," Tiffany cried. "Don't you ever stow away on a spaceship again!"

"I'm sorry," Jame replied, although she wasn't sure whether or not she really meant it, "but I was so desperate to escape."

"What happened?" Tiffany asked. "You're back early."

"Captain Ing called the rest of the trip off," Jame continued. "We explored an Earth-like planet called Atwydolyn. The Grachas are very intelligent and they build good houses. A group of Grachas is called a 'gough.' However, Crazy Max, the evil space man, is back."

"You're kidding!" cried Tiffany.

"Unfortunately not," Jame explained, "We also met a woman on Atwydolyn called Tonya. Tonya entrusted Melissa with a special light. With it, Crazy Max cannot come to Earth."

"Melissa?" asked Tiffany, puzzled. "Who's Melissa?"

"A fifth-grade girl on the ship," Jame explained. "Very friendly, understanding, loveable. By the way, how did you know I was here, Tiffany?"

"I was looking for you here," Tiffany explained. "I saw you go on that space trip, and figured you might start feeling guilty and convince the Captain to take you home. I called your parents after you left and told them where you had gone."

"You did WHAT?!" Jame yelled.

"Well, I had to tell someone," Tiffany explained. "You sparked an investigation, and someone had to know your whereabouts. Your parents will be coming by here to pick you up."

"Oh well," sighed Jame. "It was inevitable I would have to face my parents for this anyway."

In a matter of minutes, a grey car came into sight and her parents pulled up.

"Hello, Mum and Dad," Jame grinned, as innocently as she could make her voice sound.

"Get in here!" her mother yelled.

Jame had never seen her parents this angry. Her parents, especially her father, looked like a couple of firebombs ready to explode. Jame could swear they wanted to rip her apart for this.

"I'm sorry," Jame said, "look, I'll be so good and I'll never-"

"Do you have any idea how you made us feel?!" her father yelled. "We searched around your school; we went around to your friends' homes to ask where you were! We called your teachers and the principal; then, we called the police who embarked on a costly investigation! You are in big trouble!"

"I wanted to get away from you," Jame wept. "I wanted to see more than this world. I made some friends while I was out in sp-"

"I don't care WHAT you made!" Jame's mother interrupted. "We are going to MAKE YOU a better child. We are going to give you a punishment you will never forget. You are grounded from today on, until the day you don't need us anymore. While you remain living under our roof, you will not see any friends, you will have no friends coming over, you will come home immediately after school is over, you will have no holovision privileges, no desserts, you will do all chores that need doing both inside and outside the house, and you will have small portions of meals."

"You can't deprive me of desserts and meals!" Jame protested. "I'm too old for that kind of punishment. I am not a little kid anymore."

"You act like a little kid, we will treat you like a little kid!" her father exclaimed.

"But-"

"You had us worried sick!!" her father continued. "What you did was not only thoughtless, it was dangerous! If you had hurt yourself, or if you had been kidnapped, no one would have been able to help you!"

For the first time ever, Jame totally wished she had never gone on the space trip. Why couldn't she be satisfied with living in a dull household, but at least having friends, sufficient food, and rights to do what most kids her age were allowed to do? She had forfeited all of that for a few days in a spaceship where there were villains and dangers around. What was the point? For the first time, Jame felt ungrateful, short-sighted and silly.

Finally, suppertime came. Jame noticed that her supper was about half the size as the suppers of her parents. With the thought of her angry parents, and her guilty conscience, Jame couldn't eat. The food seemed textureless and bland.

She ate what she could (about a third of what was on her plate) and excused herself from the table. Jame walked into the living room. The evening sun was sinking low in the sky and there were people out on the field playing basketball. Jame wished she could be one of those people. The air outside would be growing cool, but the air inside was muggy and stale. A few birds flew over the house and into the setting sun. Jame watched as they flew into the distance, light and free; the way Jame wished she were. They grew smaller and smaller, until they were out of sight. Jame forced a smile. Someday, she would be free again. Someday, she would see all her friends again. Her heart told her that her friends would come to visit her, whether her parents liked it or not. She would receive letters from them. However, Jame felt like there was no person to blame, but herself. She had done something to shut out all of this freedom.

8 Letters

Jame was sitting in her room, out of her parents' sight, reading the letters her friends had sent her.

"Don't worry," Jame told herself. "At least I have friends to help me."

Saying this to herself hadn't worked. It seemed as though she would never be released. She peered at the letter of comfort she had received from Tiffany.

My Dearest, Bestest friend, Jame,

I am sorry your parents have shut you away. Life must be terrible for you. I just wanted to say I have thought about you and I don't blame you for going on The Horizon. I got grounded for a month when I was eleven and it was horrible. I can't imagine what it must be like to be grounded forever.

Your friend, Tiff

And the one from Melissa

Dear Jame

I feel horrible for what you must be going through. I am sorry your parents are punishing you for going on the space trip. We had many great advenchures together, at Atwydolyn and with Tonya. I am guarding her inventions well. I promise to visit you.

Take care, Melissa

Jame chuckled as she noticed Melissa had spelled "adventures" wrong. Jame had secretly invited Melissa over today, and Melissa was due to arrive shortly after her parents left to go shopping.

Before leaving for the store, Jame's father faced his daughter. "We are leaving to go shopping now and we want you on your best behaviour while we are gone. This is the only chance we are giving you to trust you to not let anything happen or for you to have anyone in the house during our absence. If we see one hint that you even might have misbehaved or might have had a friend in the house, we will lock you in your room whenever we go out from now on. Got it?"

"Got it," Jame sighed sadly.

"That's my girl," grunted Mr. Arden, giving Jame a pat on the back, which felt more like a slap.

Her mother and father opened the door and left.

Jame kept close to the door, eagerly anticipating the knock that was about to come.

After a few minutes, a knock sounded and Jame opened the door. On the other side, there was Melissa.

"Feel free to take off your shoes and make yourself at home," beamed Jame.

Melissa removed her shoes and took some steps in Jame's house. Jame couldn't help herself. She wrapped her arms tightly around Melissa and Melissa hugged Jame back. In fact, Jame hugged Melissa so tightly, the little girl gagged.

"Oops," smiled Jame. "Sorry about that."

Melissa's smile grew into a giggle, which grew into a laugh and soon the two were laughing hysterically on the landing.

"I'm so happy to see you," Jame smiled. "Come into the living room."

Melissa stepped up the stairs and they settled themselves in the living room. Melissa smiled and handed a card to Jame. "I made this card for you."

She handed Jame the most gorgeous card she had seen. It was

thin, white cardboard, and Melissa had written the following message:

"May you have the warmth of company, for the kindest friend ever."

When Jame opened the card, she saw a photograph of Melissa at Christmas time. Her father was lifting her so she could place the angel on the top of the Christmas tree. Around the picture, Melissa had drawn basketballs.

"Thank you very much. This is wonderful," smiled Jame with sincerity. "I love it."

"It was a pleasure making it," Melissa beamed.

"How are the ERL, the Dome Clothes and the Mindcoat doing?"

"They're at my house. I've locked them in the cupboard in my room to keep them safe."

"That's good," Jame replied.

"This came in our mail this morning," Melissa continued, handing Jame, what appeared to be another card, but Jame thought, "This couldn't be another card. Melissa's already given me a card and two cards, even from her, would be a bit much."

Jame looked at it more closely. It was not another card. In fact, it wasn't even from Melissa. It was from Tonya. When Jame looked it over to see exactly what it was, Jame discovered it was a picture of a treasure chest, on a grassy meadow at Atwydolyn. On the other half of the Microfoil was an explanation of the treasure, and a map of where, on Atwydolyn's surface, it was located.

Dear Melissa:

I thought you would like to be the first one to know about the incredible treasure of Latimus the Grachas are making. Since The Horizon crashed on Atwydolyn, the Grachas have been trying to restore everything back to normal. Some Grachas are making a wonderful treasure chest, to help those who have suffered from their homes being destroyed. Will you and Jame keep this map safe, apart from the ERL, the Mindcoat and the Dome Clothes? I trust that you'll be able to take good care of it.

Tonya

Jame looked over the picture of the treasure for a few minutes. "I love Atwydolyn," Jame whispered.

"Come into the kitchen," Jame smiled to Melissa.

Jame led Melissa into the kitchen, set two glasses and two plates on the table, poured milk into both glasses and set a handful of gingersnaps onto both plates.

In a minute, Jame and Melissa were sitting down at the table to milk and cookies.

"These are delicious," grinned Melissa. "Gingersnaps are my favourite."

"Are they really your favourite?" Jame asked delightedly. "Most people I know prefer oreos or chocolate chip cookies."

"There's no cookie I like more than gingersnaps," Melissa beamed, obviously enjoying herself. "I love the spiciness, crunchiness and the sweetness." Melissa washed a gingersnap down with a sip of milk.

"I'm so glad," Jame smiled.

All of a sudden, another knock sounded!

"Oh no," cried Jame. "That will be my parents for sure. Melissa, hide yourself. I will hide the map!"

Jame hid the map and the letters under the couch and Melissa hid herself behind the couch.

"Jame," Melissa asked worriedly. "When could I come and visit you again?"

"Both my parents are at work tomorrow morning. Perhaps you

could come then."

"That sounds good," Melissa replied.

"Jame, unlock this door at once!" shouted the voice of her mother from outside.

Jame ran to the door and opened it.

"My goodness," cried Jame's mother, "What took you so long? Are you going deaf?"

"H-honestly," Jame stuttered, "I heard you the whole time. I was just a bit slow."

"Slow," she shouted, "I don't believe it. You're up to something, Jame. You're as white as a ghost and you're all shaky!"

"It's just from not being able to go outside."

"Well," snapped her mother, "that's your own fault. If you hadn't stowed away on that spaceship, this wouldn't be happening right now. You should act like an eleventh grader for once."

Jame's father stepped through the door next.

"Would you two mind helping me put these groceries away?" he asked.

"Sure," replied Jame's mother.

Then, the mum started stepping up the staircase to Jame. "Tell me what's the matter."

"Nothing."

All of a sudden, a cough sounded from behind the couch.

Jame's mother stopped dead! "Who was that?"

"It was me," replied Jame.

"No, it wasn't. It came from behind the couch."

Jame's mother started to run up the rest of the stairs.

Jame cut her off. "I'll help you put the groceries away."

"First, I want to see who's trespassing in our house!"

Mrs. Arden looked behind the couch, but did not see Melissa, for Melissa had moved under the kitchen table. However, Melissa had not left, for she could not make it to her shoes without being seen.

Jame hurried up the stairs and saw Melissa under the table. "Melissa!" Jame called, in a shouting whisper. "You better go home. Don't bother with shoes. You'll have to leave in your stocking feet. My parents will go crazy if they catch you!" Jame wasn't thinking clearly at this point. She just knew she had to get Melissa out of the house.

"What?" Melissa whispered back, "but I'll get my socks dirty, and your parents will see my shoes left behind."

"Yes! Well I will tell my parents I bought a pair of new shoes!"

"Child size 10?!" replied Melissa, also in a shouting whisper. "Jame, that's silly!"

"Jame, who are you talking to?" asked Mrs. Arden sternly.

"Nobody, thinking out loud," Jame replied.

Jame's mother walked around the house, looking for the intruder. "Who is it? Who is in our house?"

At this point, Melissa decided she had better make a run for it, regardless of her shoes, and dashed out from under the table, onto the patio, spent a couple seconds with her head racing whether to scramble down the deck stairs, or slide down the wooden railing, which was old and would give her splinters in her bum.

Finally, Mrs. Arden came to the kitchen window, glanced Melissa, and nearly screamed the roof off of the house!

She grabbed Jame in her arms tight! "Who is this? What is she doing here?"

"She's just a visitor," Jame stuttered. "A friend."

"What?" screamed Jame's mother. "You have been letting visitors in when you're not allowed!"

"Jame is my friend and I want you to leave her alone!" Melissa yelled.

"Shut up!" yelled Mrs. Arden.

The Stolen Treasure

"Stop!" Jame hollered. "You leave Melissa out of this! It's bad enough that you yell at me, but now you-"

"You want to go to bed at six, Jame?"

Melissa, realizing she was no match for Jame's parents, and not wanting to get Jame into any more trouble, ran out the door.

9 The Broken Friendship

The next morning started out as an ordinary morning. Melissa awoke and dressed herself. Then, she walked from her room into the kitchen to have breakfast. It was a fine, sunny morning.

After breakfast, Melissa took the cyberlock (similar to our combination lock today, except it responds to a spoken password, which the owner would whisper closely and discreetly) off her cupboard, but when she opened it, she got the shock of her life.

The Dome Clothes, the ERL and the Mindcoat were all gone!

Melissa shut the cupboard doors and pinched herself to make sure she wasn't dreaming. Then, she opened the doors again. There was no mistake about it. All of the inventions that Tonya had entrusted to Melissa were missing.

How could this we possible? Melissa had shut and locked both her window and her cupboard. The cyberlock was quite an old one, but surely, it couldn't be this old.

Melissa examined the lock on her window. It was in ruins, as though somebody had attacked it with a crowbar. She looked at the burglar alarm and found that it was fried.

"MUM! DAD!" Melissa called.

Melissa's parents came running into her room.

"What is it?"

"They're all gone. Tonya's inventions have disappeared."

Mrs. Maguire looked stunned. "And you never took them out of your closet?"

"I haven't done anything with them except lock them in my cupboard, and I never took them out. The lock on my window looks damaged. You can take a look at it."

Melissa's mum and dad stared at the window's lock long and

The Stolen Treasure

hard. Her mum looked shocked and her dad looked horrified.

"Someone has broken into our house!" cried George. "We have to call the police."

Melissa turned to face her mother. "But the lock for my cupboard looks fine." Melissa placed the lock for her cupboard in her mother's hands.

There was a long silence as Katrina inspected it everywhere with intense scrutiny.

"I don't know," Mrs. Maguire finally whispered. "I just don't know. But there is no doubt that the lock to your window was in perfect working condition before last night."

"Could the lock to my cupboard have stopped working?" Melissa asked as calmly as she could. "You gave it to me for kindergarten, and it wasn't new then."

"It wouldn't wear out like that," her mother explained. "Locks like these have at least a fifty-year warranty. The manufacturing date on the back of this lock says 2085."

Both Melissa's parents left the room. "We will call the police and have them investigate."

Melissa looked from her window to her cupboard, to see if there was any other evidence that somebody had broken in, but she saw none. Then, she gazed outside, looking down from her window, but everything looked normal.

Then, Melissa sat down on the floor, guilty and worried. What would Tonya think if Melissa had lost all the inventions that Tonya had given to her?

***

Jame happened to be just waking up at her house. When she strode down to the kitchen to make herself her breakfast, she got a nasty shock, for sitting in the kitchen were both of her parents!

Jame stared in shock for a few seconds, before she began to speak.

"Aren't you supposed to be at work?" Jame asked.

"We would have been," replied Jame's father, "but we got a call telling us that we weren't needed today. Besides, don't you feel pleased that you have a whole extra day with us?"

"I suppose I do," Jame stuttered, though inside, she thought of her parents as evil monsters. She just could not believe this. This couldn't be happening. What about when Melissa showed up?

"I'll just go over to my room to check my treasure map," explained Jame.

She opened her drawer and it was gone too.

"My goodness. The map's gone. How can that be?"

Jame ran out of her room, to her parents.

"Somebody stole the treasure map."

"Is that so?" asked her father.

"Yes, it is so," cried Jame, "and I want it back."

"Well, you're not getting it back," shouted her father.

"You took it, didn't you?" Jame shouted. "I want it back. It was entrusted to me."

"Oh really, now who would trust you with anything?"

"Tonya."

"Tonya?" asked her father. "Who's Tonya?"

"A lady who rescued me on the space trip."

"Well, you ought to be grateful that someone would rescue you."

"Just give me the map and I won't argue anymore."

"I don't have your stupid map," he shouted, "and I'm glad. One thing got rid of, from that puny brown-haired girl trying to drive us crazy."

The Stolen Treasure

"Don't you dare insult Melissa."

"So the little slime ball has a name, does it?"

At that moment, a volcano spewing anger erupted inside Jame's stomach. She couldn't stand to Melissa being talked about like that.

"What's going on?" Jame's mother shouted, as she came into the room.

"She's claiming her stupid treasure map has been stolen," Jame's father told her.

"Oh, good riddance; it's gone at last and what about those letters?"

"The rest are still hid-" Jame caught herself, just in time, before she could finish her sentence.

"Well," her mother exclaimed. "Where are they?"

"I am not telling you. Why did you steal my treasure map?"

"We did not steal your stupid map," shouted her mother.

"I know you did. You were so angry when you discovered it under the couch."

"Now, now," explained her father. "Just take into acceptance that it is gone. It was just a map. It's no big deal."

"Yes it is. Tonya trusted me with it. It she never trusts me again, it's your fault."

"I think you are already quite untrustworthy as it is. Now stop blubbering about your silly map and get your breakfast."

Jame reached up into the freezer and pulled out a piece of bread and slipped it into the toaster.

Once it was toasted, she pulled a knife out of the drawer and spread jam onto it.

"Now listen," snarled Jame's father as Jame began to have herself her fill. "That piece of slime has buzzed in our ears long enough already. If she ever sets foot on our property again, you will make it absolutely certain that she does not feel welcome. If it knocks on our freaking door again, you get it out of the house as fast and instantly as possible. At the first step she tries to take in our house, you yell at her if that's what would work best."

"Father," cried Jame, "I could never do that. She's the best friend I've ever had."

"Your father is right!" cried her mother. "You yell the heck out of it next time you see it, Jame. It's been nosing in our business too much and has been giving you only more things to spoil your mind with. Your father is absolutely right. Next time that brat comes, you drive it away good and hard, all right?"

"I hope you understand what a bad child you have been, Jame," cried her father. "You know that we do not want people visiting you. The only reason why we are getting visitors is because you are inviting them and accepting their sappy comfort letters. You know very well that you do not deserve comfort, because of what a bad, spoiled child you are. That is disobeying your family, Jame, and that is something that we will not tolerate. I find it sickening to think that our own kid is such a disobedient brat."

Jame couldn't believe this. By the time she had finished eating, tears were forming in her eyes. The words that her parents had stuck in her mind were buzzing like vicious hornets and stinging her feelings repetitively.

Jame kept close to the door, now dreading the knock that was about to come. Jame couldn't call Melissa and tell her not to come, because Jame's parents would know who Jame was contacting on the holoputer.

Finally, after fearful, long last, a knock sounded.

"That will be it," cried Jame's father. "After yesterday, I can't believe she has come again, but, after today, she definitely won't."

Jame stuttered down the first step of the staircase and peered at the door where her father was watching with furious eyes.

The Stolen Treasure

As Jame stepped down the staircase, her body was trembling, her skin was sweating and her heart was pounding.

Finally, she had found her way to the bottom of the stairs and extended a shaking arm towards the doorknob. She couldn't believe that she would ever be afraid to meet Melissa.

After Jame had opened the door, she found Melissa Maguire standing at the other side.

Melissa's face turned slightly surprised when she noticed Jame's father at the top of the staircase, and she asked Jame, "Can I come in?"

"NO!" Jame yelled. "In fact, you are not to come to my house again! I never want to see you again?"

"But you've always liked seeing me," said Melissa surprised.

"I ... was pretending!" Jame cried. "I wanted you to think I cared so that I could really hurt your feelings when I shut you out!"

"Jame, what's going on?" said Melissa.

"You know what's going on! It's because of you I got in trouble yesterday! It's because of you I felt welcome enough on Captain Ing's ship to stay and be faced with Crazy Max. Get out of here forever, and never come back!"

"Jame," said Melissa, her face turning pale. "Stop that. Whatever you're saying, you don't really mean it."

"Oh I do!" Jame persisted. "Since you made me get in trouble, you forget you ever met me, and never see me again! You get that straight, you get that through your head!" By now, Jame was yelling so loudly and so close to Melissa's face that flecks of Jame's spit were flying at Melissa.

Melissa, now with tears in her eyes backed away, and Jame drew out her hand and slapped Melissa on the cheek.

Melissa was now sobbing on the doorstep, wearing an expression of mixed hurt and alarm.

Seeing Melissa lie there made Jame feel sick and ashamed of what she had just done. She stepped toward Melissa, just to show she was sorry and did not want Melissa to leave forever.

"GET AWAY FROM ME!!" the tiny girl screamed and Jame jumped back, alarmed and frightened.

"I'm sorry!" Jame called to Melissa. "I didn't mean that."

Melissa gave no reply except a batch of more sobs.

"WHY?!" Melissa yelled and opened the door and left.

After a few seconds, Jame heard Melissa howl in a cloudburst of tears through the door.

"'At a girl," smiled Jame's father. "You sure showed her."

Jame dashed up the staircase. "Melissa!" she wailed.

When Jame looked out the living room window, she saw Melissa stepping into the car, still shaking visibly and her face wet with tears. Her mother was wearing an expression of concern, but her father looked furious.

"From now on, you just stay away from Melissa!" he yelled at Jame through the window.

All the same, Jame looked at Melissa good and hard. "This may be the last I ever see her," she whispered to herself.

After the car had driven away, Jame felt her insides turn to ice and she ran into her room and shut the door.

"What have I done?" she wept on her bed.

Jame looked out her window at the barren street. It was all for nothing now. Just for once, Jame had gotten a dose of true kindness and love, something she could have used and held onto forever. Just for once, Jame had found a person, a young child of all people, who truly understood her, saw her for who she was and loved her. And Jame had killed all of that.

"Melissa!" she wept and dropped back onto her bed. "Tiffany! Anyone!"

The Stolen Treasure

Jame never left her room for the remainder of the day. She felt filthy, wicked and sick. She would never forgive herself, nor her parents. She hated herself. Jame knew that nothing good would come from thinking like this, but she could no longer feel any hope in her crushed heart.

10 The Fire

It had been another long and tiresome day of being stuck in the house, but bedtime was here at last. This was probably the most terrible and most wonderful night in all of Jame's life.

As Jame was getting ready for bed, she noticed a faint, weird stench hanging in the air. It smelled as though something was burning in the oven. However, when Jame looked in the oven and under the element, there was nothing to be seen.

Jame decided to ignore it and go to bed.

After falling asleep, she dreamed that she was standing by the door of Melissa's room. This house definitely appeared a lot newer and cleaner than Jame's house, but Jame could hear the heartbroken sobs coming from inside.

Jame opened the door and stepped inside, her feet feeling as though they were made of rubber.

Melissa briefly turned her face toward Jame as she entered, showing her shocked, distraught expression. Melissa soon cupped her face in her hands and persisted on crying.

"I'm not here to hurt you," stuttered Jame. "I would like to apologize."

Melissa turned away from Jame and sidled from her in an uncomfortable manner.

"I am so sorry I made you leave," Jame explained. "I care about you. I really do."

When Melissa still said nothing, Jame hugged her, trying to believe that the warmth and comfort of her arms would remind Melissa of how she would visit Jame, bringing her cards and gifts.

Melissa's trembling slowed and she turned her face back to Jame, which Jame gratefully found to appear slightly less anguished.

Melissa didn't hug Jame, but she pulled her arm gently across Jame's back.

"You see?" smiled Jame, relieved. "That's a start."

It came without warning. Melissa let out a high, agonized cry that echoed through the house. "FATHER!!"

Mr. Maguire marched down the hallway. When he saw Jame, he yelled so loudly, and so furiously, Jame though he was going to explode.

"WHAT ARE YOU DOING HERE?!! YOU'RE THAT HORROR WHO RUINED MY DAUGHTER!!"

"No, have mercy on..."

"AND HOW DARE YOU SET YOUR DISGUSTING FEET IN OUR HOUSE!!" he bellowed, his voice sounding as though it was amplified a thousand times. "GET OUT OF HERE FOREVER AND GO BACK TO YOUR HOUSE, WHERE YOU BELONG!!"

Then, Melissa's father grew bigger and all of his muscles grew so huge, they bulged. With his face vicious and furious, he chased Jame down the hallway.

The scene started to blur in front of Jame's eyes and the dream changed. Jame was now dreaming that she was inside the oven in her house and her parents were trying to stuff her in. The element was glowing red hot.

"We hate you as much as it is," cried her mother. "We want to get rid of you."

"No. NO!" Jame cried.

But her father just cackled. "Those who are garbage might as well be burned in the stove."

Her parents laughed evil laughs again.

"NO. NOOOO. You can't do this to me. I'm your daughter. I'M YOUR DAUGHTER!!"

"You're no more good to us than a pile of dog poo."

"NO. NO." Jame screamed. "HELP! PLEASE, SOMEBODY HELP ME! MELISSA! QUICK!"

"That stupid girl is not going to come for you!" shouted her father.

The elements were red and the inside was burning fire hot. It was growing hotter and hotter.

"NO. NOOOOOOOOOOOOO!!!!! SOMEBODY HELP ME. SOMEBODY PLEASE HELP ME!! HEEEEEEEEEELP!!!"

A loud beep woke her up.

It was the smoke alarm. Jame's room felt nearly as hot as the oven in her dream and the air was saturated with smoke.

All of a sudden, Jame's parents burst into her room.

"Hurry," cried her mum. "There's a fire."

Jame got down on all fours and crawled, groping through the suffocating smoke.

The heat from Jame's floor was burning her skin and everywhere she looked, there were flames.

"Hurry," Jame coughed. "I'll lead the way. Follow me."

As they crawled along the burning hallway, the air felt as though it was getting hotter all the time, and flames were bursting out from all directions.

If only Jame could make it into the next room, to call the fire department, the house just might be saved.

She crawled into the kitchen and reached up, onto the counter. Then, Jame dialled breathed to the holoputer "911."

The hologram of the operator appeared before Jame.

"Police, ambulance, or fire?" the hologram of a man asked.

"F-f-fire," Jame managed to cough through the smoke.

"And where is the fire?"

"At 213875 Wackabayashi Street."

"We will send out a firetruck immediately."

The Stolen Treasure

Jame shut the holoputer off and bolted to the door, still low on the ground.

Time seemed to be rapidly running out. The temperature was continually rising and the smoke was growing thicker and thicker.

Soon, Jame was stumbling about in the heat and flames, choking and coughing. She could no longer see where she was going.

She tried to call for her parents, but the smoke suffocated her and she was rolling on the ground trying to extinguish the flames on her pyjamas.

As Jame continued to grope her way to the door, she tried to call out again, but all that came out were coughs, for she could no longer breathe.

Finally, Jame had felt her way to the door. The doorknob was just in front of her.

She reached out, to turn the metal knob.

All of a sudden, the worst pain Jame had ever felt in all her life burst through her hand.

She tried to let go of the doorknob, but the muscles in her hand seemed paralyzed. She tried to move her fingers, but they would not budge and the pain was unbearable.

Suddenly, a horrible bumping and creaking noise reverberated from above. When Jame looked up, the burning roof was caving in and was about to fall.

Jame put all of her effort into turning the knob. She planned to open the door, and twist her arm to place her body outside.

A fiery board fell on the landing near Jame, while she frantically turned the knob and stepped backwards to open the door.

There was more sizzling and rumbling coming from the ceiling, as the wood grew yet more loose and ready to fall.

"Please let this be more of the nightmare," Jame thought to herself, even though she was certain that this was real and that she was neither dreaming nor in bed.

Finally, Jame noticed that the fire was eating away at the door and she placed herself beside it, waiting for it to collapse. It was leaning over more and more, with the burning hot metal still in her hand.

Finally, the door fell and the doorknob came off, as the burning cascade of wood tumbled to the landing. Jame ran out of the house and escaped just in time.

Outside, on the front lawn, Jame regained her air. She lay huffing and puffing on the grass for a few minutes, watching the house rapidly being consumed by flames. Jame looked around and realized that her parents had never come out.

"MUM! DAD!" she called. "MUM! DAD! WHERE ARE YOU!"

Jame looked around, but her parents were nowhere in sight.

"No," stuttered Jame. "You can't be dead. You mustn't be dead. It's not true!"

Jame kept lying there, just hoping this couldn't be true, but she knew it was true, for the house was pretty well all flames now.

"Mum," she sobbed on the lawn. "Dad. You're gone. I can't believe you're gone!"

At that moment, a fire truck arrived. Several firemen got out, with hoses, and sprayed big jets of water into the fire.

Eventually, the fire was out. All that was left of the house was the charred, wooden framework.

Then, an ambulance arrived and two men stepped out.

Jame no longer noticed how much pain her burnt skin was in. All she could think about now was her parents. It was all so terrible, she couldn't take in what had just happened. Finally, Jame fell back to sleep and had more sad and disturbing dreams.

11 A New Beginning

When Jame awoke the next morning, she found herself in a room full of doctors. Her body was in great pain and the world spun in front of her eyes.

Jame decided to look at her hand and got a big shock. It was blood red and swollen. The whole world was a big daze, as though she were fighting a really high fever.

"Look," smiled one of the doctors. "She's awake."

"My parents," Jame stuttered. "Are ... they ..."

"Yes, I'm afraid they're long gone."

Jame rolled over onto her side and tears started streaming down her cheeks.

"It must be really sad for you," replied the doctor, "but don't talk. You are very injured and sick. Your right hand has third degree burns."

But there were a lot of problems that Jame couldn't stop thinking about. She was quite grown up, but not old enough to be living on her own.

Jame's maternal grandfather had died two years ago, her paternal grandfather was in jail and she didn't have any aunts or uncles, because her mother and father had been only children.

"You should be out of the hospital in about a week," explained the doctor.

Jame closed her eyes and try to go back to sleep, but she couldn't. The pain in her body and her heart kept her awake. Jame longed to see Melissa so badly. That sweet, nurturing smile, and those innocent, sparkling eyes would brighten Jame's spirit, no matter how sick Jame felt, or what tragedy had transpired. But would Melissa want to see Jame anymore? On top of Jame's burns, smoke inhalation, and losing her parents, Jame couldn't shake the vision of Melissa lying on the landing, walking away, without even wanting to hear Jame's apology. There was nothing left for Jame to do but to lie on the hospital bed, hoping and praying Melissa would still come.

Finally, Jame heard a familiar voice from beside her bed.

"Jame, Jame, I've come to visit you."

Jame opened her eyes to find Tiffany and her parents standing there.

Tiffany's face looked sad, but still comforting. There were smudges around her eyes, showing that she must have been crying.

"How are you feeling?" Tiffany asked.

"Sick," whispered Jame, painfully. "Sick and burned."

"I'm sorry about your parents," whispered Tiffany.

"Oh Tiffany, they were horrible," Jame replied. "I know I should have told you, but they were abusive. They yelled at me a lot, treated me like garbage. That's why I never invited you to my house."

"Jame," whispered Tiffany. "You should never have let them do this to you."

"But that's not the half of it," Jame continued. "That really small girl I told you about, Melissa. The one who I befriended on Captain Ing's ship; I hurt her. I yelled at her, then slapped her in the face. My father told me to. Called me a wimp, a brat, so in the heat of the moment, I lashed out, and I did it on Melissa."

"Oh Jame!" Tiffany cried, "How could you?"

"I don't know. I knew it was wrong. I had no good excuse. She was so kind to me," wept Jame. "She was so sweet and understanding, but I hurt her. Will she still come out to see me?"

"Jame, I don't know. Even if Melissa wants to come, her parents might not let her. They might be too upset with you for what you did to their daughter. Jame, I hope your friend comes, but don't

The Stolen Treasure

count on it."

"I tried to apologize," Jame sobbed. "I felt terrible about what I had done when I saw her lying there, but she wouldn't even listen to me."

"No, she wouldn't have," replied Tiffany with confidence and sincerity. "It was too soon after it happened. No friend, no matter how loyal, would have been able to forgive that on the spot."

"Will Melissa hate me now?"

"Hate you? No, she wouldn't hate you. She may be disappointed in you, maybe even mad at you. But, if she's really your friend, she doesn't hate you; and if you can show that you are truly sorry and that you love her, I believe she can start to forgive you."

Tiffany looked like she didn't know what to say next, but sat herself down on the end of Jame's bed. Jame kept her eyes glued to the door.

A few minutes later, the door opened and three more people arrived: George and Katrina Maguire, and standing between them, much to Jame's delight and relief, was Melissa.

Melissa burst into the room, from between her parents, sobbing with fat tears pouring out of her eyes.

"Melissa," Jame whispered, a smile blossoming on her face. With a slow, trembling arm, she extended her hand to Melissa's cheek. "Thank you so much for coming."

Comforting happiness started pouring into Jame. It gave Jame even greater relief to find Melissa not rejecting or backing away, but beginning to smile.

Jame lifted Melissa onto her hospital bed and began to sob again.

"Melissa," Jame cried, "I am so sorry. Please forgive me."

"Certainly," beamed Melissa.

Then Jame turned to Melissa's parents. "I apologize to you as well," she explained. "I only want you to understand that I never really wanted to insult your daughter. It's just that my parents threatened me."

Melissa's mother still looked grieved by what had happened to Melissa, but she nodded her head all the same. "You're in my heart too, Jame," she smiled, "but that is no excuse."

"I know that I should have stood up for your daughter, but you have no idea what my parents were like. I just felt so trapped, frightened and angry. I'm sorry."

"You had better be!" frowned Melissa's father. "I can't express the shock we suffered, when Melissa came from your house yesterday."

"I'll never do anything like that ever again! I said I was sorry!" cried Jame.

"Well, she is still our child and we love her. We have been taking care of her for eleven years. We get defensive when our child's wellbeing is hindered, because Melissa," he explained turning to his daughter, "is someone we wouldn't trade for the universe."

"I was really shocked about what happened," wept Melissa, "but please don't make Jame have to suffer any more than she already has. I am just grateful that she is still alive."

"Melissa," Katrina sighed, "I'm afraid your friend has not proven herself trustworthy. Put yourself in the point of view of a parent and imagine someone confined and abused in their house saying mean things to and slapping your child."

Melissa thought and understood her mother's feelings and also, even though Melissa didn't want to feel it, she couldn't help believing that her mother had a point, that her mother may even be right. However, Jame had been kind to Melissa before their last visit and had treated Melissa like a guest and Melissa knew that Jame never wanted to be bad and that Jame never would have attacked Melissa if her parents hadn't been there.

"Jame is my friend," explained Melissa smoothly.

Even Melissa's father, who seemed to be having a harder time accepting Jame's feelings, nodded his head.

"What's done is done," he explained, turning his head to Jame, "but our daughter here must really want to help you. The very minute that she found out about last night's tragedy in the news, she forced both of us to drive her out so she could see you."

"I will never ever hurt you again," smiled Jame. "I just feel so terrible, knowing that I must have really caused you pain, not only on the outside, but on the inside as well. It must have hurt in your heart."

"That can easily be repaired," Melissa smiled.

"What can I do to make up for the pain I have caused you and our friendship?"

"Just be the kind and sweet girl that you were born to be," Melissa smiled. "Be yourself."

"You and Tiffany are enough to make me happy," whispered Jame, "but where will I live from now on?"

"You can live with us," offered Tiffany's mother.

Jame looked from Tiffany and her parents to Melissa and her parents.

Jame had known Tiffany longer, but it was Melissa who had made her see true happiness and friendship. Just the thought of living with Melissa and her family was heaven.

"I'll be happy to live with you," smiled Jame, turning her head from Tiffany's parents to Melissa's parents, "but would you really want anyone in your house who has degraded your child?"

"We'll see," explained Melissa's mother. "It's not that I don't care about you, Jame. I feel for you too. I think I even like you, but Melissa's safety and wellbeing is important to me and her father as well."

"And she will remain safe and well if I live under your roof. I learn from my mistakes. There has never been anyone who has changed my life the way your daughter has. I was not myself when I did that. I swear I will never let my anger get the better of me again, especially towards your daughter. Besides, I seriously doubt there will be any cause for me to be angry in your house."

Katrina turned to her husband who, too, looked satisfied, even charmed by Jame. The two began to talk to each other in soft voices, not quite whispers, but quiet enough so that Jame could not decipher what they were saying.

"Jame," Mrs. Maguire beamed. "You seem like the sort of child that needs a proper home; who has always needed a proper home. When you are feeling better, you can live with us."

These words rang like the bells of heaven in Jame's head. Did she really hear this? Was this real, in Jame's actual, waking life? Jame's spirit was so elated and so light, she didn't even feel sick or injured anymore. It was like Katrina's acceptance had wiped Jame clean of her burns, her grief, and all seventeen years of her suffering, like Jame could leave the hospital this minute and come to live with Melissa and her family.

"Oh Katrina!" Jame cried, with tears running down her cheeks, and a smile splitting her face. "Thank you! It's more than I could have ever dreamed!"

Mrs. Maguire stepped up to Jame and hugged her around the shoulders. Jame sat up the best she could and hugged Mrs. Maguire's shoulders in return. It felt just like hugging an adult Melissa.

"I think you and Melissa are kindred spirits," Jame beamed, "both painted with the same brush of kindness."

"I guess we are," Mrs. Maguire smiled. "You should probably get your rest now. Your body needs it."

The Stolen Treasure

As the days passed, Jame couldn't help feeling happy. Finally, after all this time in her life, she would be living with kind and decent parents. Still, as her stay wore on, her feelings of loss and emptiness regrew.

The week Jame had in the hospital was not as painful and drawn out as Jame thought it would be when she first arrived. Both Melissa and Tiffany came to visit her every day.

Slowly, even her appetite came back and the burns on her body and on her hand were healing.

After a few days, Jame was feeling up to going for short walks around the hospital corridors and after a few more days, Melissa was able to take Jame for a walk outside in the fresh air.

It was amazing, to Jame, being let out in the fresh air once again. After being a prisoner inside her own home for the two weeks following her short stay on Captain Ing's ship, then suffering the heat and smoke of her burning house, the air felt cool and distilled. The sunshine was raining down and there wasn't a cloud in the sky.

Melissa and Jame sat themselves down on a bench near the fountain. There was a mild breeze in the air blowing the fountain mist toward them.

12 The House of the Maguires

Finally, the day came for Jame to be released from the hospital.

"Good morning," smiled Melissa's mum. "We have come to take you home."

"I am very excited about living in your house," smiled Jame.

"I'm sure you'll like it very much," replied Mrs. Maguire. "You should feel at home in just a few days."

"I'm sure I'll feel at home the second I step inside," Jame beamed.

"We had better get going," smiled Mrs. Maguire. "Your new house is waiting, Jame."

Melissa, her parents and Jame made their way outside where a red car was waiting for them.

The drive to Melissa's house was very intriguing. Jame's spirit was light as she watched the sunny scenery pass by. Eventually, Jame felt it necessary to raise the subject of the missing treasure map.

"Melissa?" Jame asked.

"Yes?"

"You know all those devices that Tonya gave you? The Mindcoat, the ERL and the Dome Clothes? Have they gone missing?"

"I'm afraid they have," replied Melissa. "I checked my cupboard and they were all gone. I just don't see how. I locked my cupboard, my window and made sure all the doors were locked. Our house even has a burglar alarm. Why do you ask, Jame? Has your treasure map been stolen too?"

"The treasure map is gone as well," Jame explained. "Melissa, I have a bad feeling about this. There is a treasure thief."

"But how could he get all those devices?" asked Melissa.

"How could he have got past our burglar alarm, through my window and unlocked my cupboard and even without waking me up?"

"And what would he want with all those things?" asked Jame.

"Maybe he wants to steal the treasure at Atwydolyn," replied Melissa.

"You could be right," exclaimed Jame. "It all makes sense. What else would a thief want with a treasure map and he'd need all those inventions to protect himself from the good people who want to stop him."

"I see what you mean," acknowledged Melissa.

"But what if Tonya finds out and never trusts me again?"

"That's what I'm worried about. I hope she understands," Melissa replied.

Both girls thought about this for the rest of the trip home, while the bright, sunny scenery flashed past, their minds boggling on who would want to steal a treasure.

Finally, the car stopped at a two-storey house that was painted bright pink all over.

"Here it is," smiled Melissa's father. "The house of the Maguires."

"It's wonderful!" exclaimed Jame.

Just the sight of the house made Jame start to feel at home. This house looked a lot newer and better made than the one Jame had endured. There was even a flowerbed in front of the house full of tulips, daffodils, and many others.

"Beautiful flowerbed, isn't it?" asked Melissa's father.

"It certainly is," smiled Jame.

"Melissa planted those all by herself she did," he continued. "Why don't we go inside?"

Melissa's dad opened the door and everybody stepped into the house.

The second they had entered, Jame was lost for words at how wonderful this place looked. Jame couldn't help loving this place. The air inside smelled fresh and clean. The windows were well washed, making the sunlight dazzle through them, making the air feel warm and comforting.

"Come with me," smiled Melissa. "I'll show you my room."

Jame followed Melissa, until they came to a door near the end of the hall. On the door was a beautiful rainbow, with white clouds on either end, drawn with pencil crayons. Underneath, in big golden block letters it read 'MELISSA'S ROOM.'

"Did you make that all by yourself?" asked Jame.

"Yes, I did," replied Melissa.

Melissa opened the door and they stepped inside.

For nearly a full minute, Jame was lost for words at the room's magnificence.

It was beauty like Jame had never seen before. The walls were painted pink and below that, there was a design of a beautiful field. By the wall was a bed with a yellow and pink striped bedspread. There was even a beautiful flowery smell in the air, which came from the flowers in Melissa's garden.

"This is absolutely gorgeous!" cried Jame at last.

"Isn't it," smiled Melissa.

Below the window was a wooden cupboard with two doors. On the floor, beside the cupboard, lay a cyberlock. The handle on this lock looked long enough to fit across both knobs.

Jame picked it up and examined it.

"This cyberlock is in perfect function," she stated. Jame examined the lock. "It doesn't appear to be cut or picked anywhere. Whoever did this must be a really clever, sneaky thief. How long have you had it?"

"I got it from my mum when I entered kindergarten," replied

Melissa. "She wanted to give it to me in advance, so I could get a feeling of how it works."

"How could any thief get past this without leaving the slightest marking it the lock?"

"I don't know," replied Melissa. "I want to know just as much as you do."

A few minutes later, Jame, Melissa and her parents went to get breakfast. Melissa had corn flakes just as usual. Jame had toast with jam.

"Have the police done an investigation on who this thief might be?" asked Melissa.

Melissa's mum turned a knob on the holoputer, and them news man appeared. This is what he said:

A BANDIT UNLEASHED

The Morning News warns about a mysterious case the police are trying to solve. On a trip to outer space which had been scheduled to run from the eve of February 19 to May 21, Tonya, the great Space Explorer, entrusted Melissa Maguire with the ERL (short for Enemy Repulsion Light, a device used to keep away the evil Space Wanderer Crazy Max), a Mindcoat, (which one uses to experience other peoples' minds, or see certain moments in their own life again) and Dome Clothes, (used to keep out Colodiggan Bullets, which, when they strike the victim, turns that victim into a Space Wanderer himself). However, on the morning of March 12, these devices had all disappeared from Melissa's bedroom. Police have done an investigation, but have discovered no evidence, except that someone has appeared to have taken a crowbar to the window. Some police are wondering if Tonya's inventions could have simply been beamed out of the Maguires' house and onto the thief's spaceship, with the thief leaving the crowbar marks, as a red herring.

The same appears to have happened to Jame Arden. Jame had stowed away on this same trip. However, after the trip, she had received a map of the treasure at the Earthlike planet Atwydolyn, home of the Grachas, the most popularly explored planet in the galaxy.

"The treasure," Tonya reports, "is being made to raise funds to repair damages on Atwydolyn, caused by the crashing of Captain Ing's spaceship, The Horizon. The wealthy Grachas are making the treasure, out of the Grachas' currency, latimus, to help the Grachas in need."

It seems, however, the treasure map, entrusted to Jame Arden, has been taken too.

The police were troubled again, by an event that took place the night after. Jame's house burned down. Although Jame was able to escape, she has lost her parents, Argus and Coliness Arden, and is now living with the Maguires. The police have examined the house that burned.

"It appears to have been burnt down, not by accident, but by arson," reports officer Dan. "Nobody has any clue who has done this. All we know is that the town is not safe anymore. We will still have space trips go on, and the people will try to go about their business as normally as usual."

The Morning News conclude that Earth may not be in as much jeopardy as it seems. If there is something that Crazy Max wants, it is most likely the treasure at Atwydolyn. Max is likely to leave the people on Earth and Space Explorers alone.

The hologram of the reporter disappeared.

"Arson!" Jame cried. "My house has been deliberately burned down by Crazy Max?"

"Whoever did it must have really wanted those inventions for something," replied Melissa.

"Crazy Max must have stolen them," cried Jame.

"It couldn't have been Crazy Max. He wouldn't be able to steal the ERL."

"Then it would have had to be someone working for him," Jame replied. "If I ever find out who this criminal is, I will seriously beat him to pieces!" Her face turned angry and bitter. "He killed my parents!" Jame stammered.

Mrs. Maguire turned to Jame. "We have installed some highly advanced, indestructible alarms to protect our house. After the burning of Jame's house, I had a feeling that, if we didn't act, ours might be next."

When bedtime came, Mrs. Maguire brought a mattress and a sleeping bag into Melissa's room. There was another room next door, but Jame felt she had to spend at least the first night sleeping in Melissa's room.

Then, the light was out, and their parents had left the room.

"Good night," whispered Melissa.

"Good night," Jame smiled back.

***

The next thing Jame knew, she was walking along a bleak landscape with no colour. It was black and white like an old photograph, silent too. There wasn't even the twitter of a bird to be heard. It was a plain landscape, silent, no colour, nothing but dusty ground and grey sky.

Then, Jame heard a woman's voice, her mother's. "Jame, our daughter. Our beloved child, help us."

Jame couldn't discern where the voice was coming from. She seemed to hear it just as clearly from all around her, but there was no one in sight.

"Jame," the voice continued. "We don't know where we are."

"Mum," Jame whispered, in a panicking tone, "dad. Is that you?"

"It's too late," the voice of her father wailed. "Jame, you will never see us again. We will never see you again. If only we had been kinder to you. If only we had loved you. Jame, hear us. We are sooorrrrrrrrryyyyyyyyyy!"

The voices stopped suddenly and instantly, and Jame was lost, again, in the black and white world.

"Mum!" Jame called. "Dad!"

Silence.

"Hello!" Jame called.

More silence.

Jame woke up crying.

"Jame," whispered Melissa softly.

"It's...it's," stuttered Jame.

"It's your parents," said Melissa.

"I know," replied Jame between sobs, "but they're gone. I'll never see them again. I...I'd rather be stuck inside my other house."

"Jame, you don't really mean that," soothed Melissa. "This is sometimes the way life is. It has its lumps and bumps and bad turns, but there are plenty of happy moments in life as well, and when you're sad, you will know that, sometime, it will pass."

"Melissa, have you ever lost a loved one to death?"

"I'm sure everybody has," Melissa smiled. "It's all part of life. My grandpa Richard, my mum's father, passed away when I was six. I was very close to him. He pushed me on the swings, bought me ice cream cones, played frisbee with me, played duets on the piano with me. He never grew weak or dependant. He passed away in his sleep; went to bed happy and healthy and never woke up. I was heartbroken; couldn't stop crying for days. My mother told me he had gone on to a special place, where there was no old age, pain, or suffering, and only pure happiness, and when I grew old, I would find my way there too."

"Where are my parents?" Jame wept. "They aren't in hell are they?"

"Jame, nobody can know that," Melissa whispered. "If you loved them and prayed for them, I think God would have had mercy on them."

Melissa sighed. "When I got the Mindcoat, I thought of using it to live my moments with grandpa Richard again, but I chose not to. I decided it was best to keep him in my heart and memory and get on with my own life. I'm still here and I need to be grateful, and it wouldn't be right to get lost in memories and forget why I'm here. I see him enough in our albums anyway, and sometimes I dream about him. He was a great man."

"I don't think I'll ever completely get over my parents' death."

"Maybe not," replied Melissa, "but at least you'll always have the things you're grateful for."

"What am I grateful for?" asked Jame, thinking about all the times she had got into trouble in her life with her parents; not to mention all the rough events she had both seen and suffered on Captain Ing's ship.

Melissa smiled. "Just think."

Jame thought. "I'm grateful to have met you. I feel that my life still wouldn't be very happy if you hadn't come along."

"Good," Melissa smiled again, her face becoming warmer and fuller still, "and that you became a great basketball player and that you had your parents."

"But they shouted at me. They shooed you out. You were there. What did they ever do to show they loved me?"

"They feared for you when you left on the ship," explained Melissa. "They helped you escape your burning house. I'm sure, under all their meanness, nastiness and thoughtlessness, they still loved you, deep deep down, and you still loved them, and you had to have loved them, or else you wouldn't be shedding the tears you are shedding now."

"It's true, Melissa. I did love my parents, but now they're gone forever." Jame burst into tears again.

"They will never be gone," soothed Melissa. "Not as long as you remember all the happy moments you had with them and in your life. They will never be gone as long as they are still in your heart and I know that they will always be in your heart, just like you will always be in mine and I will always be in yours."

"I will always remember my parents," said Jame finally beginning to smile.

"Good," whispered Melissa, her warm smile now dazzling.

Jame felt a warm feeling flow through her body and tears started forming in her eyes again, not of loss this time, but of pure happiness.

13 The Inter-Family Meeting

Jame awoke the next morning to the first faint morning light streaming into the room.

Jame looked at the clock on the wall. It was only quarter to seven, but she didn't feel tired enough to go back to sleep. The excitement of moving in with the Maguires had set off her body's sleep schedule. However, Jame didn't want to get up, either. The comfort of the mattress and the dimly-lit room was overwhelming.

She lay for another fifteen minutes, with her eyes closed, but her inner clock was already eager to get going for the day. When sleep didn't come, she decided to get up.

Jame opened the kitchen cupboard, took out a bowl and dumped a pile of corn flakes into it, poured on the milk and began eating.

As Jame ate her early breakfast, she glanced out the window. The sky looked a lot more morning-like and the horizon was golden. The birds were beginning to sing and the grass was dewy.

The windows of all the houses were all still dark, partly because it was so early and partly because it was a Saturday.

After Jame had her breakfast, she took her basketball, (which was luckily by the hoop outside when Jame's house had burned down), went across the field and shot some hoops. Jame was a bit rusty, but out of ten shots, she still got eight in.

At about half past eight, Jame decided to go back into the house.

When she arrived, Melissa and her parents were just getting up, the sun was well above the horizon and the windows in some of the other houses were lighting up as well.

"Good morning," smiled Mrs. Maguire as Jame entered. "You

must have got up bright and early this morning."

Jame smiled and nodded.

Mr. Maguire stepped into the hallway next. "How do you like living in this house now that you have had a full night to decide?" he asked.

"It's beautiful!" cried Jame. "I've never seen anything like it. You must be such a proud father, raising such an adorable daughter."

"My wife and I are very proud of Melissa. She's been the sweetest of the sweet her whole life; looked so happy and high-spirited the minute she was born. I can't wait to see what a delightful lady she will grow up to be."

"Good morning, Melissa," Jame smiled, as Melissa came out of her room last, fully dressed.

"Good morning, Jame."

That morning, Mrs. Maguire made Melissa and Jame pancakes for breakfast.

"Here we are," she smiled and set the plate of pancakes down on the table.

Melissa busied herself spreading maple syrup onto her pancakes, while Jame poured raspberry syrup onto hers.

"These are absolutely delicious," cried Jame after swallowing her first mouthful.

"Why thank you," smiled Mrs. Maguire. "It's a very old recipe that has been passed down through our family for many generations."

Their parents both sat themselves down at the table.

"Now girls," explained Mrs. Maguire. "Today, I was wondering if you two would like to go to Sunny Grove."

"Sunny Grove?" asked Jame. "What's that?"

"It's a beautiful place," explained Melissa. "You will absolutely love it."

"Really?" asked Jame. "Is it as nice as Atwydolyn?"

"I'd say almost as nice," answered Melissa.

The rest of the meal remained mostly silent, with four happy Maguires enjoying their breakfasts.

After they had finished, they all put their dirty dishes in the dishwasher.

"Shall we?" asked Mrs. Maguire.

"We shall!" exclaimed the dad. "Sunny Grove is not getting any sunnier."

Everybody headed down the stairs. Finally, they came to the landing and were just about to head out the door, when the mum made an announcement.

"Why don't we ride our bikes over? It's a very sunny day."

"I don't have a bike anymore," said Jame.

"You can ride my old one," explained the father.

"Thanks," said Jame.

It was a beautiful ride over. The sun was shining brightly, making the morning dew on the grass sparkle. The air was fresh and cool, nourishing all the beautiful spring flowers around. Melissa stayed beside with Jame the whole way, as the father rode up front.

"We're here!" he announced after about half an hour.

The four dismounted their bikes and locked them to nearby bike rack.

They started walking along a trail, surrounded by many varieties of trees and flowers.

"This really is beautiful," Jame smiled as she admired the scenery, "but I'd pick Atwydolyn any day."

"It's amazing what nature can do if you let it grow in peace," stated Melissa.

"It's a very wonderful piece of woods," replied Jame, "yet now that I have been to Atwydolyn, I can almost imagine a Gracha hopping out from somewhere."

Of course, a Gracha never did hop out from anywhere. The only time they ever did see something hop was one point in which a rabbit hopped across the trail a short distance ahead of them.

"How often do you come out here?" Jame asked Melissa.

"Fairly often, about once every few months."

"Oh, look at that," said the mum, softly.

Everybody stopped and looked in the direction that Mrs. Maguire was pointing.

Just a little ways up ahead, behind a willow tree, was a mother deer and her baby.

"They're beautiful," whispered Melissa.

For the next few minutes, George, Katrina, Jame and Melissa stood still and quiet, watching the two deer, until they walked away, out of sight, behind some bushes.

"It's wonderful to see animals in their natural habitat," Melissa whispered, as the two deer disappeared.

After the Maguires had continued to walk further along the grove, they stopped to look up at a few clouds. They were in thin wisps, near the top of the sky.

"Look at that," said Melissa, pointing to some other clouds in the sky, close to the horizon.

"It appears to be Captain Ing," exclaimed Jame, "and he appears to be standing next to his spaceship."

"Maybe he's waiting for us to come with him on his next space trip," said Melissa.

"Speaking of space trip," began the mum, "it's about time we should bead back. Captain Ing is planning another trip in space to protect the Grachas' treasure. Tiffany, Rick and their parents will be coming over at two o'clock to have a meeting with us to discuss what to do."

The four turned back on their trail and started heading back.

The Stolen Treasure

It was just as pleasant a walk back. A faint wind was blowing across a nearby pond, making small waves, with the sun sparkling on the surface. The wind was also making the new spring leaves in the trees swirl around, making a pleasant, soft, swishing sound.

Then, they mounted their bikes, and rode back home.

Upon arriving home, they hurried upstairs. Melissa took all of the clean dishes out of the dishwasher and sorted them into the cupboard.

After that, they all sat themselves down on the couch and the mum put on some flute music.

Soon, a knock sounded at the door.

Melissa jumped from the couch, ran down the stairs and answered it.

Standing on the other side of the door, Melissa found Tiffany and her mother.

"Welcome, Tiffany," smiled Melissa, "we will be talking right here in the living room. We have some juice and some chocolate chip cookies set up."

"Come in," called Melissa's father, "and make yourselves at home. I'm quite sure the thief is not sneaking about this house at the moment."

Tiffany and her mother settled themselves down in the living room with the Maguires.

"So it all comes down to this," said Tiffany's mother. "There has been a sneaky thief around and someone has burnt Jame's house down. The word has been going around. I don't like the feeling of this."

"Me neither," stated Tiffany. "I think my favourite shirt has also been stolen. The one with the colourful stripes on it. I can't seem to be able to find it."

"That's because it's in the laundry," replied Tiffany's mother.

Tiffany gave a bit of a silly sigh, and looked slightly embarrassed.

"Has anything gone missing from your house?" asked Melissa's mum.

"Not yet," replied Tiffany's mother.

Melissa thought that it would be obvious that Tiffany's house wouldn't have anything stolen from it. Melissa and Jame had been guarding space inventions that Tonya had given them, but Tiffany had nothing that would be of any interest to someone who would want to steal the Grachas' treasure.

"Has anything more gone missing from your house?" asked Tiffany's mum.

"No," replied Melissa's mother.

"There's nothing more that the thief would need," explained Jame, joining Melissa's thoughts. "Tonya gave Melissa and me the ERL, the Mindcoat, the Dome Clothes and the treasure map. There wouldn't be anything else he would want to steal."

At that moment, there was another knock at the door.

"I'll answer that," exclaimed Melissa.

She ran to the door and opened it up. Jame and Tiffany followed her.

On the other side of the door was a broad faced woman, with curly brown hair and brown eyes. Her body had a fairly thin build. She was wearing grey pants with a light green T-shirt, with white polka-dots on it.

Beside her was a very handsome man, who was slightly taller. He had dark grey hair, brown eyes.

Their son, Rick, was standing in between them.

"Hi Rick; come in," Melissa smiled. "The meeting is all in the living room."

"Hi," Jame cried. "We are just starting."

The Stolen Treasure

"A pleasure to meet you," he replied, with a broad smiled. "How is it going, Jame. Melissa has told me all about you. I hear you're a basketball player."

"I'm a great basketball player," Jame smiled back casually, as though trying her hardest not to sound like she was bragging. "So far, things are going great in this new house."

"Tiffany," Rick smiled. "It is a pleasure to meet you again."

Rick held out his hand and shook hands with Tiffany and Tiffany let out a small, shy, "Hi."

Melissa's mother strode over to the top of the stairwell. "Come in Rick," she smiled, "and get yourself good and comfy in our living room."

Rick settled himself on a couch in the living room with Melissa.

"I suppose you have heard all about the nasty treasure thief Rick," began Mrs. Sterlsvern.

"I certainly have," he replied. "Melissa here has told me all about it," Rick beamed.

"This is bad," cried Tiffany's mother. "There is some nasty plan this thief has. I don't know what it is, but it is something that must be stopped."

"And what do you plan to do about it?" asked Melissa's mother. "Go back out to space to where this thief may be? Are you sure that would be safe?"

"Look Katrina," explained Tiffany's mother, picking up a cookie. "It is no more dangerous out in space than it is here. Evidently, the thief burned down Jame's house after he stole from it. Might he not try to burn down your house next, Katrina? Crazy Max could come to Earth himself with Melissa and Jame being here. I couldn't bear to imagine what would happen then."

"We have installed micro-alarms," explained Melissa's mother.

"They are much smaller and much more durable than the alarms we had before. The very second anyone suspicious comes near the house, we will be alerted and the police will be notified. Our new alarms were highly advanced and cost us a fortune, but my family's safety comes first. I told Jame about them yesterday."

"Excuse me," Melissa said to Tiffany's mother.

"Yes, Miss Maguire," she replied.

"I first received the treasure map from Tonya. It showed where the treasure was and explained why the Grachas were making the treasure. We believe the treasure is what the thief is really after."

"A treasure?" cried Mrs. Sterlsvern and Mr. Harrison.

"Yes," replied Melissa. "Houses at Atwydolyn have been destroyed by The Horizon. This treasure is a fund."

"The other Space Explorers can stop the treasure from being stolen," explained Melissa's father. "If we stay on Earth, there's nothing we need to worry about."

"George, don't you understand?" cried Rick's mother. "It goes deeper than this. The Grachas need this treasure."

Melissa spoke up again. "We are the Grachas' friends," she explained. "It is up to us to help them find their treasure."

"It was I who took the controls of The Horizon," explained Jame. "I crashed the ship into Atwydolyn and destroyed the Grachas' houses. I consider myself entirely responsible for the damage."

There was about ten seconds of silence here, in which the room held its breath and everybody seemed to be in deep thought.

"Another space trip has been planned," explained Tiffany's mother. "The Horizon will be arriving in a couple of days."

"Jame," said Tiffany, "I want to come on the next space trip. I want to see what all these mysterious planets are like and these creatures and people who live on them, rather than study them at school while the trip goes on."

The Stolen Treasure

Tiffany's mother smiled. "We would be very happy to sign you up."

"Hold on a minute," exclaimed Melissa's mother. "With this thief, it could be dangerous."

"I don't know about hat," Tiffany's mother explained. "From what I have heard, Captain Ing has a security robot who also works as his Doctor so that everyone aboard The Horizon will be protected."

"Please," begged Jame, "the Grachas need our help. It would be the least we could do to find who is trying to steal their treasure."

There was a long pause. For a moment, the room was so silent, even Melissa's mother's thoughts could almost be heard.

"All right," said Melissa's mother at last. "I see Mrs. Sterlsvern's point. It really is no safer here than it is in outer space. You'd better start getting ready, Mel."

"If there is anything I could do," smiled Tiffany to Jame, "I will come with you. I want to see what it is like on these exotic planets, along with the fact that you are my friend and I would do anything I can to keep you company."

"I'll see you on the day of the trip, then," Jame smiled to Tiffany.

"That's it," announced Mrs. Sterlsvern, finally seeming satisfied. "The plan has been made. Tiffany, we should head home. It would be a good idea to start getting packed."

"Bye, then," smiled Melissa's mother, as Tiffany and her mum headed out the door.

"Bye!" shouted Jame. "It was nice to see you."

***

That evening, Mrs. Maguire checked on Melissa who was in her room, packing.

"So," smiled Melissa's mother. "Have you got together all your stuff?"

"Yes," replied Melissa.

"Your pillow? Extra clothes?"

"Yes; I have also packed my pyjamas, some books, my toothbrush and some games."

"Excellent," smiled her mother. "Sounds like you're all set then." She turned her head from Melissa's packing bag to Jame's. They both appeared to be very full.

"I'm going to the living room to read," explained Melissa.

When Melissa entered her room, she saw the lock to her cupboard on the floor. She walked toward the lock and picked it up.

"I think I'll take this with me too," she thought. "Maybe Captain Ing, or the rest of the crew, will know how the thief got past this lock and figure out how they stole everything."

Melissa opened up her packing bag and slipped the lock in too.

"Now, I'm really ready," she told her mother.

14 Aboard The Horizon

A steady stream of students rushed out of the classroom as Melissa joined Rick.

"Jame's friend Tiffany will be coming on this trip," explained Melissa.

"Jame? The poor child. I've heard the girl's life is hard enough as it is. It must be one of the most confusing things in the world living with parents that treat her like garbage. Then, they die and she gets moved to a caring family." Rick paused. "At least she still has you Melissa," he smiled.

"Yes," Melissa smiled, "and Tiffany. From the little I have seen of Tiffany, she seems to like Jame an awful lot. It's funny though; I have always wanted a younger brother or sister. I asked my parents about three years ago, but they said that it would be too much of a responsibility."

"Good," smiled Rick, "I have always been very proud of your attitude and I'm sure your parents are too. Well, bye, Melissa. I have to head home now. I'll see you on the space trip."

"I'll see you too," called Melissa, as they parted.

Melissa opened the gate of her backyard, walked across the yard and into the house.

"Hello Melissa!" called the voice of Mrs. Maguire, from the top of the stairs. "Are you all ready to leave for the spaceport?"

"Yes," replied Melissa.

"Good," said Melissa's mother. "The Horizon should be arriving at the Grand Lodge Spaceport in about an hour."

The next person Melissa saw was Jame. Jame stepped out of her room, (the one right next to Melissa's) and down the hallway.

"So, how was school?" she asked Melissa.

"It was just fine," Melissa answered. "At the end of the day, the teacher told the class about how Captain Ing had changed his mind and decided to go on with the rest of the trip. How was your day?"

"It was quite good," answered Jame. "I got a B on my science test."

"Hello there," called the voice of the dad as he stepped out of his room. "Are you all good and excited, my dear?" he asked turning to Melissa.

"I certainly am," cried Melissa. "This trip should be fun."

"We should go," said Mrs. Maguire. "We don't want to keep Captain Ing waiting. Are you two all ready?"

"Yes!" shouted the voices of Melissa and Jame.

"Good," said the dad. "I guess we are ready then."

Melissa and Jame grabbed their bags and headed down the stairs, then outside.

They loaded their bags into the back of a car which Melissa's parents had sent for and departed.

It was a long drive to the Grand Lodge Spaceport. On the way, Melissa watched the scenery flash past. The car drove through woods, farmers' fields and towns.

"You know what?" asked Melissa as they drove along. "When you think about it, we are in space all the time."

Her mother smiled. "You are absolutely right about that."

"We just don't think about it that way because we are so used to being on Earth," Melissa continued, "but all the planets and stars are surrounded by space, and Earth is another one of those planets. I'm sure this would seem like outer space to Captain Ing."

"Atwydolyn is a lot like Earth," smiled Jame. "I think people could live there, as well as here."

"But if humans lived on it, it would become dirty and polluted just like Earth," said Melissa. "I like Atwydolyn the way it is."

Jame thought for a minute. "I suppose you're right."

Finally, the car stopped.

"Here is the Grand Lodge Spaceport," stated the father. He looked at his watch. "The ship should be arriving in about five minutes. Looks like we timed getting here just right."

Melissa and Jame stepped out of the car.

"Where are you going?" asked Mr. Maguire.

"To see if Captain Ing's spaceship is coming yet," replied Melissa.

But when they looked in the sky, there wasn't the faintest speck to be seen.

A couple of minutes later, a red car drove into sight.

"Tiffany!" Jame cried, as the car pulled up next to the Maguires.

"Are you ready for your first space trip?" Jame asked Tiffany immediately when she was outside of the car.

"Are you kidding?" she replied. "I'm dying to see all these amazing new planets. Hey look."

Tiffany was pointing up into the sky.

Jame looked up to where Tiffany was pointing and saw a tiny black dot.

"That must be Captain Ing's spaceship!" Jame cried. "I think he's coming at last. We're going to be in space soon."

At that moment, a blue car pulled up.

"Rick!" cried Melissa, as the car parked on the other side of where the Maguires were.

Rick opened the door and stepped out.

"Melissa!" he cried. "It's wonderful to see you."

"It's wonderful to see you too Rick."

"Look!" he cried. "The ship is nearly here."

When Melissa looked up into the sky, she couldn't understand how she hadn't noticed it since Tiffany had pointed it out. The black speck had transformed into the outline of a ship.

"It's getting really close," stated Rick's mother.

Everybody's eyes were focused on the ship. "It's going to land!" cried Tiffany.

Seconds after she had said this, the ship settled down onto the spaceport and out stepped the Captain.

"Greetings," he called out to the three families.

"Greetings," everybody answered back.

"You must be Captain Ing," exclaimed Tiffany. "I have been so anxious to meet you."

"I am indeed Captain Ing," he smiled back. "I suppose you are all looking forward to a wonderful trip in space."

Melissa and Jame both grabbed their bags out of the car.

"Have a good time," whispered Mrs. Maguire, pulling Melissa and Jame into a big hug and kissing them both on the cheeks. "I'll see you in a couple of months."

Melissa and Jame glanced over and saw Tiffany and Rick's parents giving their farewells.

Melissa, Jame, Tiffany and Rick all walked together into the ship, as they watched all the cars drive away.

"At least you're not so hard pressed rushing into the ship this time," Tiffany stated as they stepped up the staircase leading into the ship.

Jame let out a soft giggle. "Let's just say that I'm not in huge trouble this time," she answered back.

When everyone had reached the top of the stairs, Tiffany was speechless at what she saw in front of her. They were all in a room filled with machines and computers. On the floor were plenty of chairs.

The Stolen Treasure

"Captain Ing?" asked Rick, "where are the crew?"

"They're at their stations, getting the controls ready for the trip," replied Captain Ing. "They will be along in just a few minutes. I assure you they will be the exact same people as on the last trip."

The topic was suddenly changed by the sound of many feet coming closer.

"That will be the crew," announced Captain Ing. Surely enough, the Ensign, Lieutenant, Engineer and Doctor appeared in the Bridge.

"Good to see you again," Captain Ing smiled to them all. "Tiffany, let me introduce to you to our robot Doctor Eric, our Engineer Len, Lieutenant Linda and Ensign Lucy. Everybody; this is Tiffany Sterlsvern, a new passenger on this ship."

"I am pleased to meet you all," smiled Tiffany, giving a slight bow.

Captain Ing clapped his hands. "Everyone back to your stations!" he called.

Everyone departed down various corridors of the ship, except Captain Ing, who walked up to the end the centre of the Bridge and started pressing some buttons.

The ship started to rise off the ground slowly; then coasted low for a few seconds. Then, it blasted away.

They were in space!

15 A Threat Brought Back

A few minutes after they had blasted off, Jame showed Captain Ing's board of space chess to Tiffany and asked her if she would like to have a game.

"That sounds awesome!" Tiffany exclaimed. "What's that? Are the pieces space objects or something?"

"They are indeed," Jame beamed.

"Cool! Certainly, I will play you a game!"

As Tiffany sat down, Jame told her what each piece was, and they started to play.

"Commander Finks is coming!" Captain Ing announced.

Tiffany and Jame stopped their game of Space Chess, Rick stopped trying to solve a scrambled picture puzzle, Melissa put a book she was reading and everybody turned their heads toward the door.

"Mandy?" asked Jame, "do you or Captain Ing have any idea who is trying to steal the Grachas' treasure?"

"I do know," Mandy replied, "a terribly vicious monster by the name of Alcarsh. I have been doing all I can to catch him and stop the treasure from being stolen."

"Alcarsh!" cried Jame. "Is he the one who set my house on fire and stole all of Tonya's devices?"

"That's what we understand," replied the Commander. "I'll show you more about him at dinner."

"So what's so fascinating about this Commander, or Commandress I should say?" asked Tiffany.

"Call me Commander," smiled Mandy Finks. "It's more formal."

"I met Mandy here when she had heard about me and came to

visit me on my ship about three years ago," explained Captain Ing. "I could immediately tell, by her uniform, that she was a Latimus Prospector. She showed me her talents and almost immediately, we became friends."

"Surely, you don't prospect for Latimus in that uniform!" exclaimed Tiffany.

"This?" she asked, "Oh no, I made this myself. I am good at making clothes and cooking. I even made my own Prospector's shoes. They make us stand tall so we're important. I'm very talented."

"Just you wait until supper," smiled Captain Ing. "You won't believe what delicious food she can cook."

Tiffany figured, being the new passenger on the ship, it would be formidable to introduce herself. "My name is Tiffany," she explained, as she stepped forward, "and I am Jame's best friend. I am sixteen years old and new to this ship."

"So I understand," stated the Commander, "but you will know your way around here in no time after a bit of exploring and that will start right now. Come on. I'm going to show you around."

"Wait!" exclaimed Captain Ing. "Here is your zapshot. I recharged it after it burned out."

"Thank you, Captain Ing," she smiled, as he handed her her zapshot.

Mandy's expression turned forlorn.

"What is it?" asked Captain Ing. "What is the matter?"

"Oh, nothing," she replied. "Nothing."

Mandy smiled again and stood up confidently.

"Good," smiled Captain Ing. "I think that will do. Come on everyone. Let's get supper. I'm starving."

They all departed from The Lounge and hurried into the kitchen.

When they had arrived in the kitchen, the Commander reached into the oven and pulled out a rich, juicy steak.

Captain Ing started scooping mashed potatoes onto everybody's plate, while the Commander poured gravy on the potatoes and set everyone's plate with some spaghetti.

Then, she took a large plastic juice container from the shelf, which contained a purple liquid.

"What's that?" asked Rick.

"This?" asked Mandy. "It's Ulbarberry juice. It's a kind of berry from Atwydolyn. It has a lot of vitamins."

She poured some into everybody's glasses one by one.

Rick took a small sip of his. It tasted sort-of sour, but after he had swallowed it, it left behind a sweet aftertaste.

"Let's eat," said Captain Ing as he sat down.

They all dug into their food, which was very well cooked. The meat as very tender and chewy and the mashed potatoes melted in their mouths.

"This is a very delicious dinner," Melissa smiled to Captain Ing and Mandy.

"Thank-you," Captain Ing smiled back.

"Captain Ing?" asked Jame. "Can you show us more about Alcarsh?"

"Certainly," replied Captain Ing. He stood up, walked to a screen that was hanging on the wall and turned it on. A man's face appeared.

"This is Joseph John Obelston, one of my companions on my planet," the Captain explained. "He will tell us about Alcarsh." Joseph John began speaking:

A Threat Brought Back

Captain Ing's Company and other spacemen grow panicked

about something that has been forgotten for five years. The evil monster Alcarsh, (meaning 'Ravenous Beast,' in Gracha tongue) has returned.

Alcarsh was first ever seen after wickedly devouring Robert Noin, (pronounced No-in), who was one of history's greatest Space Explorers. Mr. Noin's remains were discovered in the woods on planet Earth by Detective Freefall, an inhabitant of Arshga, and close friend to Captain Ing himself. Since that day, Alcarsh has never been seen again, up until now.

"Detective Freefall, Samantha, and I saw him again on March 12 at 04:17, mountain time on Earth, carrying the ERL, (Enemy Repulsion Light) a device used for blasting away Crazy Max," reported Joseph John Obelston, one of Captain Ing's companions. "Nobody knows where he was taking it, but what we do know is that the Space Explorer Tonya left it with Melissa Emily Maguire, an eleven-year-old female human. We suspect that Alcarsh wants to steal the Grachas' Latimus fund at Atwydolyn. Freefall tried to arrest him, but unfortunately the monster escaped."

"The Grachas' treasure has been safe, until Alcarsh told Crazy Max about it," reported Latimus Prospector, and ship Commander, Mandy Finks, to us and her fellow Prospectors. "We have been taking extreme measures to make sure Crazy Max can't detect it, but now that this evil beast has let the secret out, the treasure is no longer safe."

In the meantime, however, all explorers must use caution, while Space Explorer Captain Ing, the Latimus Prospectors and ourselves try to arrest Alcarsh and keep him under control, so he can no longer hurt anyone, or rob the Grachas.

On the top left of the screen was an icon of what did indeed look like a ferocious monster. It was all covered in thick death-black hair. In its mouth were nasty, sharp fangs and it had blood-red eyes.

Captain Ing turned the news off and everyone looked at him.

"Alcarsh!" cried Jame. "I wonder why the news back on Earth never mentioned anything about him."

"I wanted to show you," explained Captain Ing, "but I thought it wasn't time yet. I didn't think it would be right to show you more bad news, when your life was so full of terrible events already. You didn't need one extra thing to worry about."

"You have a group of companions who are trying to help imprison Alcarsh?" asked Tiffany, "and make sure we're safe from him?"

"I certainly do," smiled Captain Ing. "Detective Freefall is leading them at the moment. He always knows what to do."

"Could we see these companions of yours sometime?" asked Tiffany.

"Maybe later in the trip. Right now, is a time for us to get used to my ship and get you settled."

After everyone had finished their supper, Commander Finks strode back to the oven and pulled out a pie.

"This is Ambleberry pie," she explained. "It's a berry from Arshga. I made it myself."

Mandy set the pie down on the table, while Captain Ing took out a knife from the drawer and started to cut it.

This pie had a bright red filling that made it look a lot like cherry pie.

Captain Ing and Mandy started serving everybody their pieces. After everybody had been served, they took their first fork-full.

The pie tasted very sweet, like a cross between cherries and strawberries. When they were done, they slipped their dishes into Captain Ing's dishwasher.

"Just as I demonstrated," smiled Captain Ing. "Click the switch and slip the dishes in the left slot."

Everybody ran up to the machine and Jame turned it on.

Immediately, the sound of the motor came on and, one by one, everybody (except the Doctor who didn't eat being a robot) started slipping their dishes into the dishwasher:

First Tiffany, then Jame, then Melissa, Rick, Engineer Len, Lieutenant Linda, Ensign Lucy, Commander Mandy and finally Captain Ing.

For a couple of minutes, everyone listened as the water swished inside, with an occasional 'clink,' from the plates and cutlery.

Finally, bit by bit, it started coming out the other side, cleaner and shinier than a diamond.

Everyone started placing the plates back into the cupboard and hanging the cups by their handles on their hooks, coming from the ceiling of the bottom shelf.

"Wow!" cried Tiffany. "That dishwasher is so cool. I wish the one at our house did that."

"I'm sure your family would find that very fascinating indeed," smiled Captain Ing, "but I'm sure your kitchen is not big enough. Now," he yawned. "I think it is about time for bed. The Commander and I have installed cameras that will watch the ship for Alcarsh."

It was only eight o'clock, but it had been a long day and everyone was tired.

They departed from the kitchen and headed up the staircase to their sleeping quarters.

When they had reached the two doors, everybody watched as Mandy led the rest of the crew into their bedroom.

Then, Tiffany, Jame, Melissa followed the Commander into their room, and Rick followed the Captain into his.

"Tiffany," the Commander announced. "I need to give you your bed. There are only three beds in this room, and, since you're new, I need to give you yours."

"How are you going to do that?" asked Tiffany puzzled.

"I will show you," smiled Commander Mandy.

Mandy pushed the button on the wall that Captain Ing had pushed when he gave Jame her bed. The same thing happened, and Tiffany's bed appeared on the other side of the wall.

Tiffany stood amazed.

"Oh my goodness! I have never seen anything like that!"

"Who wants to use the washroom first?" asked Jame.

"You can," replied Tiffany.

"No," objected Jame. "I'm in no big hurry. Would you like to get ready first, Melissa?"

"Not unless somebody else wants to go," she replied.

"No, you go," came the voices of everybody else.

So Melissa grabbed her pink pyjamas, toothpaste and toothbrush and her yellow towel (pink and yellow were Melissa's favourite colours) and disappeared into the bathroom. Sounds of brushing teeth and showering came from inside the door. Soon, Melissa stepped out of the bathroom, clean, in her pyjamas and ready for bed.

"I'll go next," said the Commander and disappeared behind the door.

Melissa sat down on her bed and peered out the starry window.

"How are you liking this space trip so far, Tiffany?" asked Melissa.

"I think it's great," she answered back. "I never knew this ship would have so many surprises. I love surprises."

"Wait until you see the bathroom then," smiled Melissa. "It's really cool."

"Really?" asked Tiffany. "Then I guess I'll get my fair share of surprises for the day."

A few minutes later, the Commander stepped out of the bathroom, in her dark purple pyjamas, covered in planets.

The door opened and shut and before everybody knew it, Tiffany was the one inside.

There were a couple of minutes of silence before they heard Tiffany's voice again.

"Wow! This is really cool. Look at all these toothpastes."

Mandy chuckled as Tiffany said this.

"I'm glad she's having a good time," grinned Commander Mandy.

Soon, Tiffany was also out of the bathroom.

"Wow!" she cried. "You won't believe what's in there. I never knew they had ambleberry and ulbarberry flavoured toothpaste."

"I have lots of flavours of toothpaste. I formed them all myself," smiled the Commander.

"I'll go next," said Jame.

She shut herself behind the door and started to get ready for bed.

Several minutes later, she stepped out in purple pyjamas.

"You're right Tiffany," Jame smiled. "I picked the grape toothpaste and soap."

Finally, everyone climbed into their beds.

Melissa clicked the light switch beside her bed and a soft comfortable darkness filled the room.

"Good night," she whispered to everybody.

"Good night," they all answered back.

Everybody curled up in their bedspread and slept.

Tiffany stayed awake for a few minutes with her warm bedspread making her as comfortable as she could ever wish for. She was truly happy now. She just knew that this was going to be a great space trip.

16 The Mind Deck

"So how was your night?" Captain Ing asked his new passenger at breakfast. "How do you like your room?"

"It's just great," replied the Tiffany. "There's plenty of space and the beds are soft and cosy."

Everyone dug into their breakfasts, which was just as delicious as yesterday evening's supper.

The eggs were rich and creamy and the bacon was crunchy and juicy.

"Mandy," smiled Captain Ing. "These are really good."

"Thank you," she replied. "I am very proud of my talents."

When breakfast was finished, they cleared the table and slipped the dishes through the dishwasher.

As they were putting the dishes away, Captain Ing began to speak.

"We should go over to Atwydolyn and check on the treasure," he explained.

"What treasure?" asked Rick.

Then, he remembered. "Oh, the Grachas' treasure."

He had been so focussed on getting used to the ship that he had completely forgotten about the main reason they had gone.

"But Captain Ing?" asked Jame. "How are you going to know where to land? We don't have the map."

"I remember where the ship crashed," he replied. "I know exactly where to land."

"What? Atwydolyn?" exclaimed Tiffany. "You mean the beautiful planet Jame keeps telling me about?"

"Yes, that's the one," said Captain Ing, "and I suggest we get over there before more time runs out. Come on. Let's head off to

The Lounge."

Captain Ing busied himself pressing buttons, clicking switches and moving the controls, just as he did yesterday.

"Jame!" called Tiffany. "Let's finish our game."

Jame joined Tiffany at the table and they continued the game of Space Chess they had started the day before.

Melissa and Rick looked out the window of the ship and watched all the stars drifting by.

"Aren't they beautiful?" whispered Melissa.

"They certainly are," said Rick. "You can see a lot more of them when you're aboard a ship. They don't get blurred by the atmosphere."

"I don't know," Melissa replied. "Sometimes, it may be better to see less. You can see a lot more shapes and pictures in them that way. My parents have taken me out stargazing since I was about four years old. They try to show me the constellations, but I could never really understand them. I like to try and make up my own instead."

"What did you see when you looked at the constellations with you parents?" asked Rick.

"There's Floris, the daffodil," began Melissa.

"Floris," said Rick. "That's a beautiful name for a constellation."

"Thank you very much," replied Melissa.

"Have you discovered any other constellations?" Rick asked.

"I have named more. There is Hoppy the rabbit and Astron, the spaceship."

"A spaceship?" asked Rick. "Does it look anything like The Horizon?"

"Now that I have seen Captain Ing's ship, it does sort-of, a bit."

"Melissa," smiled Rick. "You have an amazing imagination."

"Checkmate!" exclaimed Tiffany from across the room.

"You got me," smiled Jame.

When Melissa and Rick looked at the Space Chess board, they saw Jame's sun on the side of the board trapped by Tiffany's moon, which would be in danger of the comet if the sun took the moon.

"Glad to see you're enjoying that game," beamed Captain Ing at the two friends.

"Captain Ing," explained the Commander. "I do believe Atwydolyn is coming up."

As the planet drew nearer, Captain Ing pressed a black button on the control board. Before everybody knew it, the ship landed.

"Everybody out!" called Captain Ing.

As everyone headed out of the ship, Tiffany stopped at the sight of some purple berries.

"Are these Ulbarberries?" she asked.

They were spherical and about the size of grapes.

"They certainly are," replied Captain Ing. "They are the exact berries our juice was made from at supper."

"Cool!" Tiffany smiled. "Can I taste them?"

"I'm sure you could, but they don't taste very good raw."

Tiffany picked a berry off and popped it into her mouth, but it tasted terrible and she spat it out.

"Captain Ing," continued Tiffany. "Where are the Grachas?"

"They're probably near the treasure. Tiffany, tell me what you see."

Tiffany looked ahead.

"There's a large object," she observed.

"That's the treasure!" cried Jame. "I recognize those trees. They were in Tonya's map."

They continued to walk the rest of the way to the treasure, and when they reached it, they found it was a stone chest.

"Looks like the Grachas' treasure is safe after all," observed

The Stolen Treasure

Jame.

"I wouldn't be too sure of that," corrected Captain Ing. "Alcarsh is probably waiting for the right moment to come after it. He wants us to think it's safe first."

One of the Grachas hissed suspiciously as the crew and passengers stared at the splendour.

"It's okay," soothed Melissa. "Were not going to hurt you. We're friends."

But the Gracha continued to hiss all the same.

"I don't think he understands English," explained Rick.

"Do these Grachas always guard the treasure?" continued Rick, as he turned to face the Captain.

"Whenever the Grachas are not using the treasure, they shut it and it can only be opened with a password."

"Look at that!" cried Jame, looking just over to her right.

It was the broken down Gracha houses that The Horizon had struck.

"If The Horizon hadn't struck those houses, it wouldn't have been for the treasure, and if it hadn't been for the treasure, Alcarsh would have never stolen Tonya's inventions."

"All we can do is keep our eyes on the treasure," explained Captain Ing. "Blaming circumstances beyond our control is not going to do us any good."

"Are these coins really Latimus?" asked Tiffany, admiring the treasure.

"They certainly are," replied Mandy. "It's what I and my fellow Prospectors mine for. Isn't it beautiful?"

"It certainly is," beamed Tiffany. "I've seen my mother's 24-carat golden wedding ring, but his stuff appears priceless."

Captain Ing looked up from Jame and glanced over at everybody else.

"We had better head back to our ship," he told his passengers and crew. "We can't stay on Atwydolyn forever."

As Captain Ing led everyone back to the ship, the distant silhouette of the ship looked like a tower against the clear blue sky. About halfway back to the ship, Rick suddenly stopped walking.

"Captain Ing?" he asked. "Have you ever considered why this monster is after the treasure?"

"All that space monsters ever concern themselves with is money and wealth and Latimus has been known to have healing powers."

"Healing powers? Has he been wounded?"

"I don't know, but I'm sure he has been in lots of fights."

Rick was skeptical though. He knew it went deeper than this.

They returned to the ship about five minutes later, and made their way up the staircase leading inside, which shut after they had reached The Bridge.

After they had arrived in the Bridge, Captain Ing started pressing the usual buttons.

Things happened much the same as they had just yesterday. The ship rose off the ground first before blasting away.

Captain Ing turned to his passengers and crew.

"Come on, everyone," he smiled as he clapped his hands. "There is a part of the ship that I haven't shown any of you yet, that I thought I might save for later. Follow me."

Captain Ing led everyone out of the Bridge, as the Commander rose from her table to join Captain Ing. They walked along the same corridors as yesterday. The Captain, crew and passengers headed up the staircase, along the hallway, where the crew's rooms were located, turned left along the hall where the passengers' rooms were located, and stopped at the end. Everybody stood puzzled, for, at the end of the hallway, was nothing more than a blank wall.

"Everybody stand back!" the Captain called as he pushed on the wall.

To everyone's astonishment, the wall fell forward to reveal a dark room with nothing inside.

"What is that?" cried Tiffany as she stared into the room.

"This?" asked Captain Ing. "It is my Mind Deck."

"What is a Mind Deck?" asked Tiffany in a confused voice.

"I will show you in a minute," beamed Captain Ing as he walked down the ramp that used to be the wall and into the darkness leading everyone inside.

"Wow!" exclaimed Tiffany. "I never knew I would be walking along a wall in my life."

After they were all inside, the ramp rose and shut back into the wall it had been, leaving everyone inside in total darkness.

"Captain Ing," inquired Rick. "What are we supposed to do now that we are standing here as though all our eyes are shut?"

Captain Ing gave a slight laugh before he spoke again.

"Think and imagine," he explained.

"Think of what?" Rick asked.

"Whatever you want," Captain Ing explained, "and it will appear in this deck. On this deck, all you have to do is think of what you want and the computers will create it. You will notice, here, that the images projected are not tangible, but when you are finished, all you have to do is clap your hands and you will all notice something very fascinating about how the images disappear."

Melissa closed her eyes and started thinking of the wonderful meadow where the treasure was situated on Atwydolyn, but nothing happened.

"Captain Ing," she explained. "Nothing is happening."

"Oh, so sorry. I haven't turned it on yet."

Nobody could see what Captain Ing was doing in the pitch

darkness, but there were a few seconds of a cracking sound and before everybody knew it, a faint green light was shining from Captain Ing's fingernails.

"Cool!" everyone cried.

With the light projected from Captain Ing's fingernails, everyone could see a green button on the wall.

Captain Ing pressed the button, but nothing appeared to happen.

It was only when Melissa closed her eyes and thought for the second time, that things really started appearing.

At once, a bright and brilliant view of Atwydolyn, so dazzling that everyone had to squint for a few seconds appeared in the room.

"It's amazing what you can do with sophisticated technology," stated Rick.

The only tangible part of the projection, however, was the ground and even though it looked like an earthy surface, it still had the feeling and texture of the metal floor of the deck.

"Look!" cried Tiffany. "A gough of Grachas."

She ran up to them, just as she had tried to do at Atwydolyn, but these ones didn't seem to notice her, nor any of the others, for that matter. These Grachas just stood there, guarding their treasure, some keeping close watch on the chest, with others gazing up into the sky to see if there was anything suspicious coming.

Tiffany tried to lean herself against a nearby tree, but fell over onto the ground, her body passing right through it.

"Remember what I said," Captain Ing reminded her. "The images are transparent to the real objects."

"Aren't you going to make them tangible?" asked Tiffany.

"Maybe," replied Captain Ing, "but I have had other priorities."

At that moment, however, Tiffany closed her eyes, while immediately, a fair distance from them, Atwydolyn ended to show the schoolyard at Tiffany and Jame's school, where they always liked to

The Stolen Treasure

hang out.

They both ran across the last bit of Atwydolyn ground toward their school ground with Captain Ing and the others behind.

It was fascinating that a straight line divided Atwydolyn from the schoolyard, and, when Tiffany and Jame stepped across this line, they could see Atwydolyn just behind them.

Just ahead was Tiffany and Jame's favourite hangout spot. They both broke into a run for their corner. Jame arrived first, just before Tiffany.

As Jame sat down next to Tiffany, she peered around at the students walking around outside the school, who didn't seem to be paying any attention to the landscape of Atwydolyn just beyond them.

"The Grand Lodge Spaceport is somewhere way off over there," smiled Jame, as she peered over her shoulder just behind the school.

The scene suddenly became even more complex, for just to the left of he school, the schoolyard and Atwydolyn ended to show a dusty, red surface that looked a lot like Mars.

"Is this your planet, Arshga?" cried Tiffany, facing the Captain.

"It certainly is," smiled Captain Ing.

Tiffany and Jame both ran from their corner by the school and onto the new alien landscape on which Captain Ing lived.

"This certainly is an amazing invention, Captain Ing," continued Rick. "When did you invent it?"

"I installed it a couple of Earth years ago," replied Captain Ing. "I wanted an easy way to express my thoughts and see other planets more conveniently and quickly, so I installed this Mind Deck."

"It's wonderful!" cried Rick. "Can you close your eyes now and imagine all these amazing friends of yours?"

"Not now," explained Captain Ing. "I want to show them to you in person when I am ready. You will see them when I think the time is right."

Captain Ing gazed around him at the three images they had created, and the lines which divided them. The point in which Earth and Atwydolyn stopped to show Arshga was where all three surfaces met.

"It is time to go back to The Lounge," explained Captain Ing, looking around at all the others. "I think we have about had enough experience with this deck by now. Remember what I said earlier. All you need to do is clap your hands."

Everybody clapped their hands, pretty well in unison and the most amazing thing began to happen.

The scenes from all around them suddenly whirled away and disappeared into each person's head, as though being sucked into a black hole.

"Wow!" everyone cried, except Captain Ing who was obviously used to this sort of phenomenon.

Jet-black darkness immediately replaced the brightness of the scenes that had been there before.

The wall that led into the deck opened, to show the hall which contained the sleeping quarters, shining some light into the deck.

"This way!" Captain Ing called and everyone followed him back up the ramp that led into the Mind Deck.

"That was indeed the most fascinating experience in my life," Rick beamed as the wall shut behind them, looking as much as an ordinary wall as it had before.

He wondered what other surprises this trip might bring as he followed Captain Ing back to The Lounge.

The Stolen Treasure

17 A Monster in the Night

Jame had another nightmare that night. She was back on Atwydolyn, but the sun wasn't bright or beautiful this time. Instead of the pleasant warmth it usually brought, it felt petrified and icy and in place of its golden sunlight, it cast long, dark and spooky shadows and the light it cast was red as blood. The air also had a dead and decaying stench in it.

Jame turned her shaking body around in every direction in the hope of finding The Horizon to get her away from this spooky place, but the ship was nowhere in sight.

Jame looked forward and saw the Grachas' treasure, only, this time, it was in the shape of a coffin.

The Grachas guarding it didn't look like ordinary Grachas either. Instead, their fur was black and their eyes were red, like the picture of Alcarsh in Tonya's and Mandy's newsfeeds.

It was then that Jame noticed the black dot in the sky. Hoping it was Captain Ing, Jame started waving her arms.

The ship did not take the shape of The Horizon, however. Instead, it was black all over and along the side, in red letters, which appeared to be written in blood, it read, 'THE DEATH MACHINE.' Jame started to watch who might start stepping out of it.

Someone, or more like something, did start emerging from the horror-ship, but it definitely wasn't Captain Ing. It wasn't Alcarsh either.

It was a hand; a ghastly skeleton of a hand, with no flesh on it, which held a sharpened axe.

Jame stood there, petrified, waiting to see what was going to happen next.

Immediately, the hand made its way over to the Grachas, who

started growling and snapping.

The event that followed was terrible to watch. The bony hand started slaughtering the entire gough with its axe!

Once all the Grachas were dead, the treasure started to rise off the ground.

"Stop!" Jame yelled. "No!"

The treasure didn't stop, of course. Inside the terrifying ship, a sliding door opened and the treasure floated inside.

"Nothing more," Jame thought longingly. "Please don't let anything more happen. Please let Captain Ing come."

The ship, however, did not go away and neither did the hand. Instead, the hand started approaching the person Jame wanted it to approach the least of all! Herself!

Jame ran from the hand as fast as her legs could possibly carry her, but the hand with the axe came after her at breakneck speed.

When Jame looked behind, she saw that it was gaining on her, no matter how fast she could make herself go and had itself positioned straight at her neck.

Jame screamed and awoke in a freezing sweat!

She sat up in bed shaking and peering around in the darkness.

There was the sound of the movement of sheets all around her.

"Are you all right?" came the voice of Tiffany from beside her.

"I had a terrible nightmare," Jame replied breathlessly, her body still shaking and trembling.

"It's all right now," soothed the soft and gentle voice of Melissa from her other side.

But Melissa's words were immediately proven wrong by the sound of part of Jame's dream coming true, for at that moment, Dr. Fact showed up in the doorway.

"We have an intruder on board!" he exclaimed.

The passengers jolted upwards in their beds.

"Maybe, we should investigate," Tiffany stuttered.

Tiffany climbed out of her bed, while Jame and Melissa followed.

When they peered out the door, the first person they saw was Commander Mandy, who had already run out first. Captain Ing ran out of his room next.

The rest of the crew ran out of their sleeping quarters, while the passengers hid behind the doorway of their room.

The creature who came striding out last was the one all the passengers had been dreading since they had heard the crew's screams.

It was the enormous, death-black-haired monster, with blood-red eyes and terrible fangs, whose head practically touched the ceiling like Mandy's.

Alcarsh was on the ship!

For a few seconds, the passengers concealed themselves behind the doorway of their sleeping quarters, as the crew passed with Alcarsh after them, until Jame made an announcement.

"Let's go and see what he's up to. I want to get him if it is the last thing I do."

All passengers ran down the hallway, where they could see Commander Finks running as she approached the staircase. Then, she stumbled and off came her right high-heeled shoe. The Commander crashed down the stairs and landed on the bottom, with her other shoe still on.

Alcarsh picked up the fallen shoe as he passed it, while Tiffany, Jame, Melissa and Rick followed everyone else down the stairs.

"Back to bed!" ordered Mandy, when she saw them coming. "I don't want you getting involved in this."

Alcarsh chased Captain Ing and his crew back into the Bridge.

Then, he turned his angry, red eyes to their Commander, then started to approach her with slow, malicious steps.

Mandy's face grew as white as Jame's had in her dream and her body started shaking as Alcarsh tried to corner her.

At one point, Alcarsh managed to trap Mandy in the corner.

Although no one could see their Commander at the moment, being that she was blocked by the monster, they noticed that he made a violent movement with his right arm. It appeared to be a big slash up Mandy's uniform.

She gave a cry of pain at this, which made Captain Ing absolutely furious.

He approached Alcarsh at a huge sprint and jumped onto his back, trying to pull him away from his friend.

But he was nothing compared to the huge monster, who jerked Captain Ing off his back and onto the floor. Then, Alcarsh drew out his zapshot and shot.

Captain Ing lay on the floor, motionless, while all crew and passengers stared at him, with their mouths open in shock.

"Is he dead?" asked the Ensign.

The Doctor took out a scanner and examined him.

"No, he's just stunned."

It was what they saw next, when they looked up at Alcarsh, that really got their attention. From under his right arm, he pulled out two objects that looked very familiar:

The treasure map and the Mindcoat. From his left, he pulled out the Dome Clothes.

"Tonya's inventions!" Jame cried after she had regained her words.

Before anyone could do anything, Alcarsh lifted up a hinged piece of the floor, like a trapdoor, and jumped inside.

Alcarsh remained out of sight, as the trap door closed. Then, all of a sudden, a tiny ship that was practically only a cockpit, barely

The Stolen Treasure

big enough to fit the beast, sped away. It had been attached to the bottom of the Bridge.

"Where is that ship going?" asked the Lieutenant, as Alcarsh piloted it off.

"It appears to be destined for Atwydolyn!" cried the Engineer.

"ATWYDOLYN?!" everyone gasped at once.

"Exactly," he continued. "We have to follow him and stop him from stealing the Grachas' treasure."

"Order!" shouted a voice from the other side of the room.

It was Mandy. She struggled to her feet, put her shoes back on, and dusted herself off. Her face was wretched with anger and her uniform was stained with blood.

"Commander!" cried Jame, "that monster is the creature who stole Tonya's inventions, and is now on his way to the Grachas to steal their treasure and you say 'Order?'"

"I can deal with the monster myself!" Mandy cried, "and make sure the treasure isn't stolen. Just leave it to me. I am a Latimus Prospector. I know what I am doing. Go back to bed."

"But Mandy!" continued Jame, "we all really should go out there to see what is going..."

"Do you dare to criticize my Commanding?" she cried, her face growing yet more angry. "I am the Commander. That was a command. Go to bed!"

Everyone did as they were told. While the passengers left, they glanced over their shoulders to see their Commander slip a big, transparent, sphere over her head, attach a rocket to her back, press an orange button on the rocket and beam herself out of the ship.

The Doctor stayed behind to watch over Captain Ing.

18 Tonya's Story

When the breakfast bell rang at nine o'clock the next morning, the passengers and crew were anxious to know what had become of the treasure and Alcarsh.

One by one, everyone got dressed. Once outside their rooms, they could see the crew leaving theirs, only this time, their Commander was not with them.

"Where is Commander Mandy?" Tiffany asked.

"We were just with her," explained the Lieutenant. "She is with the Doctor. It looks like she got quite an attack last night."

"Is the treasure all right?" asked Rick. "Is Alcarsh caught?"

"The Doctor should know the answer to that," explained the Engineer. "He is in Sickbay right now treating Mandy. Why don't you go down the hall and ask him?"

Finally, Captain Ing appeared.

"Captain Ing!" cried Melissa. "Are you all right?"

"What happened last night?" he asked. "I think I must have fallen back to sleep."

"The monster stunned you with his zapshot," explained Rick. "It was then that we noticed that he was carrying Tonya's inventions. Then, he disappeared off to Atwydolyn and Mandy went after him."

"Mandy!" he cried. "Where is she now? Is she all right?"

"We just got word from the crew that she is with the Doctor."

"The Doctor?" he cried. "Come on. We are going to see her."

Captain Ing led his passengers and crew down the hallway. When they reached Sickbay, he knocked on the door.

"Come in," came the voice of the Doctor from inside.

Captain Ing pushed the door open and everyone looked inside the room.

When they looked at their Commander, they got quite a shock.

Her skin was scratched and bitten all over and she was bleeding. Her uniform had tears.

"What happened?" cried Tiffany.

Mandy rolled over onto her side to everybody and eyed them one by one, as though she were thinking of how best to answer Tiffany's question.

"Alcarsh," she gasped.

"He must have attacked you!" cried Captain Ing. "Did you get him? Is the treasure safe?"

"I tried to protect the treasure from him," she stuttered, "but he's too strong. He attacked me, and the treasure..."

Mandy paused, as tears started building up inside her eyes.

"What happened to the treasure?" asked Captain Ing.

Mandy gasped, as though struggling to find the courage to say the words.

"It's ... it's," she cried.

"It's what?" cried Captain Ing.

"IT'S STOLEN!!" she shouted out at last.

"Stolen?!" cried Captain Ing.

"I knew it," frowned Jame. "All of us should have gone after Alcarsh. That way, none of this would have happened."

Captain Ing's face was indeed very cross that his best friend would think that she could take on a hideous monster this size by herself and hold him under control, but he looked at Mandy with a somewhat satisfied look on his face.

"What's done is done," he explained. "Getting angry is not going to do us any good. All we can do now is go back to Atwydolyn to check this out."

"You should go," explained the Doctor. "I need to treat your Commander."

"Come on," called Captain Ing.

It was a bit different, following Captain Ing without Mandy up front. Since they had first met Mandy, everyone had gotten quite used to both Captain Ing and the Commander leading, but now, she was with the Doctor and Captain Ing was by himself at the front.

"I knew this would happen," Rick explained to Melissa when they had reached The Lounge. "It is the typical event that could come from a situation like this. A treasure gets made and there's a nasty monster around. Put two and two together and what do you get?"

"What I don't understand is why the treasure wasn't stolen when we first checked on it and why Alcarsh would attack Mandy in particular before he took it," puzzled Melissa.

"It's obvious. Mandy is a Latimus Prospector, isn't she, and what is the treasure made of?"

"Latimus, but..."

"Correct, so the answer is easy; because Mandy prospects for Latimus, she would want the treasure to be stolen the least. You heard what she said, in her own words, in Captain Ing's news. Therefore, being that Mandy Finks would be the one trying to stop the treasure from being stolen the most, Mandy would be a great target for Alcarsh to get rid of, so that he would be clear for stealing the treasure."

"I see your point, but remember that there are a lot of other Latimus Prospectors and why would Alcarsh take Tonya's inventions onto Captain Ing's ship for us to see? If he were the thief, he wouldn't want us to know he had stolen the inventions Tonya had given us."

"Maybe he was afraid that, if he left them on his ship when he attacked Mandy, someone would take them back and maybe he did attack the other Latimus Prospectors like he did Mandy. We haven't seen them so we wouldn't know."

"You're right, Rick. Things just aren't making sense. That's all."

Suddenly, Captain Ing turned his back away from the cockpit and toward his crew so he could make sure they were all paying attention.

"Atwydolyn is coming up," announced Captain Ing. "Time to land."

Captain Ing clicked a switch and the landing feet came out of the bottom of the ship. The ship cruised along the surface of the planet a little ways before it touched the ground.

"Everyone out!" he called.

When they were out of the ship, the most shocking sight met their eyes.

"Will you look at that!" cried Captain Ing, eyeing the horrible scene.

In the clearing, there was a large rectangle imprinted, where the treasure had been.

"The treasure really is gone!" cried Captain Ing, staring at the bare patch of ground. Around the space of the treasure, there was a line of huge footprints.

"Monster tracks!" cried Rick, "and look over there. It looks like we had some witnesses."

Around the space that the treasure chest used to be was a whole gough of Grachas. They were obviously the ones who had been guarding the treasure. However, they were all stunned and motionless, like pieces of driftwood on a beach.

"The Gracha guards had a crack at Alcarsh too," muttered Tiffany.

"Just as I dreamed last night," stated Jame. "The villain slaughters the Grachas and makes off with the treasure."

"But what we don't know is where he has taken it or why,"

came a voice from over their shoulders.

Captain Ing turned to see who had spoken these words.

It was Tonya herself. She was sitting on a nearby boulder, next to her ship, and eyeing the scene with as much concern on her face as Captain Ing and Mandy.

"Tonya," the Captain puzzled, eyeing her in admiration.

"Yes, it's me," she beamed, gazing at them all. "The minute I heard the treasure was stolen, I immediately knew you would be showing up next."

"Surely, you were here to see this happen though," stated Rick.

"I'm afraid not," she explained mournfully. "Atwydolyn is not my planet. Earth is my planet. It is just a place I come to from time to time to admire, just like all of you."

"You must have more information about Alcarsh, though," inquired Captain Ing.

"Alcarsh," muttered Tonya, quietly and pensively to herself. "Now that is quite a story."

"So you do know more?" asked Captain Ing.

"More? I know practically everything. I am from Earth too, you know. I also happened to live just across the street from where the incident happened."

"Tell us!" everyone cried, with anxious ears.

"I still spend much more time on Earth than on Atwydolyn, as Earth is where I was born. I was good friends with the neighbours across the street: the Gordons," Tonya began. "I knew their children very well, but I never liked their daughter, Percia. Their son, Michael, was quite a nice guy though.

"Michael was the first one born. He was a very good-natured, well-behaved little boy. The other child was born just over a year later. Percia Gordon was nothing like her brother. She was certainly no girl made of sugar and spice. She was selfish, greedy and spoiled.

The Stolen Treasure

As a baby, she cried way more often than any ordinary child, and much louder as well."

"She sounds horrible!" exclaimed Jame. "What about when she got older?"

"When she got older, her behaviour did not mature with her age. She thought of herself as the one important person, while everyone else were just frills. She threw tantrums, blamed others, and cried when she didn't get what she wanted. The one person she envied most of all was her brother. She was furious at her parents, because she thought that they tended to Michael more, and gave him better honours for what he did."

"Did you hear about Alcarsh when he was seen five years ago?" Captain Ing asked.

"Oh yes. Percia ran away one day, you know, when she was eighteen years old. Some people believe that the night she ran away, Crazy Max came back, and that was when Alcarsh ate Mr. Noin."

"Crazy Max!" cried Captain Ing. "You mean that he was already back when you knew the Gordons?"

"From what I heard," replied Tonya. "I was with Mr. Noin just before he was eaten, which also happened to be the same night Percia left. Mr. Noin told me that Crazy Max had returned. I remember that he was running as though he was in a hurry. He didn't have time to talk to me properly."

"Mr. Noin!" cried Rick, "Does that mean that Crazy Max sent Alcarsh to devour Mr. Noin that night?"

"That's the way it seems," explained Tonya. "People say that Crazy Max genetically created Alcarsh to devour Mr. Noin, because Crazy Max thought Mr. Noin was watching him too closely. I and a lot of my friends also believe that Percia played a key part in making Crazy Max come back. Alcarsh now patrols space, making sure that no one stands in Crazy Max's way and attacks anyone who he thinks would."

"That's terrible!" cried Captain Ing. "We can't give up here, though. Alcarsh may be delivering the treasure to Crazy Max."

"It's possible," said Tonya. "You and Mandy can investigate further, but make sure your passengers get their entertaining voyage. Catching Alcarsh is only the first step to conquering Crazy Max, remember."

"Why didn't you tell us this when we last saw you on your ship?" asked the Ensign.

"Remember Captain Ing's news story?" said Tonya. "Alcarsh hasn't been seen for five years, so we haven't been worrying about him."

"I suppose you're right."

"You had better start making your way again," explained Tonya, her face finally brightening. "It is not a good idea to get stuck on a problem and forget to enjoy your trip. I'm going to leave you now. I hope I meet all of you again later."

Tonya climbed back into her ship. There was the rumbling of the motor for a few seconds and a few puffs of steam before she blasted herself away.

"Tonya's right," Captain Ing explained to his passengers and crew. "Come on. It is time to depart.".

Once everyone was aboard, Captain Ing piloted the ship and, even after they were in space again, the passengers glanced out the ship's window for a last glimpse of Atwydolyn, before the ship blasted into Space Swoop.

19 The Latimus Prospectors

Commander Mandy stayed with the Doctor for the next few days, while Captain Ing shared fascinating stories with his passengers in The Lounge.

On the day after Tonya had told them of the Gordons, Captain Ing had told them about the day he had met the first of his Companions on Arshga.

"It was quite an ordinary day," he began, "when I met my first extra-Arshga friends who came from Earth to my planet. They told me their names were Samantha and Joseph John. Somehow, I had had the intuitive sensation, beforehand, that visitors would be coming. The minute they had arrived, I tried to make them feel as at home as possible."

"Did they adapt well?" asked Rick.

"Well, Samantha was the adventurous one. She wanted to live on my planet. Joseph John nearly left though. He was very reluctant about the journey of coming where I lived, but they both adapted and we're now friends. For the next few days, the stories that they had both decided to stay spread to Earth and others came to live on my planet too. After a while, they all became my Companions. I started to teach them methods of fighting evil. Now that is what they have helped me do all these days."

"What became of their spaceship?" asked Tiffany.

"The ship," beamed Captain Ing, "now is the most fascinating part of the story. When my friends decided they were staying, they pledged their ship to me, so I could learn to be a great Space Explorer and take passengers with me wherever I wanted. That ship that they arrived at my planet in is The Horizon now."

"Does this mean that Arshgans were not space-faring until your friends arrived?"

"That's right. They are the ones who inspired me and the rest of my race to explore more of space."

"Cool!!" everyone cried.

The next day after that, Captain Ing brought in a bowl of water with purple spheres in it, each one about the size of a pea.

"What are those?" Jame asked.

"These? They're Furlica eggs. The Furlica are a type of fish that grow in the tropics of Arshga."

Captain Ing had recently transferred the Furlicas, which had already hatched and grown a few centimetres long, to a fish tank.

Their names certainly matched their appearance. They were covered in short and stubby hair that look just like what covered most mammals on Earth.

"They're curious creatures," stated Rick as he peered into their tank which had some sort of blue alien coral.

"I think they're quite fascinating," commented Melissa.

Two days later, Rick and Melissa were busying themselves by discussing what Tonya had told them back at Atwydolyn.

"It is strange," began Melissa as she sat down beside Rick. "If Crazy Max really were to create a ravenous beast, it would take years for it to grow."

"Maybe he already had it growing all the time, just in case someone stood in his way," replied Rick, "or maybe he has a fast growth formula."

Jame changed the subject. "Why don't we go up to Sickbay and see how our Commander is doing?"

"We could do that," smiled Rick. "Come on."

The passengers and Captain Ing departed from The Lounge, along the kitchen corridor, up the spiral staircase and followed Captain Ing into Sickbay.

The Stolen Treasure

Captain Ing knocked on the door. There were footsteps as the Doctor strode over to the door and opened it.

"Hello there!" called a voice, from inside, as the door opened.

The Doctor was standing on the opposite side of the door, looking bright-eyed and cheerful.

"Come in," he beamed. "I suppose you would like to see your Commander."

"Yes, we do," explained Captain Ing. "How is she doing?"

"Come here and you'll see."

The Doctor pulled aside the curtains around the second bed from the door.

"She is looking a lot better today," smiled Captain Ing as he looked down at Mandy. "Is she going to leave here soon and rejoin the ship?"

"It looks like it," he replied. "After a few days of care and relaxing, she is recovering quite nicely."

The Commander really did look almost like herself again. Her wounds had practically healed and the blood on her skin had been washed away.

The Doctor had also mended her uniform.

"How are you feeling today, my old friend?" asked Captain Ing.

"I'm feeling quite fine," Mandy replied. "You were right. It was my fault that the treasure was stolen. If we had all come after Alcarsh, this never would have happened."

"It's all right," beamed Captain Ing. "You were trying to do your duty. When we find the treasure, just try to give your crew more of a chance."

"What do you want to do, once you leave Sickbay?" asked the Doctor.

"I was thinking of taking you to where I prospect for Latimus," explained Mandy, her face turning happy and excited again. "The Latimus Prospectors. They will be very proud to see me back for a few hours and they are always open to visitors."

"What a good idea," beamed Captain Ing in agreement. "We will go whenever you feel like it. How do you feel now?"

"I feel quite fine now. Do you think it's time for me to leave Sickbay?" she asked, turning to the Doctor.

"I think you could leave now," explained the Doctor, looking Mandy in the face with sincerity. "Why don't you step over to the controls and take us to this planet of yours? I've been wanting to see these Latimus Prospectors you've been talking about quite a lot myself."

As Mandy Finks climbed out of the Sickbay bed, she slipped her shoes back on.

"It's time to get up and running," she grinned as she joined Captain Ing to follow her passengers out of the room.

It was a bit different having the Commander piloting the ship instead of Captain Ing. However, Mandy seemed to know what she was doing and Captain Ing seemed to have his full confidence in her piloting.

"Where is this place where they prospect for this mineral called Latimus?" asked Tiffany as Mandy turned on the Space Swoop.

"It's called Uberdan," explained Mandy. "It has lots of devices that the Prospectors have invented to help them do their prospecting."

"How do you know where the Latimus is?" asked Jame.

"We don't," replied Mandy, "but it is usually concealed up the walls of canyons, and even when we get there, there probably won't be any. We have scanners in the hats we wear to try and detect the Latimus and whatever Latimus there is, it will be very little. It's so rare that it is noticeably harder to find now, than when it was first discovered over fifty years ago by Arst."

The Stolen Treasure

"Arst?" asked Rick. "Arst who?"

"He doesn't have a last name," explained Mandy. "Nobody from that planet has a last name; nobody except myself, that is. The few inhabitants on that planet, who are Latimus Prospectors, are native there. I'm the only one who isn't."

Rick took a closer look at the Commander, who looked like a fairly typical Earth woman.

"Are you from Earth, then, just like us?"

"I certainly am," she replied. "I learnt about Latimus when I became a Space Explorer and decided to take the job."

"I don't understand," Rick continued. "If it took many years for the prospectors to mine enough Latimus for the Grachas to make their treasure, how have the Grachas been able to make their treasure in a matter of days?"

"Oh, Latimus has been on Atwydolyn all this time," Mandy replied. "If there was a giant storm on Earth that blew your house down, you can bet that people far and wide would organize funds for your family for repairs. Still, that same money used for you will have been in existence on Earth long before the storm even happened. It's the same situation with the Grachas."

At that moment, yet another planet started appearing through the window, with oceans of grape purple, rather than the blue and green ones on Earth. The land portion of the planet appeared primarily orange.

"It's time to land this baby," beamed Mandy, as she pressed the landing button.

After the ship had landed, Captain Ing and the Commander led the crew and passengers out of the ship. The most unusual landscape met their eyes.

Fine, orange soil covered the ground. Around the land was a large purple ocean, and the trees divided into many branches and

129

sprouted leaves of a very odd shade of orange and the sky matched the colour of the leaves.

"Good to see you're here again, Mandy," came a low and booming voice from off in the distance.

"That will be Arst," explained Mandy. "The chief."

The Commander ran up to Arst as Captain Ing and the rest of his troop tried to catch up with her.

Up ahead was an alien whose skin was a fairly fleshy colour, with a slight tinge of green.

"Arst is the boss," explained Mandy. "He knows where to dig best."

"Long time, no see," grinned Captain Ing, as he shook hands.

"Long time no see you, either," he grinned.

Everyone else gathered around as they watched to see what was going to happen.

The strange creature called 'Arst' strode over to a vertical wall of rock which had a black and orange striped pattern. It was so high it appeared to touch the sky.

At that moment, several others of these strange creatures gathered around the rock and drew small chisels and hammers out of their uniforms.

Much to everyone's surprise, Arst and all five of the others, really did have immensely high-heeled shoes on their feet but they were not wearing uniforms like Mandy's. Instead, each one was wearing a yellow uniform that appeared to be made of some kind of extraterrestrial fabric.

"Excuse me Arst," began Captain Ing, "but have you, or any of your other Prospectors, ever been attacked by the newly returned beast Alcarsh?"

Arst stared up at Captain Ing and shook his head.

"That's curious," explained Captain Ing, "because he has

recently stolen the Grachas' treasure at Atwydolyn. The treasure is a fund for repairing the Grachas' houses that were wrecked, when The Horizon crashed into them."

"No," Arst explained. "He doesn't seem to want anything to do with us."

"My friend, Mandy Finks here, was attacked by Alcarsh, during night hours, a few nights ago. After that, we noticed that he had Tonya's devices, and before we could stop him, he stole the treasure from Atwydolyn."

"Maybe your friend was closer at hand and more able to stop him. We are farther away, remember, and if we heard he was about to steal the treasure, it would take longer for us to get to your ship and try to stop him."

"You have a point there," acknowledged Captain Ing.

At that point, Arst glanced over his shoulder at his fellow Prospectors.

"Excuse me, Ing," he smiled, "but you're making us forget our tasks. Maybe you could talk to us later."

"Oh sorry," said Captain Ing as he backed away from the rocks.

"Begin your prospecting," Arst announced after Captain Ing had cleared away.

Arst and all his fellow Prospectors put on domed hats. Then, at that instant, the most fascinating sight of all met everyone's eyes.

All the Latimus Prospectors, including Mandy, squinted and levitated off the ground and into the air.

Many of the others gaped and 'wowed' at this sight.

The passengers waited to hear if someone's helmet beeped, signalling Latimus in the rock, but it never happened.

"Aren't they ever going to find anything?" asked Rick, who was getting impatient.

"Maybe," Captain Ing said, "but probably not. Latimus is very rare, remember."

More time started ticking by. Soon, it added up to ten minutes, fifteen minutes and finally twenty minutes.

Eventually, it had been half an hour and even Melissa was growing impatient.

"All of you!" Captain Ing (who was growing restless himself) yelled up at the rocks. "If none of you find anything in the next five Earth minutes, we will get into the ship and go, no excuses."

It was a good thing they had decided to wait a little longer, for about three minutes after Captain Ing's admonition, a tiny beep sounded from high up on the rock face.

"I think I've discovered something!" yelled the voice of Mandy from way up high, where they could barely hear.

She picked a small chisel out of her pocket and began to chip away at the rock.

Everyone watched as the orange and black dust fell into her yellow bucket, wondering if there could really be Latimus in there, the very substance that made up the Grachas' treasure, the treasure they were trying to find.

Her hat continued to beep, and her picking and chiselling continued, until her bucket was half-full. Then, the beeping stopped.

Finally, she and her other Prospectors began to descend from the rocks and back down to the ground, so Mandy could show Captain Ing what she had.

After Mandy had reached the ground, she ran up to Captain Ing and showed him her bucket.

"Very good," he beamed, when he saw what was inside. "It is amazing what can come from a little bit of waiting and a bit of chipping away at rock. That's quite a nice find you got there. Come on. We'll go back into the ship and see what comes from it."

"Now," declared Arst, "We are going to extract the Latimus

The Stolen Treasure

from what Mandy has collected."

Arst handed Many a large sieve and a large pan.

Mandy held the metal pan under the sieve, and turned around with her bucket that contained the rock dust, poured its contents into the sieve, and began shaking it.

After a few minutes, she stopped shaking the sieve. Mandy lifted the metal pan and showed it around.

"Mandy!" cried Tiffany in astonishment. "You didn't get anything!"

"That's not quite true," Mandy explained. "Look over there in that corner."

When everyone gathered around and peered into the corner to Mandy's left that was away from her, they saw a tiny twinkle of yellow glitter that was barely larger than a grain of sand.

"That's all you got?" cried Tiffany. "After all that work?"

"I'm afraid so," explained Mandy. "I told you Latimus was rare."

"I had no idea it was that rare!" cried Rick. "It's no wonder it took years to find enough to make a treasure that size. Only that from half a bucket-full. It's no wonder you would show such concern over the treasure."

Mandy led Captain Ing and his crew, as she turned around for a split second, to wave goodbye to Arst.

"Goodbye," grinned Captain Ing, as he climbed into The Horizon with his crew and passengers behind him.

Captain Ing pressed a few buttons and the ship left the surface of the planet, showing its distant purple seas once again.

The Commander strode over to the table in the centre of The Lounge, leaving Captain Ing in The Bridge to the controls for the rest of the voyage.

20 Family Conflicts

Commander Mandy stayed with the passengers in The Lounge for the next few hours, while Captain Ing tended to some of his priorities elsewhere in the ship.

Tiffany, Jame and Melissa spent most of their time gazing out the window at the stars, (Melissa, probably trying to name more constellations) as Rick asked more questions about Mandy's occupation.

"How long have you been prospecting for Latimus?"

Mandy looked up and glanced at Rick with her usual daydreaming face.

"I first heard about Latimus Prospecting when I became a Space Explorer," explained Mandy. "Mining for a rare and precious mineral sounded like a great honour to me."

At that moment, Captain Ing showed up carrying black chips.

"What are those for?" asked the Ensign.

"I have been spending the past few hours constructing some safety plans," explained Captain Ing. "Because of recent incidents, we will set these new precautions into the ship. The crew and I will set force fields around all the doors and entrances, which will be programmed to open only to a certain password, which I will show all of you in a minute and we will install hidden alarms, which will alert us of any danger. Alcarsh's picture is programmed into the alarms, so they will go off if and only if he enters. If all goes well, we should not have any more attacks on this ship.

"'Furlica Food' is the password," explained Captain Ing after everyone had taken a good look at it. "It is top secret, so only those aboard this ship are permitted to know it."

Jame and Melissa glanced over to Captain Ing's Furlicas, who had grown to about twice their length since Mandy had taken the crew and passengers to Uberdan.

"We will all install these," explained Captain Ing, holding some tiny, black, devices in his hands, which were only about a centimetre across. "They are hidden burglar alarms. If Alcarsh dares to enter, they will go off and alert us all."

He passed by all of the members of his crew and handed one to each person. However, after he had distributed them, he still had one left in his own hand, for himself.

"Now listen up good," explained Captain Ing, "because here is the plan. I will stay here, in the Bridge, and install the alarm, password and force fields. Mandy, you will tend to the kitchen; the Ensign, sleeping quarters; Engineer, the hallway bathrooms; the Doctor, Sickbay; and the Lieutenant will see to the Mind Deck."

Everyone kept their eyes up to Captain Ing, waiting for what he was about to say next.

"Everyone break!" he called, clapping his hands.

The crew disappeared down the hallway, while the passengers pondered whether they should go with them or stay in The Lounge.

"All passengers will stay here," explained Captain Ing.

All the crew started installing force fields in the doors, just as Captain Ing had instructed, and hid the tiny burglar alarms in various obscure places in the rooms.

Lieutenant Linda pushed the Mind Deck wall aside.

After she had done so, however, a great surprise met her eyes.

Instead of being dark like the room usually was, dazzling light filled it, and a scene was already happening.

Nevertheless, Linda hopped down into it all the same. Suddenly, the end wall rose and closed, leaving her trapped inside what was happening.

This image appeared to be back on some place on the surface of planet Earth and Linda was standing by a street, with houses all along it.

Immediately, she did the obvious thing, which, as Captain Ing had instructed, was to clap her hands to make the image go away, but this time it didn't.

Then, she tried shutting her eyes and picturing the doorway, through which she had entered, but no door or wall appeared.

Finally, she decided that the best thing to do would be to make use of what was going on and see what all this could be about.

The Lieutenant turned to face the houses behind her. In the front yard of the house that had been behind her before was a young woman with brown hair, who was watering her flower garden.

"Tonya!" cried Linda.

But Tonya acted as though she didn't even notice Linda was there, just like the Grachas in the one image Melissa had made.

All of a sudden, a thought occurred to the Lieutenant. Back at Atwydolyn, Tonya had explained that she had lived just across the street from the Gordons.

Linda turned to face the houses on the other side of the street and noticed a wooden sign hanging from the second storey, on the brown house that was just across from Tonya's, which had 'The Gordons' etched in it.

The sun was sinking low and casting long shadows, while the evening breeze was rustling the leaves in the trees.

Linda walked across the street to the front of the Gordons' house and waited to see if anyone's face was going to appear through the window or step outside.

Knowing that they wouldn't even notice her presence, she decided to step inside and investigate.

Lieutenant Linda made her way to the door and stuck her foot up to it, which went straight through the door as if it weren't there.

The Stolen Treasure

Then, she moved her whole body forward which slid straight through the door without the slightest disturbance in the wood.

Just ahead of Linda was a flight of metal stairs, which she wondered would be transparent to her body also. Knowing there was only one way to find out, she set her right foot down on the first stair. Much to her relief, she was able step up the first stair, then up all the rest of the stairs.

A man whose skin was slightly tanned appeared. He had short stubs of black hair on the top of his head and a roundish face with brown eyes.

The two who followed were a girl and a boy. The girl appeared to be in her late teens. She was followed by a young man who looked to be either in his late teens or early twenties.

The young man, who was obviously Michael Gordon, had short and stubby hair, just like his father, only Michael's was a middle shade of brown and his head had a fair point to it. He was dressed mostly in blue.

The girl, who was obviously his wicked sister, Percia, had brown eyes and long, tangled, matted brown hair. Her lips were covered in red lipstick and she had a face which pretty well matched the lipstick.

Next, a woman appeared at the top of the stairs. She was obviously Michael and Percia's mother. She had long, rippling brown hair like Mandy's, brown eyes, red cheeks and a pointed chin. She was wearing a shirt that looked like it had once been beautiful, for it was a bright pink with daffodils of a happy shade of yellow. However, it also bore spots of bleach and paint, marring its once happy, wonderful appearance. Her pants were a light shade of blue.

Linda stepped up the rest of the stairs and into the second storey of the house, where she noticed that the one that was obviously Michael was carrying a large sheet of canvas, which showed a beautifully-done painting of the Gordons' house. On the bottom was the title that Michael had given it.

'The House of the Gordons.'

Every detail was included. It had a background of a beautiful blue sky with a dazzling yellow and orange sun. Even the trees and bushes surrounding the house were amazing to look at.

"Wow!" cried his mother when she admired it. "Did you draw this all by yourself?"

"I certainly did," grinned Michael, "but my instructor doesn't seem to think much of it."

His mother turned the canvas over to see the comment written at the other side:

"You need to improve your ability to blend your colours and you must choose a more original image to draw." Jamie Lookalike.

"That's an outrage!" cried his mother. "I am going to give him a big talking to, but I like it all the same. Don't listen to what others say. Just draw what makes you feel good."

Percia presented her mother with some small loaves of bread.

"What about the rolls I baked in cooking class today?"

"They look okay," her mother said, eyeing Percia's bread without the enthusiasm in her voice she had used for Michael.

The mother took a bite out of one of them.

"Not bad," she commented casually.

Percia immediately blew her stack.

"What is the matter with you? Why in the world do you give my brother all the attention and completely ignore me? For your information, my teacher marked me high on those rolls, while Michael's instructor gives a poor comment about some dopey picture of a house. So what. Anyone can draw a house, while it takes talent to get great marks in school."

"Percia!" cried her mother sternly. "I have paid for your

brother's art lessons. He chose to take them on his own. It is one of his great talents. Any kid can go to school. Now apologize to your brother."

"No!" she yelled and made a rude face at Michael.

"Percia!" bellowed her father. "Say you're sorry right now, or you can darn well go to your room."

"Fine!" she yelled as she stomped out of the kitchen. She thumped her way down the hall and into her room, slammed the door and made a cloudburst of tears on her bed.

"Honestly!" cried Percia's father. "I can't believe what a filthy attitude our daughter has. It's as though she expects everything to blossom in her favour."

"I couldn't have put it better," Mrs. Gordon remarked as she left the room, favouring her right foot slightly. "If we want rolls, we can simply buy them from the bakery."

"Are you sure you don't want your foot checked?" asked the father. "It's been hurting like that for the past couple of weeks."

"No, I'm fine," she explained as she left the room.

Suddenly, the scene began to change. It started off in the distance, as far as Linda's eyes could see and then came closer, bordered by a line as though it were pulling the new image along.

Before Linda knew it, she was standing in the driveway of the Gordons' house, beside the rose bush that grew in the front.

Linda watched as the family stood beside a car. The weather was blazing hot sunshine and the air was so muggy it made her sweat.

"Now come on," stated Mr. Gordon. "We must take mum to the hospital."

The father sat down in a car as his wife sat down beside him. Michael sat in the seat behind his mother.

"I'll stay here," insisted Percia. "I don't want to be dragged out to the hospital for nothing."

"You will come with us," insisted her father. "Now get in the back."

Percia frowned and sat down in the seat beside her brother.

Linda watched as the car, as it drove down the street and out of sight. She was slightly disappointed now. She was now curious about what was happening and wanted to see more.

Her disappointment soon ended, for off in the distance, a line started moving along, changing the scene.

Before Linda knew it, she found herself standing in the foyer of a hospital.

"Fred Gordon, I presume," beamed the red-haired triage nurse at the other side of the desk.

"I certainly am," he smiled back. "I am here to see about my wife, Alexandra. She has been having a pain in her right foot."

"Well make yourselves comfortable in our waiting room," beamed the nurse. "A Doctor will examine Alexandra in a few moments."

Linda continued to watch and see what was going to happen next, until a Doctor appeared at the end of the hallway.

"Come on up," he called.

Linda followed as the Gordons strode down the corridor, following the Doctor.

"My name is Doctor Stonewall," he explained as they walked along, "and I understand that your wife has a pain in her right foot," he stated turning to Mr. Gordon.

He stopped at the nearest hospital bed that was vacant and Mrs. Gordon lay down on it.

"This will only take a moment," explained the Doctor as he took out a scanning tool and started examining her foot.

Then, he opened his mouth with terrified shock and his eyes became wide.

The Stolen Treasure

"I'm very sorry to tell you this, Fred Gordon, but I'm afraid your wife has a serious infection."

"What?" he cried going even more horrified than the Doctor. "A bone infection?"

"That's the unfortunate truth," he explained. "It's a superbug, Strodificus Botulinus. It's been known for about ten years, there's no known antibiotic that can treat it, and it may have spread through her whole body by now. If that's the case, amputating her foot will not save her."

"Will she make it?"

"She might," explained the Doctor, "but it already looks fairly severe. I wish you had come sooner."

"She's got a pretty tough immune system," Mr. Gordon insisted.

"And this is a very tough kind of superbug," sighed the Doctor. "We will do what we can to save your wife, but we cannot promise she will live."

"I tried to encourage her to check this out at the hospital," explained Mr. Gordon, "but she didn't want to go."

"Mother!" cried Michael. "I will do anything I can to spare your life. I will stay with you."

Out of the blue, Percia burst into the issue.

"No we won't. We are not going to spend all our long hours stuck up in this room in this hospital. We now know what is wrong. We can go home now."

"Percia!" Mr. Gordon yelled. "Not so fast. Your mother has a fatal disease and you should show at least some respect for her."

"Yes dad," she sighed.

At that instant, the scene froze and another change began happening. This one turned out to be a very small change.

In the new image, Linda was standing in the same room in the same hospital. The only differences were a few minor details in the scenery. The porcelain dogs that had been on the bedside table before had vanished, the window was now open, but the most fascinating change of all was that the picture that Michael had drawn was now on the wall and Mrs. Gordon was admiring it.

However, Mrs. Gordon no longer looked healthy. Her face had gone pale and her eyes were dull and misty.

"Mother," said Michael, close to tears and stroking her hand.

"Is she going to live?" he asked the Doctor.

"It does not look like it," explained the Doctor, shaking his head. "It looks like this lady is in her last minutes."

"Your company is enough," she gasped. "I am very pleased that you have all been here to support me and encourage me to keep going. If it weren't for all of you, I don't think I would have made it this far."

Then, she turned to Michael.

"Take this, my son," she smiled, slipping the golden bracelet off her right wrist. "It is a gift for supporting me in all the awkward situations and for your virtues of being such a wonderful child all these years."

"Thank you mother," he cried, his voice in awe and gratefulness. "It's more than I could ever have imagined. I never dreamed you would part with your golden bracelet."

"It is yours to keep," she beamed. "Take good care of it."

"What about me?" asked Percia. "Don't I get anything?"

Her mother shook her head. "Those who do not willingly support others do not get presents. Perhaps, if you had come to watch over me without your father dragging you out all the time, I might have willingly split the bracelet between the two of you to own, but your brother has taken every opportunity he has been given to think of and help others. He, alone, deserves the bracelet."

The Stolen Treasure

"But I'm your daughter!" she cried. "I'm your child too. Don't you love me as well?"

"You are indeed precious, no matter what your personality is. Maybe, in the days to come, you will learn to love and care for others. Then, maybe, people will send you their valuable possessions in your honour."

"But I don't want to have to work for honours!" cried Percia, getting angry. "I want them now!"

It was too late. Mrs. Gordon rolled over onto her side, stopped breathing and remained motionless as all her life drained from her.

Mr. Gordon stretched out his right hand, brushed it gently against his dead wife's face and burst into tears.

"It's all right," stuttered Michael. "There is nothing we can do about it now."

But even the tone of his voice sounded as though he were trying his best to prevent sobs.

He opened his right hand, where he was holding his new bracelet, and slipped it onto his arm.

It was a perfect fit.

As suddenly as a volcano erupting, Percia exploded with fury. She stamped over to her brother and yelled at him.

"How dare you accept that bracelet! You know all to well that mother only gave that thing to you because she favoured you more and paid no attention to me."

"Percia!" cried her father. "That is certainly not called for."

"Whose side are you on anyway?" shouted Percia.

"Your behaviour is completely inexcusable," yelled Mr. Gordon. "I am going to have a big talk with you when we get home."

At that moment, the surroundings began to change and this time, Linda found herself standing in the Gordons' house once more.

"I am disgraced in you, Percia!" yelled Mr. Gordon from the

top of the stairs, when his daughter arrived upstairs. "You have shown total disregard for the fact that your mother, my wife, has died."

"She gave all her love, if she ever even had any, and attention to my pig-faced bratty brother. That's what she did. I hate him," she roared. "I positively absolutely hate him, from the top of his head, to the tips of his toes and all through his body."

"Your brother has been amazingly tolerant with you and you ought to be ashamed of yourself for treating your own dead mother with such disrespect."

"She was a selfish, heartless creature who paid no attention to anything I did," bellowed Percia. "Just listen to Michael. Don't you hear him weeping and wailing like a baby?"

"He is mourning the death of his mother," snapped Mr. Gordon, "just like you should be."

"I am going to give him a huge talking to this instant, so I can really express my feelings," she cried.

Lieutenant Linda followed Percia the firebomb down the hallway as she marched into her brother's room, where Michael was sobbing on his bed.

"What is the matter with you?" she cried, scowling at her brother.

"Mother's gone," he sobbed.

"Oh, shut up, you crybaby," she whined in a high voice. "You ought to be proud after what your mummy has done for you."

"You shut up," he roared. "What is the matter with you anyway? Our mother is dead. Don't you get it? D-E-A-D dead. Don't you feel the least bit of grief over her passing?"

"Oh, well, at least you can spell," chided Percia. "There is only one way we can end this conflict right now. Give me that bracelet!"

"No," he yelled. "Mother gave it to me. Honestly, I hope that someday father throws you out of this house and tosses you onto the street."

"At least you don't have to worry about that," she scowled at him. "You are the one who is loved in the family and that is a wonder. Do you see me crying like a little baby like you are right now? I'm too grown up to cry. What's the point of weeping over your mummy if it's not going to bring her back?"

Michael did nothing then, but to make a loud growl at his sister. Percia left the room.

In the next scene, the Gordons were leaving a church. The sun was low in the sky and setting behind a bank of clouds, shining its last golden light on the scenery around.

At this sight, Linda knew that this was the end of Mrs. Gordon's funeral and they were about to head back home.

"Percia!" yelled her father, as they headed out the church door. "I don't think I have ever felt so furious in my entire life. It is bad enough thinking of your mother as spoiled and selfish, but letting it out in front of the entire congregation, when you were giving the eulogy of her funeral, is a totally different story. I am shocked that my own daughter could say something like that. You have both hurt me and humiliated me."

"I gave her what she deserved," hissed Percia. "Her funeral was the best place to let out how horrified I am about this incident, and her Michael-oriented life, to everyone. If you ask me, she can bloody well go to h..."

"Don't you dare say it," yelled her father.

Linda (who easily guessed that Mr. Gordon was referring to an outburst at the funeral about Mrs. Gordon's giving her prized bracelet to Michael) tried to follow the Gordons. No car was anywhere to be seen, so it looked like they would be walking home.

"It's been quite dry these days," stated Michael. "Do you

reckon it's going to rain soon?"

"If it does, I want it to be a great downpour," cried Percia. "I can almost feel my skin burning. Let's have some thunder and lighting. It's been super quiet around here lately. There's nobody to play with."

"You could invite Lisa over," suggested Michael.

Michael's suggestion turned out to be a huge mistake, for, at that moment, Percia's face became red and her body shook all over in fury.

"Lisa!" she roared, "forget Lisa. Don't you remember what happened when she came over for my twelfth birthday party? She didn't give me a present. Since that day, I've sworn I am never being friends with her again."

"That's not the attitude, Percia," corrected her father sternly. "The only reason why you don't have any friends is because you have driven them all away with your anger."

"The only reason why I don't have any friends is because they have not been generous enough for my satisfaction."

"You had better watch out, Percia," admonished her father, his face growing even more serious, "or someday I might drive you away with my anger."

There wasn't any further conversation exchanged as they walked. Finally, on one of the streets (Underbridge Street, as the sign on the side read) Linda caught sight of a poster on the window of what looked like a cross between a house and a mansion. The sign on this building read 'The Black Bear Inn.' Then, in a flash, Percia, too, caught a glimpse of what the poster read:

Space Explorers Day Costume Party

We are proud to announce that we will be holding a great party here, in honour of ourselves (Captain Ing and Mr. Noin) and all other honourable space heroes. We will have plenty of food and drink, music and fantastic entertainment for the night. We will see you all here, at The Black Bear Inn, with your costumes on August 22, at 7:00 PM to midnight.

Final note: There is a special prize for the best costume.

Sincerely, Captain Ing and Mr. Noin, your hosts.

"Captain Ing and Mr. Noin," whispered Linda to herself, after she had read the last part of the sign.

"Can we go?" cried Percia after she had finished reading the poster. "Michael and I?"

"Certainly, you can go with Michael," smiled Percia's father, showing the first smile he had worn since they had left the funeral. "You have one week to get ready. Do you think you can get your costumes together in that short a time?"

"Certainly!" cried Percia, "I can whip up a costume in a flash."

"Brilliant!" beamed her father, "Your mother would be proud that you two are finally learning to come together. Maybe you really will be a wonderful daughter of mine at last."

A scene change happened here. In almost no time, Linda found herself standing in front of the Gordons' house.

In the living room, Linda saw Michael constructing himself a fine mask of a man with short and stubby grey hair and a proud and handsome face.

Percia was creating something completely different. In her hands, she was clutching a great, black and hairy cloth that looked like the skin of a great, vicious beast. In its mouth were long, sharp fangs.

"What do you think?" asked Percia.

"It looks creepy!" opined her brother. "It looks like it came straight out of a horror movie."

"Brilliant!" she cried, "wait until I get to the party. They will actually think I'm a real monster. My costume will be first place for sure."

"Don't get your hopes up sis. Remember that this is not a Halloween party."

"I know, but somewhere in space, I'm sure there's a monster like this, or perhaps will be. Besides, a good scare always works up the energy."

"Or gives me the creeps that anything dreadful could happen to me," shuddered Michael.

"Relax," said Percia in a false soothing voice, "It's not real. I'm not really a monster."

"You are inside," replied her brother. "I can feel it. I just know you are up to something. There is a reason why you are going to this party and it's not good. Maybe, I shouldn't go."

"Come on!" cried Percia. "What are you anyway? Chicken?"

She put her hands up her armpits and started to flap her elbows about, making chicken noises.

"I am no chicken!" announced Michael. "I will come with you to the Black Bear Inn at seven o'clock tonight. Gotcha?"

"Good!" hissed Percia, "and I forgot to show you these."

She was holding some clear red chips between her fingers.

"What are those?" asked Michael.

"Watch," she grinned and started slipping on her costume.

"Oh my goodness!" exclaimed her brother once Percia was wearing the costume. "It's almost as though you've transformed."

"But watch now," she grinned and started slipping her red chips into the eye holes in the head.

Linda stood there aghast. This was exactly what Alcarsh had looked like.

"Oh my gosh," Michael murmured, in horror. "You *have* transformed. You ought to really give the others at the party a freak. They'll actually think there's a real monster in the building."

"You will be there, won't you?"

"Certainly, dear sister," he grinned. "I think it will be fine. You're right. Costumes are not real. Why was I even scared in the first place?"

"What about your costume? Is it ready?"

"I think it is," beamed Michael as he lifted the mask of the handsome man. "Give me a moment in my room while I change."

Michael appeared back in the living room in a matter of minutes to show his costume to his sister.

"Wow!" she cried. "You look like a prince."

"I'm Mr. Noin," he smiled. "I have heard about him and I admire him. I have heard that he has been to many planets that few people even know about and has discovered a few new ones."

"Sounds terrific!" grinned Percia. "It looks like we're all set for tonight then."

"I can do art and costumes," beamed Michael, "and you can work with fabric. Put them together and what do you get?" smiled Michael as he adjusted his mask.

"I'm taking off my costume for the moment," explained Percia. "I don't need it right now and it's getting awful stuffy in here, being black and all."

"Keep it on for a few more minutes," exclaimed Michael. "I want to show dad."

"All right," replied Percia.

"Dad!" Michael called as he ran down the stairs, pulling his sister along behind him. "Look at us."

Their father looked at Michael and Percia from painting his wooden sculpture of a dolphin and grinned.

"Brilliant costume Michael," he smiled as he looked at his son. "You look just like the real Mr. Noin."

"Always got your heart set on beasts and monsters huh, Percia," he commented as he peered at his daughter. "Girls are supposed to be beautiful and graceful you know."

"Someday, I might be," she answered, "but now, I think it's time to be mean, before I go fascinating and pretty."

"You know, my daughter?" Mr. Gordon smiled. "I think you are starting to grow up. Both of you know the way to the Black Bear Inn, don't you?"

"Certainly," grinned Michael. "It isn't far from here at all. I could find my way there blindfold with both hands tied behind my back."

"Brilliant," Mr. Gordon grinned. "Have a great time tonight then."

21 The Costume Party

The world started changing in front of Linda's eyes and the view that replaced the Gordons' house was a dance floor. The door was wide open and guests of all ages were rapidly filling the place. Some were children who looked as young as six. Others were seniors who could fit into the category of the eighties. All of them were dressed in costumes of various spacemen and creatures. There were even a few who were dressed as planets.

Linda continued to stand by the door until Michael and Percia appeared.

The Black Bear Inn was decorated with many colourful streamers and ribbons; holographic images of spaceships and planets were floating in the air near the ceiling, and the room was what appeared to be one large chamber with a few doors in the sides, and a flight of stairs leading downward in the North corner.

"Come on," beamed Michael. "The party is on."

After both the brother and sister were inside, Linda followed them into the building to see what sort of activities would be taking place.

"Welcome! Welcome!" came a voice, from the front of the room, that sounded very familiar.

Linda turned to the source of the voice, and there was Captain Ing and, at his side, was the very character of whom Michael was dressed.

Mr. Noin!

"Greetings to you all," beamed Captain Ing, "and what a fine turnout we have this evening. I will make sure that there is plenty of entertainment for all of you. Both of us are here to make sure that none of you receives a single minute of boredom. This is a day we have set aside to celebrate how thankful we are of all our space heroes and travellers out there. If super space technology had never been invented, we would never know about all those amazing planets and creatures in different worlds.

"I will also remind you, in case you didn't catch it on the notice, that there is a grand prize for whoever has the best costume. I will not tell any of you what it is or it will no longer be a surprise.

"In our crowd tonight, I also see that there are some really young children here. I must note that this party officially goes until midnight, but for those of you who are young and have certain bedtimes, you are welcome to go home anytime you wish."

Then, Captain Ing turned to face Mr. Noin as though wondering whether or not he might want a few words.

"I just wanted to say," began Mr. Noin, "that we have supplied plenty of music for you to dance to and food as well. A lot of the music we have is from other planets, like Captain Ing's planet Arshga, which will be quite a new experience for me, being an Earth man myself. Some music will also be from Uberdan where the Latimus Prospectors work, Atwydolyn where the Grachas live and a tiny bit from Earth. I'm sure some of you have also noticed that we have a spaceship set up, just outside. It is a model of a ship that can give you a simulated space tour."

Mr. Noin paused as he put his hands on his lap and gazed around at the crowd.

"Any last announcements?" asked Captain Ing.

Mr. Noin just grinned at everybody and announced, "Without further ado, let the party begin!"

At that moment, the air was filled with the most peculiar music Linda had heard in her life. It sounded as though it really was from a completely whole new planet.

Once the music had begun, everybody started to dance.

The Stolen Treasure

Linda decided that, since she was now here, she might as well participate in the events of the party and think of her Lieutenant uniform as her costume for her own sake of being a participant.

The music started out slowly and was soft and muted, while everyone, including Linda, danced singly.

However, after a few minutes, the music grew faster and the participants started pairing up:

Captain Ing danced with Mr. Noin, Michael danced with his sister, (though Percia was starting to carry a hateful expression again) and several of the little kids began to take some steps with their parents, while the elders helped teach the children a few moves they had learnt in their lives.

After another few minutes, the music began to change once more to the sound of stones being clacked together, beating on logs and sounds of somebody blowing on some reeds. It was practically all rhythm and sounded a lot like the type of music cave people might make.

Linda knew at once that this must be music from Atwydolyn.

"Grachas sure are talented," thought Linda.

When the music from Atwydolyn began, everyone began to dance lively, happily and fast.

There was music that was from another alien planet. It was soft and dreamy and sounded slow and sleepy. Linda recognized it as the music from Uberdan.

They spent the first hour at the Black Bear Inn dancing to all kinds of space music, with a tiny bit here and there from Earth.

Finally, the music came to a stop and Captain Ing and Mr. Noin reappeared at the front. Captain Ing cleared his throat.

"Before we start our Space Explorers Day costume party feast, I would like to award the prize for the best costume we have here tonight."

Everybody cheered and Percia grinned conceitedly to herself as though she knew it was going to be her.

"I would have saved this for the end," called Mr. Noin, "but I saw a costume that looked so spectacular that I wanted to give the prize for it as soon as I could."

Percia started jumping up and down on the spot and wiggling around friskily as though she had to use the bathroom desperately.

"Get down," cried Michael. "You're making an idiot of yourself."

It was true. Some of the guests were staring at Percia, as though wondering who this crazy person was.

"And the prize goes to..." Mr. Noin paused, "Michael Gordon, who dressed in a costume that makes me feel greatly honoured and is amazingly well done. His costume is actually me."

"I am deeply pleased," grinned Captain Ing proudly.

The whole crowd broke out in cheers. Percia sat down sharply.

"Come to the front," smiled Captain Ing to Michael.

Percia's face went red. "I HATE YOU, MICHAEL!" she yelled, but all the same, she patted her pocket and whispered in a voice so soft that Linda had to strain her ears, "but for the last time."

Linda watched as Captain Ing handed a glass cube to Michael. It contained what looked like a gold nugget, but obviously, it was Latimus.

"A whole nugget of Latimus," grinned Captain Ing proudly. "It is extremely rare, so take great care of it. Let's thank our prized miners, shall we, the Latimus Prospectors of Uberdan, who mine it and keep it safe."

Hundreds of cheers erupted from the crowd yet again.

Michael started to make his way back to his seat. However, just as he was about to sit down, his sister stuck her foot out and tripped Michael.

The Latimus nugget flew through the air. Percia ran out and caught it just before it hit the ground.

Everyone cheered.

"Here," smiled Michael. "Give it to me."

"No!" cried Percia. "I caught it. It's mine now."

"Percia Gordon!" cried Mr. Noin. "Your brother won it. Let him have it."

"No way!" she yelled.

"Percia!" yelled Captain Ing.

"Just give it to me and it will be over with!" cried Michael.

"It's mine!" cried his sister.

In the middle of their quarrel, it flew out of Percia's hands, through the window (thank goodness it was open) and onto the street, where the glass cube smashed.

"The nugget!" cried Michael.

However, when he peered out the window, it was nowhere to be seen.

"Where did it go?" asked Percia, as she too looked out. "I was sure it landed there."

"Grab that broom, get out there and clean up that glass!" cried Captain Ing, pointing at the broom in the corner.

"I will not!" she yelled.

Avoiding more arguing, Captain Ing was forced to excuse himself, go outside and dispose of the shattered glass in a nearby garbage can.

Even though the party was quite disturbed, it was time to eat. Linda followed all of the participants to a long, wooden table, which was already set with the choicest of foods.

There was ham and pineapple, mashed potatoes, peas, long cooked carrots, steak and even a few Ulbarberries and round, red berries that Linda recognized as Ambleberries, the very berry of which Mandy's pie had been made on the trip.

"Dig in," grinned Captain Ing, who was sitting at the head of the table across from Mr. Noin who was at the other head and everyone started eating.

Linda knew, at once, what the purple liquid was that everyone was pouring into their glasses. It was Ulbarberry juice, which came in clear jugs.

Her stomach gave a loud rumble at the sight of the intangible food and her mouth began to water. Why did she have to stand here being tantalized?

As Linda watched all the guests sitting in their seats, Percia made a loud hiss at her brother from across the table and her face (she had removed her mask so that she could eat) was turning yet more menacing.

Michael did nothing in response to his sister, except to scoop some fried Furlica onto his plate.

Linda grimaced from where she stood as Michael cut his first piece of hairy fish into his mouth.

An hour later, when the feast had finished, most of the party headed outside to test the simulated spaceship that Captain Ing and Mr. Noin had set up for them.

The only ones who stayed behind were Michael and Percia, along with a few others who stayed to explore the Black Bear Inn a little bit.

Percia gave a slight tug on Michael's sleeve and started whispering to him.

"Come downstairs with me," she said, trying to make her voice as friendly as possible.

"Why?" asked Michael. "There's nothing set up for us down there."

"Come on," she whispered. "I have a surprise set up for you."

"Will I like it?" Michael asked.

"Oh Michael," replied Percia, her voice growing ever more coaxing, "it is positively heavenly."

"All right," Michael replied. "I'll come down with you, but this had better be a pleasant surprise, all right?"

Michael started following Percia down, as the stairs creaked and strange, spooky noises echoed through the darkness, while the air was filled with a terrible, rotting stench.

Linda ran down the staircase behind Michael and Percia. As they strode along, the staircase grew darker and darker and the air became as cold as ice.

"Where are you taking me?" asked Michael.

"You will see in a minute," replied Percia.

As Linda followed, she trembled constantly harder as they came nearer and nearer to the basement and, by now, her heart was pounding so hard, she was afraid it would burst.

Finally, Percia had led Michael into the cellar, where the air was icy and dead, and the floor was hard, cold stone.

Before Michael could say another word, Percia whipped a sharp dagger out of the pocket of her costume and stuck it hard into her brother's chest with all of her force as fast and suddenly as lightning.

Linda buried her face in her shirt, shut her eyes tight and stuck her fingers in her ears, but she could hear the horrible, bloodcurdling, scream of Percia's brother all the same. Then, the screaming stopped and a heavy thump sounded.

Linda unplugged her ears and set her eyes toward the stone floor to see what was going to happen next.

Percia was slipping the bracelet off her brother's arm and putting it on her own. Michael was lying motionless on the cold stone, an expression of shock still etched in his face. A bloody pool from his chest was growing on the floor.

Michael was dead.

Linda broke out in tears. What would she do? She wished she could call the police, but she knew that what she was seeing was in the past, and could not be changed.

Without wasting a second, Percia shoved her brother's dead body into the corner and slipped her knife back into her pocket.

"Have a pleasant happily-ever-after with your mother," Percia smirked.

Then, Percia scrambled back up the steps, opened the door, and ran out of the inn, down the street.

Linda's body shook with shock and fury as she, too, ran out the door and chased Percia. If she couldn't call the police, the least Linda could do would be to find out where Percia was heading.

Percia's run was very fast and Linda had to do all she could to catch up with her, but she swore that she would never quit until Percia stopped.

Finally, after several minutes, Linda arrived at a scene that was fairly familiar.

It was the Gordons' street and just four houses ahead was Percia's house.

Percia's run slowed into a walk as Linda followed her along their driveway, up the stairs and through the door.

When Percia entered, Mr. Gordon glanced at his daughter, with a puzzled expression.

"Percia," he called, "Is that you? What are you doing home so early?"

"The party wasn't as much fun as I thought it would be," she replied. "I got so bored, I decided to come home."

"I see," said her father, his face still in a puzzle. "Where is your brother?"

"He enjoyed it a lot more than I did," she explained. "Isn't it bizarre that he actually likes to eat hairy fish?"

"Not really," replied her father. "Different people like different things."

At that moment, Percia turned away from her father and headed down the hallway. Then, she opened the door of her room and stepped inside.

Linda watched as Percia removed her costume, to reveal her wicked and bitter face once more.

Once her monster costume was off, she took a long gaze at the shiny, golden bracelet on her wrist, but the sight of it only gave her a shudder, instead of the breath of relief that Percia had always wanted since her mother had given Michael the bracelet. Percia was now a murderer and, when Michael didn't come home, her father was bound to find out what had happened.

She opened the pocket in her costume that contained her knife and slipped it back out. The blade was stained with blood.

Percia threw the knife onto the floor and began to weep on her bed. Why did she do this? Just a bit of jealousy and a bit of hatred and she had to murder her own brother?

Linda kneeled over by Percia's side and watched her body tremble slightly. It felt very odd, but deep inside, Linda couldn't help feeling a tiny bit of compassion for Percia.

"Don't be so silly, Percia," she told herself, turning her head away from the knife. "Now that your father has no one but you now, he'll give all the attention to you. That's what you have been wishing for all your life."

Telling herself this didn't help though. She just knew her father was going to come in and ask her more about Michael any moment and the police would find his dead body.

Percia turned toward the door and watched to see if she could catch any sign of her father. She dashed off her bed, and sat down in front of the knife to cover it with her body.

The door did open after a few minutes and the person who entered was the very person for whom Percia had been watching.

It was her father.

"What is it?" Percia stuttered as he stared at her at the doorway. "What do you want now?"

"I was just wondering if something was the matter, my dear. You seemed awfully shaky and I just want to know what's wrong."

"It's nothing that concerns you," she cried. "It's a very private and personal matter."

"I'm a father," he said sternly. "My job is to be concerned."

"Just go away," she sobbed.

"I wonder if there is something you're hiding from me," puzzled Mr. Gordon.

"No there isn't!" she yelled. "Just go."

"Wait a minute," he stated. "What on Earth is Michael's bracelet doing on your wrist? Did you take it from him?"

"No," she stuttered.

"Something is bothering you! What is it?"

"It is nothing!"

"No, it's not. There is something in here you don't want me to know about!" he cried and marched into Percia's room.

When he looked behind Percia, his mouth dropped and his face turned white as he took a look at Percia's knife.

"What in cockamamia is this?!" he cried.

Percia burst into tears on her bed.

"Is this the reason why my son is not coming home?"

"No, father!" she cried.

"Yes it is. You killed your brother, didn't you? You murdered him, just so you could get your mother's bracelet."

The Stolen Treasure

"I'm sorry dad!" wailed Percia.

Mr. Gordon immediately snatched the knife off the floor and pointed it at his daughter's chest.

"Should I kill you?" he yelled. "Should I stab you with this knife and show you what it is like?"

"No!" she bawled, tears running down her face, "no, father, don't hurt me."

"Don't you dare call me 'father!'" he yelled, throwing the knife aside, which stuck into the wall it hit. "I don't even know you."

"Please!" she bawled. "I'm still your Percia, aren't I? If the police show up, you'll protect me from them, right?"

"I most certainly will not! You are nothing but a filthy piece of trash. You're just a brainless murderer who has killed my son and just when I thought you two were finally beginning to get along."

"I didn't kill him. Michael just gave this bracelet to me and the knife is just another part of my costume."

"Don't lie! Michael would have never parted with that bracelet, especially to filthy vermin like you."

"Vermin," she stuttered, "but I..."

"Get out of this house at once!" yelled her father in a rage. "I never want to see you here or anywhere else ever again!"

"Father!" she cried. "No!"

"IT IS TOO LATE!" he bellowed. "I WILL TURN YOU IN TO THE POLICE, PERCIA, AND I'LL MAKE SURE YOU'LL GET CAUGHT!!"

"NO! NO, FATHER!!"

"GET OUT!!"

"Please!"

"OOOOOOOOOOUUUUUTTT!" hollered Mr. Gordon at the top of his lungs.

Linda followed behind as Percia's furious father kicked and

161

beat his daughter down the hallway and down the stairs. It was sad and horrible to watch. It was as though she were being abused.

"AND STAY OUT!!!" he yelled as he opened the door and pushed her out.

Mr. Gordon slammed the door behind Percia.

"AND YOU'RE NOT MY DAUGHTER ANYMORE!!!" he yelled through the door.

Percia ran away from the house and back down the street, tears still in her eyes, as Linda chased her again.

It was a long chase to find out what was going to happen to Percia Gordon. Percia continued to run farther and farther from her house, down the long and dark streets, while Linda's legs were aching more and more from the long chase. Wouldn't Percia ever get tired?

Finally, when Percia had left the populated area of the houses and was running deep into the woods, the sound came; the very sound that Linda had been anticipating. It started off as quiet, like someone sliding a trombone back and forth in the distance. Then, it gradually began to grow.

It was sirens. A police car was coming for Percia.

Percia, who had obviously heard these sirens, started searching around desperately for a place to hide.

However, at that moment, a miracle occurred. There was a loud, whirring noise in the sky and what appeared to be a huge machine stopped and hovered several metres above the ground.

It was a spaceship.

With the sound of the sirens drawing yet nearer, Percia ran closer to the ship. Then, the most amazing thing happened.

A slot in the bottom of the ship opened and Percia started to rise toward the inside. Whoever was in the ship was beaming Percia aboard!

It was then, that Linda noticed that this was no ordinary ship.

On its side was a picture of a gun with a star with a "C" on the side.

It was The Equator, the ship of Crazy Max himself!

In almost no time at all, Crazy Max had beamed Percia inside The Equator. After she was inside, the ship continued to hover.

Linda couldn't believe this. It was true, then. Crazy Max really had returned five years ago.

Mr. Noin came rushing forward and he glared up at Crazy Max's immense, black ship. Crazy Max had obviously seen Mr. Noin coming.

"So, we have Mr. Noin here," cackled Crazy Max. "You look like our only witness. Don't try to run, because you can't resist me."

A wicked and evil chuckle echoed through the air from Crazy Max's ship and there was an evil whooshing noise like a furious hurricane.

Linda stared at Mr. Noin, then up at the spaceship. She knew exactly what was going to happen next. Crazy Max was going to set Alcarsh on Mr. Noin to devour him.

"No, wait!" yelled Mr. Noin, his face suddenly startled. "Please don't do it, Crazy Max. Anything but that."

"It is too late, Noin," boomed the evil and dry voice from above. "It is too dangerous. I'm afraid I'm going to have to set it on you. You are the only one who knows the true story."

Linda's head jerked up toward Crazy Max's ship as though touched by an electric spark. She watched to catch Alcarsh jumping out.

Linda saw no such thing, however, even though all her senses were tuned to The Equator.

The only thing that broke her attention from the ship was a ferocious growl coming from her side.

When Linda glanced over her shoulder to see what was going on, she got the fright of her life.

Mr. Noin was nowhere to be seen and Linda was just able to catch a glimpse of a terrifying black-haired monster disappear into the grass. No matter how hard Linda looked to see if Alcarsh was carrying Mr. Noin's remains, she saw none, for Alcarsh's back was turned.

The cackle of Crazy Max sounded again. Then, the ship sped away.

Linda stood there, petrified in the woods, her mind shuddering over what Alcarsh was about to do next. At least Linda now knew what had happened to Percia.

A line started to move along the sky toward Linda from the horizon, pulling what looked like finally a new event behind it.

As it turned out, the new scene was a huge contrast from the last one. Linda now found herself on another street with warm sunshine and brightly coloured houses everywhere.

The house that was directly across from Linda was mostly pink.

Standing behind the house was a very young girl, who appeared barely older than a toddler. She was holding a bag of daffodil bulbs, and throwing them onto a bare patch of earth, while on the ground, by her feet, were packages of other flower seeds.

Linda immediately knew, by the black-patched, blue-eyed stuffed dog that the girl was cuddling under her arm with the bulbs, that she must be a younger Melissa Maguire.

The younger version of her looked quite different from the Melissa that Linda already knew. Her hair was more of a blond colour, rather than light brown, and it wasn't done up in lots of tiny braids, but hung down loosely, and in place of her bubble gum pink shorts, and her yellow T-shirt, she was wore a pink skirt with flowers all over it.

"Come here, my sweet!" called a voice from Just in front of the house.

The Stolen Treasure

When Linda glanced up, she noticed a young woman with light brown hair standing on the doorstep, who was obviously Melissa's mother.

"Yes, mommy?" Melissa called as she put her bag of bulbs down, and stepped toward her mother, hugging the dog close to her chest.

"Melissa," the woman smiled, "I would like to show you something I got for you. I am giving it to you now, so you can have an opportunity to get used to working it."

She reached into her pocket and pulled out a cyberlock. She took a small sheet of microfoil from her pocket, and began to write the password, before ripping the small sticker off on the back, which contained the password, before handing the lock to her daughter.

The little girl took it gently from her mother's hand, and began to turn the knob on it.

"You will find it to be very useful for keeping your possessions safe, so take good care of it. Here, you can write your name on it," smiled her mother, holding out a tag and a pen.

Melissa took the tag and pen, and began to write her name on the paper, spelling it slowly and thoughtfully, as though she hadn't quite learnt to write her name yet.

"Thanks, mom," grinned the girl.

"My big girl is going into kindergarten," smiled the mother, hugging her daughter tightly. "My Melissa is growing up so fast!"

Linda wished she could see the beautiful house a little longer. However, the scene started disappearing; not changing to into something else as usual, but being whirled away completely, just as they had seen on the Mind Deck before, when everyone had clapped their hands.

The trees, the rocks and the streams all became swept away, like they were in a whirlpool, and into nothingness.

Soon, Linda found herself standing on the floor of the Mind Deck, in the total blackness in which the room had been when Captain Ing had shown it to his crew and passengers.

The door opened and light poured into the room once again.

Captain Ing was standing just outside the Mind Deck door, eyeing Linda as though he were wondering what was taking her so long.

Linda ran out of the Mind Deck to join Captain Ing as the door shut back into the wall it had been.

"Linda!" the Captain cried. "What have you been doing? It's been three hours."

"Sorry," replied the Lieutenant. "I got very distracted."

"I see," puzzled Captain Ing. "Did you get those safety alarms and password put in?"

"No, I didn't. The most bizarre thing happened. When I went to install your alarms, there was already an image going on inside the Mind Deck."

"An image!" cried Captain Ing, "but that's impossible. Who could have turned the Mind Deck on?"

"I don't know," replied Linda. "Perhaps, before Alcarsh attacked us, he turned it on."

"But what did you see?" inquired Captain Ing.

"I saw the Gordons," explained the Lieutenant. "Percia Gordon noticed a poster advertising a Space Explorers Day costume party. At the party, you and Mr. Noin were there. You were both the hosts. Then, Mr. Noin gave Michael a prize for best costume: a Latimus nugget in a glass cube. Michael and Percia fought and it smashed on the street, but it mysteriously disappeared. Then, I saw Percia lead Michael down to the cellar and kill him. After her father had driven Percia out of his house, Percia ran away into the woods. I saw it then. I saw what happened to Percia. Crazy Max came out of the sky and beamed her aboard. Mr. Noin came running and while I was staring at Crazy Max's ship, he set Alcarsh on Mr. Noin."

Captain Ing smiled. "What you saw was correct. Mr. Noin and I were indeed the hosts. That must be what happened to Percia. Because Crazy Max took Percia away, I couldn't have known about all of this because I was hosting the party. However, I was wondering why Michael and Percia weren't there anymore. At the time, I simply thought they had gone home. Mr. Noin was skeptical, however. When he saw that they were missing, he wanted to find out what had happened. I let him go, while I decided to continue to host the party. However, the party had to be shut down early, when police arrived with Fred Gordon and announced they had reason to believe that someone had been stabbed somewhere in the inn. That must have been when it happened. You have filled me in on some very puzzling questions, my Lieutenant."

"But there was more," she explained. "After that, I saw Melissa. I saw a younger version of her. She was going into kindergarten. Her mother was standing on the doorstep, and she gave her a cyberlock."

"A cyberlock?" asked Mr. Ing. "What about it?"

"Melissa's mother was giving it to her for Kindergarten," explained Linda, "but I wonder what that would have to do with the Gordons."

"Very interesting," said Mr. Ing. "Who knows?"

"Where are the rest of the crew?" asked the Lieutenant.

"They're all in the Bridge," replied Captain Ing. "Commander Mandy is watching over them. They have all finished installing their safety devices. All we need to do now is install yours and our ship will be completely Alcarsh free."

Linda picked the tiny burglar alarms out of her pocket, lifted up the Mind Deck door and looked inside the Deck again, hoping for all of space that there would not be another image. When she saw there was no mind activity going on inside, Captain Ing left the door open so Linda could press the button to turn the Mind Deck off. Then she busied herself installing the burglar alarms and password.

Once Linda had finished, she said "Furlica food," and left the Mind Deck again to join her crew in the Bridge. Once she was out of the Mind Deck, the force field replaced itself.

That evening at supper, everyone gathered around Linda as though welcoming her back after she had been gone on a long holiday.

"I have some news for all of you," explained Captain Ing. "A very strange thing happened to our Lieutenant, when she installed the password and alarms in the Mind Deck. There was a scene going on inside and, apparently, it was about the Gordons."

Linda explained to the crew and passengers all that she had seen in the Mind Deck. She told them about Michael's painting and Percia's bread rolls, how the Latimus nugget had vanished at the party after it had fallen through the open window, and about Percia's gruesome murder of her brother.

"And what happened to Miss Gordon after she ran away?" asked the Engineer after Linda paused briefly.

"Percia Gordon was abducted by Crazy Max after killing Michael," explained Linda.

There was a row of excitement at this statement.

"That's it!" cried the children in amazement.

22 Captain Ing's Companions

When the next morning arrived, the passengers were all anxious to discuss more with the Lieutenant about what had happened in the Mind Deck the day before.

"It would be a good idea to ask the Lieutenant for more details when we see her," explained Rick. "I already have many questions."

"Breakfast time," announced the Captain.

Then, from the female crew's room, there came a scream.

"SHE'S GONE!!"

"What?!" cried Captain Ing, snapping awake and jumping so high from his start that he nearly hit his head on the ceiling.

Captain Ing and Rick left their room and made their way to the crew's room. The rest of the crew and passengers were already there, and a shocking sight met their eyes.

Lieutenant Linda was missing.

"That's impossible!" cried Captain Ing. "We installed burglar alarms and passwords."

"Perhaps our ship is being watched," suggested Rick.

"Maybe," said the Captain.

Mandy dropped onto her bed and started weeping softly.

"Where's the Doctor?" Jame asked. "He was supposed to be guarding the ship."

"Come on," directed the Captain. "We will go to Sickbay."

When the Captain, passengers, and crew arrived at Sickbay, Eric was collapsed on the floor with all his circuits fried.

"He's been zapped with a zapshot!" the Captain exclaimed. "Somehow, the abductor knew we had a robot guarding our ship and where we had the robot stationed."

"Captain Ing," Tiffany suggested, "I'm beginning to have a bad feeling. I think I know how the thief took our Lieutenant away and I know I may sound crazy but you've got to believe me."

"What?" asked Captain Ing.

"It was someone already on this ship who took her."

"Somebody on the ship? Who would do such a thing?"

"It's only a theory," persisted Tiffany, "but how could a thief, or kidnapper, possibly make it onto our ship with the alarms, passwords and force-fields we installed, and our robot Doctor watching?"

"I didn't abduct our Lieutenant," explained the Engineer.

"I didn't do it," stated the Commander.

"Nor did I," said the Ensign.

"Maybe Alcarsh has someone working for him, who Alcarsh sent to kidnap the Lieutenant," suggested Rick. "Perhaps Alcarsh has bugged our ship, knows the password, and sent his servant to our ship to take Lieutenant Linda away."

"And perhaps this servant that Alcarsh is using is this member of our ship," continued Tiffany.

***

Over breakfast, everyone was discussing how the Lieutenant could have gone missing.

"I don't get it," said Jame at the breakfast table. "How could an image already be going on in the Mind Deck with the Lieutenant just entering it? She would have had to turn it on first."

"Somehow, the thief is getting around our ship unnoticed," hypothesized Captain Ing, munching on a piece of plant from his planet. "He must have turned invisible, turned on the Mind Deck, then betrayed our Lieutenant after we had gone to bed. When he returned to his ship, he would have had to become visible again and..."

"Captain Ing," observed Tiffany. "If Alcarsh could turn invisible, he would have been invisible when he attacked Mandy on the ship."

"What do you suppose Crazy Max did with Percia after he took her onto The Equator?" asked Rick.

"How should we know that?" asked Tiffany. "Maybe she's just been helping him out ever since that night she killed Michael."

"But how could anyone kill a sibling?" cried Melissa. "All my life, I have wanted one and Percia kills the one she has, and for what? A bracelet. How could anyone be so cruel?"

By now, Commander Mandy was shuddering. "I don't know; I really don't, but I think it all boils down to jealousy and hatred."

Captain Ing did many hours of scanning to try to detect The Equator, in hopes of locating their lost Lieutenant, but nothing came from it.

"Have you found anything?" asked the Engineer, looking up from repairing Eric.

"Nothing," replied Captain Ing.

"Captain Ing," inquired Melissa, in a more hopeful tone. "Are you absolutely certain that we can do nothing? Are you sure that all hope is gone? Just last week, weren't you telling us about some people who were your friends, that you would one day take us to meet?"

Captain Ing's eyes brightened. "My Companions!" he cried.

"Now, you're thinking," smiled Melissa.

"It would be a perfect time too. On Arshga, there will soon be a spectacular show going on in the sky called The Blue Clouds."

"What are the Blue Clouds?"

"They occur once every few Arshga years, or about once every ten Earth years. Special chemicals combine in the air and create interesting patterns. We will set a course for Arshga. My Companions will be going to see it as well."

Captain Ing manipulated the ship's controls and changed the ship's course to the planet that many patient friends had longed to see, and launched into Space Swoop.

"My planet should be coming up soon," explained Captain Ing a little while after he had activated the Space Swoop. "We should prepare to land."

A planet that looked similar to Mars was approaching.

After the ship had landed, the door on the side opened and everyone jumped out onto red ground. They peered around on the rusty red landscape to see if they could find any human life that might be Captain Ing's Companions.

"Are you sure you landed in the right place?" asked Tiffany, after she had seen no one.

"I'm certain," explained Captain Ing. "They're just not here yet. They're likely off discussing some business about the treasure using information they've gathered from Detective Freefall."

The sky was a dull orange. No blue clouds, or patterns, had appeared. As a matter of fact, nobody could see any clouds at all.

"Where are these Blue Clouds that you were talking about?" Tiffany asked.

"We will see them shortly," the Captain answered.

After five Earth minutes, some clouds started appearing along the horizon that were a deep shade of blue.

"Those must be the Blue Clouds!" cried Tiffany.

They moved across the sky, covering it quickly.

Soon, the clouds had covered the entire sky, and at that moment, very fascinating events started to occur in the clouds.

First, bright golden sparks started flashing and dancing. Then, other sparks, of all sorts of colours appeared, including red, orange, yellow, green, blue, purple, pink, white, grey, black, brown, and ochre. Next, swirls of wind started making the clouds form different patterns. There were spirals, ripples and ellipses. For a brief moment, a green triangle formed and danced around the sky. Sometimes, the sun would catch the clouds and turn them bright orange.

"Amazing!" cried Captain Ing.

After fifteen minutes, the clouds started drifting away.

"Brilliant!" remarked Rick.

"Wonderful!" cried Jame.

"That was the most spectacular show I've ever seen!" grinned Tiffany.

Captain Ing looked around.

"Where's Mandy?" he asked.

Much to everyone's surprise, their Commander had disappeared.

"Crazy Max, Alcarsh, or this servant of Alcarsh better not have taken our Commander away too," cried out Captain Ing.

"Wait, there she is!" cried Melissa. Just above them, Commander Mandy came landing back onto the planet's surface with portable rockets on her back.

"Where were you?" asked Captain Ing. "What were you doing?"

"Oh, I was just doing some more scanning for our Lieutenant," she replied.

"Speaking of our Lieutenant, look!" cried the Engineer in horror, as though he couldn't believe what he saw.

Floating above them with a rocket was their Lieutenant, or rather the person whom they had been used to as their Lieutenant from the beginning of the trip to the previous night. However, her face now looked evil and menacing and, on his right arm, he now had

173

a C with a star beside it.

"The symbol of the Colodiggan Gun!" cried Captain Ing. "Our Lieutenant's a Space Wanderer now. It's just as I have feared. Crazy Max has finally got a new being on his side with his horrific gun."

Linda was soon out of sight.

"Hello there," came a voice from beside them.

A thin man presented himself to the Captain. He had a long, rectangular face, with curly-brown hair. His uniform was green and grey.

"Hi there, Joseph John Obelston," smiled Captain Ing taking a bow.

"Come with me," he smiled back.

Joseph John led everyone along the surface of the planet, to where they met a group of several other Companions.

"Here they are," grinned Captain Ing proudly. "My friends, since these two arrived at my planet."

Captain Ing turned from Joseph John to a woman in the front of the crowd, with long brown hair and a thin face.

"Meet Samantha and Detective Freefall," smiled Captain Ing.

"Greetings," smiled the black-haired man, whom Captain Ing had introduced as Detective Freefall. "I am very pleased to meet you all. How can I help you?"

"I have very bad news," stated Captain Ing. "Our Lieutenant has been taken by Crazy Max and made into a Space Wanderer. Do you know what we could do?"

"The best thing for you to do now is to get yourself a new Lieutenant."

"How are we going to do that?"

"We'll make arrangements."

"Do you have any idea where the treasure is?"

"Not its exact location," replied Joseph John. "However, in our

The Stolen Treasure

scanning, we have detected Alcarsh with Crazy Max."

"That's predictable," replied Captain Ing. "How do you suppose we could find the treasure?"

"The best you could do would be to scan for it," replied Samantha, "and try to keep your ship safe from the monster."

"But we've been trying to keep our ship safe ever since these thefts started."

"Don't give up," stated a blonde-haired companion in the crowd, nodding her head. "Try the little advice we have given you and keep in mind that you will soon have a new Lieutenant."

"When will we have a new Lieutenant?"

"Come back here in an Earth week," replied Samantha. "You could do guard shifts during the night hours."

"Our Doctor, who is also a robot, was keeping watch, but he got fried when our Lieutenant was taken," the Captain explained.

"One of your crew will have to keep watch then."

"You mean that we'll have to stay up all night?" cried the Ensign.

"Look," stated Captain Ing firmly, finally beginning to get serious. "Are we worried or not? Would you rather be tired or be Space Wanderers?"

"You're right," sighed the Ensign. "I suppose it would be worthwhile."

"We will develop a schedule of who will keep watch, during the night hours, for either Alcarsh or Crazy Max," continued the Captain. "It would probably be both if Alcarsh is already on The Equator."

"What about us?" asked Rick.

"Don't worry," replied Captain Ing. "Only the crew will do the watching and it will be one at a time. You kids can get your sleep."

"But what if I am right and someone on our crew is a traitor?"

175

asked Tiffany.

"We could have two crew members watching at a time then," the Captain explained. "If one of them does something suspicious, the other will stop him or her and report, to me, what happened. It's time to head back to the ship."

Captain Ing and the Commander led the crew and passengers back to the ship, as usual, but they were still questioning the meeting that they had just witnessed.

"What was the point of that?" asked Rick. "We didn't learn a single thing from these Companions."

"Sure we did," Melissa. "We now know, for sure, that Alcarsh is with Crazy Max. That means that, if we ever encounter Crazy Max, Alcarsh is going to be there too and if Alcarsh is there, then what other valuable object will he have that we want to find?"

"The treasure!" cried Rick.

"Captain Ing," explained Tiffany. "They didn't know where the treasure is, remember, and if it were with Alcarsh, I'm sure they would have detected the treasure on The Equator."

"He's probably got it hidden," stated the Captain.

"I suppose you're right," acknowledged Rick, as he followed Captain Ing, the crew and the passengers back onto the ship.

23 A New Crew Member

Shortly after they had left the planet, Captain Ing turned to his crew.

"I would like to develop a plan for who will be guarding the ship," he began. "Who would like to guard the ship first?"

Captain Ing waited but nobody nodded or raised a hand.

"No volunteers? I'll pick one then. The Commander and Ensign from the female crew's room can watch first."

"All right," replied the Commander.

"The Engineer and the Doctor can watch next. We will repeat this routine until the treasure and inventions are recovered and Alcarsh is caught."

"Can't we use video cameras?" asked the Ensign, "and what about when our next Lieutenant arrives?"

"All our video cameras were destroyed when Linda was taken and video cameras will not alert us when the villain comes," replied Captain Ing. "When our next Lieutenant comes, he or she will watch too."

"How come you're not staying up?" asked the Doctor.

"I will be doing checks around the ship from time to time."

The Engineer spent all the rest of that day repairing the Doctor.

The next week on The Horizon seemed very long and drawn out. Even though the crew were all guarding the ship, there was still fear at night of abduction, which was constantly relieved in the morning, by everyone being safe and sound.

By the end of the week, only the worries were dying on this ship. Everyone getting their panic up in the evening and being gratefully snuffed in the morning when no one was gone seemed to be becoming no more than a boring routine.

Tiffany and Jame were becoming bored of playing Space Chess and Melissa was finally beginning to lose interest in searching for constellations.

Captain Ing had been spending much time in The Lounge with the passengers, teaching them about plants and animals on other planets and where to find them. There were the Paragulas, who lived in the solar system next to Atwydolyn's. They looked a lot like anteaters, only they grew to the size of two-storey houses from being the size of a dog at birth.

Captain Ing told them about the Worlog trees three solar systems from Uberdan that grew what looked like cabbage, but it would give whoever touched it terrible blisters that lasted for weeks. The Worlog trees grew as tall as skyscrapers.

They learnt that Atwydolyn's sun, Ollium, had twelve planets and that Atwydolyn was the fourth.

Captain Ing's Furlicas had now grown about seven inches long each and they were eating the powdered fish food, in great quantities, that Captain Ing kept for them.

Right now, it was an hour before supper and Jame was playing Space Chess with Melissa, who seemed to be winning.

The rest of the crew had been discussing a lot about who the new Lieutenant might be.

"I sure hope that it will be good," stated the Ensign. "Maybe whoever it is will be the one to find the treasure."

"Maybe it will be Arst," stated the Engineer. "Then, we can have another Latimus Prospector on the ship."

"You got me," grinned Jame from the table in the centre of The Lounge. "Good game Melissa," she smiled as they shook hands.

"May I play with you, Melissa?" asked Rick.

"I would love a game," she replied.

Rick sat down at the opposite side of the table from Melissa

The Stolen Treasure

and they began to reset the board.

At supper that evening, the Commander served what looked like a plate of noodles, but were a plant from Arshga, that Captain Ing called, 'The White Worms.'

They tasted quite delicious, unlike their name, but Captain Ing had told them about how a lot of members of his planet ate food that resembled worms.

Rick had won the game he had played with Melissa. He had found it really fun, given the suspense for the upcoming Lieutenant.

Everyone had now grown used to the ship's special dishwasher, making the enthusiastic cheers at the beginning of the trip no more than a distant memory.

Even though Captain Ing had spent plenty of time scanning for The Equator, which supposedly contained the treasure, everyone was overjoyed when Captain Ing finally announced that they would collect their new Lieutenant the next day.

"I'm relieved," smiled Jame. "We will soon have something new happening on this ship at last."

Everyone was beginning to sleep easier, since their old Lieutenant had been abducted, and the sleep that came was much more smooth and sound than it had been several days before. In almost no time that night, there were quiet rooms full of sleeping passengers and crew, preparing tomorrow's energy for the new Lieutenant on the ship.

***

The next day started out as the usual morning routine on The Horizon. Everyone got up and dressed and Captain Ing and the Commander led them to the kitchen to get breakfast. They brushed their teeth and waited, while Captain Ing set a course for Arshga.

Unlike most trips to planets, there was no conversation exchanged on the way to this one. Everyone had already spoken what they had wanted about the arrival of the Lieutenant and they were all anticipating it in their minds.

Finally, the planet moved into sight and Captain Ing prepared the ship to land.

"Everybody out!" he called when the ship hit solid ground.

A short distance away, they saw Detective Freefall, Samantha and Joseph John, along with the other Companions and perhaps even the new Lieutenant.

Detective Freefall greeted them joyfully when they arrived. "Hello there," he grinned, "I suppose you've come for your Lieutenant."

"We have," replied Captain Ing. "Is he here?"

"He certainly is," grinned the detective, turning his head. "Come here."

A man who appeared to be from Earth bowed to Captain Ing. He had short and stubby black hair, brown eyes and a round, darkish face, which looked troubled and bothered, even though he was trying to smile.

"Hello there," he announced. "I have come to be your new Lieutenant. I am Fred Gordon."

"Mr. Gordon?!" cried Captain Ing, "You travel in space and became a Lieutenant?"

"It was the only chance of happiness that I saw left in my life, ever since my family got ripped apart," he muttered. "I used to be an artist and costume designer, but deep down, I have always wanted to be a Space Explorer."

"Come on," said the Ensign, "Let's go back to the ship. We will talk more there."

"Thank you," beamed Captain Ing as he waved goodbye to

Detective Freefall.

"I'll be seeing you," replied the detective.

After the ship had left Arshga, Mr. Gordon sat down at the edge of the Bridge and the crew began to introduce themselves, while Captain Ing pointed out their rank.

"Here's our Ensign," he smiled, pointing at Lucy.

"Greetings," Mr. Gordon beamed, shaking hands with the Ensign.

"This is our Commander," beamed Captain Ing, pointing at Mandy who was next to the Ensign. "I am delighted to announce that she is the best friend I have ever had. She is even a Latimus Prospector. I suppose you've heard that that's what the Grachas' treasure is made of."

"Wonderful!" cried the new Lieutenant as he shook hands with the Commander. "I think that Mandy is a wonderful name."

"I-I think so too," she stuttered as her body shook a little. Her eyes watered slightly and her cheeks turned red.

In turn, the Engineer and then the Doctor introduced themselves, as they bowed and shook hands with Mr. Gordon and then the passengers.

"Nice crew you've got there," smiled Mr. Gordon to the Captain. "I see they're all from Earth."

The Ensign offered the new Lieutenant her insight. "We think that we have some information about what happened to your daughter."

"I don't have a daughter," Lieutenant Gordon protested. "My wife and I never had a female child. I had a son but he was murdered."

The Ensign kept trying to explain. "My friend, Linda, our old Lieutenant, who was abducted, claims to have seen Percia being taken away. She saw it on our Mind Deck."

"Percia is no daughter of mine," grunted Mr. Gordon. "She is my son's killer, nothing more."

"Anyway," continued the Ensign, "on the Mind Deck, it showed Crazy Max taking Percia away after she had run away from you, because of the murder of your son. Linda also noticed that at the party, the Latimus nugget that Mr. Noin had given to Michael disappeared. Percia fought with him to get it, but it fell out the window and vanished."

"She fought did she?" said Mr. Gordon. "That's predictable. You see, people believe that the night of that party was the night that Crazy Max returned."

"Are you serious?!" cried Captain Ing.

"Unfortunately, I was a complete idiot that night," the Lieutenant continued. "I swore to turn Percia over to the police for murdering Michael, but I had lost all logical thought because of what she had done. I never wanted to see her again, ever. Instead of making sure she couldn't get away from the police, I drove her out of the house. When the police arrived to arrest her, I realized what I had done. I had helped her to escape. Thankfully, the police didn't take offence. They assured me that this sort of crime is an extremely rare occurrence, and that the circumstances of what had transpired had driven me into a moment of insanity. They took me to the Black Bear Inn and searched everywhere inside to make sure that Michael was really dead. When we found Michael's body in the basement, I was completely numb my worst fear had been confirmed. They called for backup to gather more evidence from the inn. Mr. Noin had already gone out to look for Michael and Percia. I pointed the police in the direction Percia had fled, and we were just on the verge of catching her, but that was when we lost her."

"Do you know what is even more peculiar?" Lieutenant Gordon asked.

The Stolen Treasure

"Tell me," cried Captain Ing. "I'm dying to hear any more information that you carry."

"For the past few years, the Latimus Prospectors have been discovering that they are missing Latimus that isn't accounted for, while Crazy Max is growing stronger, but the Prospectors don't care. I only know this because I heard it on Space News."

"It's Alcarsh!" cried Captain Ing. "He's a dirty thief. At the beginning of my trip, Space Explorer Tonya gave us a Mindcoat, for seeing thoughts and images, Dome Clothes, for repelling Colodiggan bullets, and an Enemy Repulsion Light, to repel Crazy Max. They have all been stolen. Plus, he has robbed the Grachas and the Latimus Prospectors. Tonya cannot make any more of her devices because Crazy Max erased her memory."

"Is that so?" asked Mr. Gordon. "Do you have any idea where these devices might be? Have you seen or detected them?"

"We saw them with Alcarsh," explained the Engineer. "He came onto our ship in the night last week. Then, we saw him go off to steal the treasure."

"That's extremely informative," stated the new Lieutenant. "Have you seen the monster since?"

"No," replied Captain Ing, "however, we believe that he has been walking in our ship without our knowledge, because somehow our Mind Deck got turned on to show that image we told you about, and even though we installed burglar alarms and a password in the doorways, he was somehow able to take away our old Lieutenant. The password is 'Furlica Food,' by the way."

"Furlica food," grinned Mr. Gordon, nodding his head. "I can remember that."

Melissa was the next to speak up. "Captain Ing," she began, "our Commander is..."

"Right here," beamed Mandy as she entered the room.

183

Captain Ing had never noticed that she was even gone, so he was surprised to see her enter.

"Were you preparing lunch?" he asked.

"I was going to," replied the Commander, "but I thought that I would do some more scanning for the treasure and guess what?"

"You found it?!" cried Captain Ing, his face breaking out in a grin so big it barely fit his face. "Did you actually find the treasure?"

"I certainly did," she replied.

The room erupted with cheers.

"I'll take you there," she smiled, stepping toward the controls. "I can pilot the ship there."

Captain Ing moved away, leaving the controls to the Commander.

After a jump to Space Swoop, Mandy landed the ship. However, when it touched the ground, it appeared to hit what looked a lot like snow and there were blizzards outside the windows.

Getting impatient, Captain Ing spoke up. "Mandy, I sure hope you're right about this."

"I'm positive," she explained. "This is the North Pole of Uberdan."

"Well, let's get out then," called Captain Ing. "We had better make this fast."

The crew followed Captain Ing and the Commander out of the ship.

Next, the Commander turned to the Lieutenant. "I think you should stay and watch the ship while we do this, Lieutenant Gordon," she explained.

"Why?" he asked.

"Who knows? The thief might come back and take the ship away for all we know," she replied.

"I guess you have a point," said Mr. Gordon as he disappeared

The Stolen Treasure

back inside the ship.

As Captain Ing and the crew trudged through the blizzard, the icy cold burnt against their skin and the snowlike substance that was falling from the sky seemed more like powder than snow and it didn't scrunch together under their feet.

"How much farther until we reach the treasure?" asked Captain Ing.

"We will be there in a little bit," stated Mandy.

"Wait a minute!" cried Captain Ing, pointing ahead. "What's that?"

A short distance ahead was what appeared to be a dark, stone chest.

"THE TREASURE!" everybody cried and they all broke into a sprint.

The crew and Captain dusted the snow of it.

Surely enough, when it was bare, it looked exactly like the treasure chest that Tonya had sent in her picture and when they had seen it for real at Atwydolyn.

"I can't believe it!" cried the Ensign, jumping up and down, (extra high due to less gravity). "We found it. We found it! We found it!!! It took a lot of adventures and bravery to get to this moment, but after patience and search, we finally did it."

"It will be very heavy indeed," explained Captain Ing. "It will be a lot of work getting it back to the ship."

"Wait a minute!" cried the Engineer. "What's happening?"

The treasure chest seemed to be moving on its own, only it wasn't moving toward the ship. It seemed to be growing taller.

"What in the world, I mean the universe, is going on?" yelled the Ensign, taking a step back.

Soon, it even sprouted arms and legs and, yet more shockingly, developed a face. The face was in no stretch of the imagination sweet or friendly, but evil and malicious. The texture of rock was also disappearing and seemed to be being replaced by what looked like leathery flesh. Before everyone's shocked eyes, an evil spaceman was standing on the planet, where the treasure used to be.

"I've got you now!" he cackled. "There is no escape."

24 Chased Again

"Crazy Max!" Captain Ing cried.

"I have come to assimilate you all," he grinned. "Your Lieutenant was only the beginning of it."

"Max!" the Captain cried. "I implore you to remember who you truly are. You are one of my people. Come back to my planet."

"I am not one of your people," Crazy Max growled. "I used to be, but that was long ago when I was young and naive. I have achieved powers that have made me a strong, wise leader of space."

"What are you up to?" yelled Captain Ing. "If you had wanted all of us in the first place, why didn't you shoot us all when you took away Linda?"

Crazy Max gave a nasty cackle. "I wanted to," he replied, "but I couldn't, without being caught. Because other people were around, I thought that it would be safer if I disguised myself as the treasure."

"Why would you worry about getting caught?" asked Captain Ing. "Everybody knows you're evil."

"But not everybody knows that a treasure chest could be evil, right? You see, it wasn't a matter of me being caught, Captain Ing. It was a matter of my assistant being caught. Even though I wanted to get all of your ship members, I noticed a certain Ensign stir. I knew that if you had all awakened and caught me, there would be a crisis in your ship, with everyone running out of the bedrooms as fast as their dirty, rotten legs could go, with walls and corridors in the way, and I wouldn't be able to shoot anyone.

"However," grinned Crazy Max, with his wicked grin broadening, "there is plenty of open space here. Don't you understand? I made plans with this friend of mine to come out here, to get all of you. You all know the truth about Percia. So, just like I dealt with Mr. Noin for knowing what happened to her, and dealing with your Lieutenant for finding out about her, I am now going to deal with all of you. Because your Lieutenant was the first to know, I thought that she should be assimilated first. I rescued Percia in order to repay her for her service to me. With that unprotected Latimus nugget, with no shield protecting it, or people seeing it, I was able to take it away unnoticed and get at least some of my strength back."

"So that's what happened to that nugget at the Black Bear Inn," cried Captain Ing, "and just how did you find the nugget?"

"I was stalking Tonya. When I found she wasn't at her house, I remembered Space News advertising the costume party at the Black Bear Inn and figured that's where she'd be. I arrived at the Black Bear Inn just as the cube smashed on the street."

"And who is this assistant of yours? Is he Alcarsh?"

"Not Arcarsh in this incident," laughed Crazy Max. "After what you have seen, I'd have thought that you would have known better. Percia is my assistant. She has been helping me ever since I beamed her into my ship. However, I have had Alcarsh on my ship for a long time now and I give him great credit for my assimilating Linda."

"Alcarsh took you over to our ship, then, when Linda was turned evil," cried Captain Ing, "but neither you, nor she, could have entered my ship. I had a password. How could you have done it?"

"That is a part of the secret that I will certainly not reveal," cried Crazy Max. "You must not know how I took your Lieutenant away."

"And why not?!" yelled Captain Ing, "You've just been helping yourself to the Grachas' treasure that Alcarsh has delivered to you."

"If only it were true," growled Crazy Max. "It doesn't want to open. I lift up the lid with all my might but it's jammed shut. I shoot at it but it won't blow apart either. Nothing works."

The Stolen Treasure

A light bulb flashed on inside Tiffany's head. She had just remembered Captain Ing saying that the Grachas had shut the treasure with a password.

"You don't have the power to blow apart the treasure?" cried Captain Ing.

"I'm afraid I don't," admitted Crazy Max, "but I do have the power to shoot all of you, and so does my new helper behind me."

Much to everyone's shock, their former Lieutenant appeared from behind Crazy Max with her evil eyes glowing, and two Colodiggan Guns in her hand. She handed one of them to Crazy Max.

"I have lacked helpers for long enough now," grinned Crazy Max. "I remember going into my Mind Deck and making fake mind images about good people from reality doing evil things, particularly this little shrimp over here," Crazy Max yelled, pointing a gangrenous, warty finger at Melissa, who jolted at this statement as though she had been struck with an arrow.

Crazy Max laughed. "Those days are over now. This will be for real. Come on, Linda. Let's get this over with."

Captain Ing, the crew and the passengers broke into a run for The Horizon, as Crazy Max and Linda aimed their guns at them.

A loud cry sounded before the first gunshot.

When Captain Ing looked back, he saw the now evil Linda standing back onto her feet. She had slipped on some ice and the bullet had soared high above everyone's head.

Crazy Max pressed the trigger on his Colodiggan Gun, but nothing happened. The gun wouldn't shoot.

"Drat!" he cried. "Mine has run out. Give me yours."

Linda handed her gun to Crazy Max who began to run fast, for Captain Ing and everyone else were already a great distance away but he too slipped on the ice and the gun flew out of his hand.

By the time Crazy Max had picked up the gun, Captain Ing, the crew, and the passengers were already back in the ship.

"Quick!" cried Captain Ing as he pressed buttons on the control board, "Let's get out of here!"

Captain Ing began to manipulate the controls and switches. The Horizon soared above the ground. Then, Captain Ing clicked a switch and the ship flew into space once more, away from the North Pole of Uberdan.

"That was close," sighed Captain Ing.

However, the Engineer turned to the Commander with fury in his eyes. "That was a trick, wasn't it?" he yelled. "You were trying to turn us in to that madman and treacherous Lieutenant."

"It was not a trick!" the Commander cried. "Honestly, I had no idea that the treasure was really Crazy Max in disguise. I never meant any harm to happen."

"You lie," hissed the Engineer.

"Both of you!" exclaimed Captain Ing, "let's settle this at once. Commander, did you really believe that you had tracked down the treasure and not Crazy Max?"

"Yes, I did," she replied.

"It's settled then," explained Captain Ing. "Mandy's taking us to Crazy Max was all a misunderstanding."

"Hold on a minute!" exclaimed the Ensign. "What's that?"

In the distance, a pair of lights were approaching The Horizon.

"It's The Equator!" yelled Captain Ing. "Space Swoop, fast."

Captain Ing blasted the ship away, but so did Crazy Max, and he started shooting at The Horizon with fire-red torpedoes.

"He's going to catch us!" yelled Captain Ing.

"Faster!" cried the Ensign. "He's gaining on us."

"If I go any faster, I'll burn out the engine," yelled the Engineer.

The Stolen Treasure

"Let's try going in zigzags," suggested the Ensign.

Hurriedly, Captain Ing piloted the ship from right to left many times, very quickly, in the hope of dodging Crazy Max's shots.

At first, it seemed to be a success. Crazy Max's shooting did miss The Horizon. At one point, a bright flash appeared right outside the window, a signal that a torpedo had narrowly missed the ship.

"He nearly got us!" called Captain Ing. "We must make faster and bigger zigzags if we don't want our ship to be blown apart."

Captain Ing turned the ship back and forth even more briskly.

Suddenly, there was a loud zap.

"A torpedo scraped the edge of one of the side wings!" cried the Engineer. "The ship now has minor damage."

In the light of the two ships, the Ensign noticed another object approaching Captain Ing's ship. It looked like a large monster with an air bubble on its head and a portable rocket attached to its back.

"It's Alcarsh, Captain!" cried the Ensign.

Captain Ing sped the ship on, but the monster drew nearer and nearer.

When he was close to Equator, he slowed down slightly.

"What's he doing?" asked Captain Ing.

"It looks like he's going to join Crazy Max in the ship," replied the Ensign.

However, the most astonishing sight met their eyes when Alcarsh got near Crazy Max's ship. Crazy Max's ship suddenly started moving away in the opposite direction.

Captain Ing stared in astonishment. "What made it do that?" he pondered to himself, as though he thought he were hallucinating.

"Now, I have seen everything," said Captain Ing softly to himself.

Next, Alcarsh was setting his black-haired hands on the window of The Horizon, with his eyes tight shut, as though he were focussing really hard on a thought.

Next thing Captain Ing knew, Alcarsh had beamed himself inside The Horizon.

"Oh no," Captain Ing yelled, "not you again. There is no way that I am going to let you hurt anybody here. Out at once."

However, Alcarsh removed his portable rocket and took the air bubble off his head and set them on the floor.

Captain Ing stood at the controls as though he wanted to go to Arshga to report this to his companions.

"But ... but why did you save us?" stuttered the Ensign.

Alcarsh eyed everyone on the ship as though he were trying to get everyone's attention.

"I will explain," he muttered.

25 The Secret Is Revealed

Several seconds of silence passed on The Horizon. Captain Ing and his crew were in complete disbelief of what was happening now. Maybe this was part of another trick.

"Just what are you up to?" asked Captain Ing. "After all that you have done with the treasure, why have you saved us?"

"I need you all to listen very closely to me," explained Alcarsh. "If you don't, you will never be able to recover the treasure."

"Get rid of him!" yelled the Ensign. "He's trying to trick us. We know that he devoured Mr. Noin. We know that he stole the treasure. We saw him, remember?"

"The treasure?" Alcarsh asked. "That is what you misunderstand the most. I need all of you to understand that I would never commit such a theft. I have been trying to protect the treasure as a matter of fact."

"You're a liar!" Captain Ing yelled. "We saw you hurry to Atwydolyn to take it. We witnessed you with our own eyes."

"But did you ever actually see me lift it off the surface of the planet and take it away?" Alcarsh asserted.

Captain Ing made a blank expression and shook his head slightly.

"You're right. You didn't see me. That's because I never did take it away, Captain Ing. You see, I hurried to Atwydolyn to protect the treasure and see if I could stop it from being stolen, but still, the true enemy came after me."

"What do you mean?" cried Captain Ing. "Who came after you?"

"Someone you have always trusted for three years," he replied, "Someone whom you have remained loyal to all through this trip.

She has cooked your meals, commanded your ship, and roomed with Tiffany, Jame and Melissa. Never mind that she has also stolen Tonya's inventions, told Crazy Max about the treasure, and taken the treasure from Atwydolyn's surface."

"What?! Our Commander Mandy?" cried Captain Ing in disbelief. "She is my friend."

"She is also a traitor and a thief," explained Alcarsh. "It is she who has been working against you and your crew all this time."

"You're mad!" Captain Ing exclaimed. "You're crazy if you think that you can fool us by trying to turn Mandy Finks away from me."

"I rescued you from Crazy Max, remember?" Alcarsh growled. "I need you to trust me. It's the only way you'll get the Grachas' treasure back and end my five-year burden of being feared by everyone."

"Why shouldn't people fear you?" asked Captain Ing. "You're a repulsive black and hairy beast, who has taken the Grachas' treasure, stolen Tonya's inventions and eaten Mr. Noin."

"Mr. Noin?" he asked. "Mr. Noin is with me wherever I go and he does whatever I do and when I do it. When I am eating, he is eating. When I am sleeping, he is sleeping. When I went to guard the treasure, he went to guard the treasure."

"What do you mean?" asked Captain Ing. "What are you trying to tell us?"

"I am Mr. Noin," replied Alcarsh. "You see, I didn't eat him. I was transformed into a monster by Crazy Max when I knew about Percia. Crazy Max returned to the forest shortly after and disguised himself as my remains, while Percia piloted Crazy Max's ship. I don't know how Percia learned to pilot a ship so quickly, but Crazy Max must have done something to her."

"But that's insane!" cried Captain Ing. "You can't be Mr.

The Stolen Treasure

Noin. It isn't true."

"It is true," he explained. "You see, when I was made a monster, nobody trusted me. They all feared me. When everyone believed that I was a monster, I had no choice but to stay in hiding in the woods, drinking water from streams and eating vegetation and berries. I knew that, if anybody caught me and held me captive in a prison, or worse, put me to death, I would be powerless if any serious emergency situation occurred.

"I have stayed hidden, until my time has come, which is now. If Crazy Max regains this treasure, he may become too powerful for us to conquer. My only hope is to recover the treasure, so that the Grachas can keep it safe from Crazy Max and use it. Only then, everyone will see who I truly am and hopefully feel terribly guilty for being so prejudiced in the first place.

"You must remember that I am just another Earth man. Even my own parents believed that a monster had killed and eaten their son and they swore that they would do anything, even risk their lives, if it meant catching the killer."

"I am really sorry," sympathized Jame, stepping toward Alcarsh. "We will follow through with your plan."

"Get away!" cried the Captain. "Do you want him to bite your head off?"

Jame made a mild gesture of disappointment and sat back down.

"I have never had anyone be so kind to me," said Alcarsh. "I have never had anyone understand me, ever since I became this monster."

"You are a monster!" yelled Captain Ing. "You can't deny it. I happen to know Mr. Noin and he would never steal valuable devices."

Alcarsh lifted his hands from behind his back. "You mean these?" he asked, pensively, showing everyone the Mindcoat, and the

195

Dome Clothes.

"You stole those!" cried Captain Ing. "That is why you have them here."

"I didn't steal them," he explained. "I recovered them. I took them all away from your Commander the night that I attacked her. It was she who had them to start with, not me. I only took them away to keep them safe."

"If that really were the case, why didn't you give them back to us?" asked Jame.

"From what I have already told you, I thought you would have already been able to guess the answer to that. I knew that wouldn't be safe with the real thief on board your ship."

"I am not a thief!" yelled Mandy. "Everyone, don't listen to him. It's all a slander. He's trying to fool us. I have been helping you. I have been trying to prevent the treasure from being stolen."

"That will be quite enough thank you," stated Alcarsh. He lifted up his zapshot and shot.

Mandy lay there, stunned.

"What did you do that for?" yelled Captain Ing.

"We can't let her interfere with our plan," explained Alcarsh.

"What plan?" asked Rick.

"I will get to that in a few minutes," replied Alcarsh.

"Excuse me!" cried Rick, "but, on our Mind Deck, our old Lieutenant witnessed a re-creation of Percia being taken away. Lieutenant Linda said nothing about your being transformed, and she would never have left out something like that."

"She saw my thoughts?" asked Alcarsh, worried. "What happened to her?"

"She was shot by Crazy Max's Colodiggan Gun and assimilated with Crazy Max," explained Tiffany.

"Then, that's my fault," sighed Alcarsh. "I didn't know that

The Stolen Treasure

mind images could be transferred to other Mind Decks."

"Just explain why Linda didn't talk about Crazy Max's transforming you," continued Rick. "Why did she still think that Mr. Noin got devoured? See if you can get yourself out of that one."

Alcarsh stood there, thinking for a few seconds, before he answered.

"Sometimes, thoughts can be deceiving," he replied finally. "If I were your Lieutenant in this incident, I would have looked up toward The Equator, to watch for Alcarsh coming down from Crazy Max releasing him, to devour Mr. Noin. What really happened was all on land. Crazy Max must have focussed his thoughts really hard, or something, to transform me. All your Lieutenant would have seen, at the most, would have had to have been me running away, ashamed of my new appearance. She would never have seen my transformation, while looking up at the ship."

"All right," growled Captain Ing, "I'll let you win on this one, but now explain this!" he cried switching on the news hologram, titled, "A Threat Brought Back." It was the exact same one that he had shown to everyone when their Commander had first told them about Alcarsh.

"What were you doing with the ERL?" asked Captain Ing, turning the news hologram off.

"That will be easy to explain," replied Alcarsh. "You see, I happened to catch Mandy the night she stole from Jame and Melissa's houses. Mandy had a Portable Rocket and she was transporting herself there. My Space Swoop wasn't working and I couldn't make my ship go fast enough to reach Mandy in time to stop her, but with Tachyon Imagery Magnification, I could see her take the Mindcoat. She stuffed the ERL in the Mindcoat, and stuffed the Mindcoat and Dome Clothes in her uniform. You won't believe this, but she had the map rolled and hidden up her high-heeled shoe. I tried to contact

Detective Freefall. Unfortunately, I was delayed by Gerbulans and Arts, which I suppose were sent by Crazy Max, when he saw that I was following Mandy. Mandy had made an agreement with Crazy Max that she would bring Tonya's inventions to him so that he could destroy them. That was why I knew I had to come and recover them from your ship, where Mandy had them concealed after stealing them from the homes, the first opportunity I had so that I could stop her from taking them to Crazy Max."

"You're...you're kidding," cried Captain Ing.

"However, as you can see, I have the map now, so there's no point in checking your Commander. After Mandy had stolen Tonya's inventions, the ERL slipped from inside the Dome Clothes. Then, I moved my ship really close to it, so that I could beam it inside and I did. I went to Atwydolyn to put the ERL on top of the treasure so that it would blast Crazy Max away if he came near it, but Detective Freefall saw me, and the ERL that was inside the ship, before I made it to Atwydolyn, and assumed I was the thief. He tried to arrest me, but I outmanoeuvred him.

"Don't you see? Mandy has been watching what the Grachas have been doing closely since their houses got destroyed to see if they used their Latimus to make a treasure chest fund. When she found that they were, she told Crazy Max about it. Then, she told Captain Ing's Company and the Latimus Prospectors that I told Crazy Max."

"Tell us about when you came onto our ship, for the first time, and attacked our Commander," inquired Jame.

"Because I knew where your Commander was keeping the Treasure Map and the Mindcoat, I was at an advantage," explained Alcarsh. "Do you remember when Mandy tripped at the top of the stairs and her right shoe came off?"

"I think so," replied Rick.

"In half of a chance, I was lucky that it was the right shoe.

The Stolen Treasure

Therefore, it was easy to take the map out of it.

"It was the Mindcoat, however, that I really had to fight Mandy for. I managed to get it out with that big swipe up her uniform. However, my body was in the way, so you couldn't see me retrieve the Mindcoat.

"Then, I went through the cabinets and drawers in your ship in hope of finding the Dome Clothes. However, I only found them after I had stunned your Captain. Nobody saw me find them in one of the drawers in the wall and take them out, because you were all preoccupied with worrying about Captain Ing.

"Do you understand? Even though I took all of the devices from Mandy, it was unlucky that nobody actually saw me do it. If anyone had caught any of these, you would know, by now, how guilty your Commander really is."

"That's amazing!" cried Jame.

"But why didn't you just explain?" asked Rick.

"I knew that you wouldn't believe me," replied Alcarsh. "I knew I had to receive your trust before I had any hope that you would. Even after I have saved you, you still have trouble understanding my situation."

"Hold on a minute," inquired Tiffany this time. "We went to Atwydolyn before the treasure was stolen and there was no ERL there."

"Yeah," said Jame in mildly suspicious tones, "how would you explain that?"

"I had been watching over the treasure too. Because of its brilliance, the Grachas thought that they could use the ERL as another part of the treasure and shut it inside. They used the password, 'Row-shee-doo.'"

Rick spoke up again. "Our Mind Deck needs to be turned on to work. How did you turn it on, so it would display mind images, without us noticing?"

"I didn't turn it on," explained Alcarsh. "I didn't even know that these images were going on in your Mind Deck. Are you sure you turned it off the last time you used it?"

"I ... I think I did," replied Captain Ing. "I'm not sure whether I did or not, now that I think of it. It's too long ago now."

"That could be why," sighed Alcarsh.

"If Mandy really is the thief, then where did she take the treasure?" asked Jame.

"I can't say," replied Alcarsh. "Even I don't know everything. However, I do know that, after I had reached Atwydolyn and Mandy came after me, a large gough of Grachas attacked her. Then, Mandy used her Latimus Prospector shoes, which she had put back on, to float down to steal the treasure and she shot them all. Then, she took a hand-made monster foot out of her pocket and stamped it on the ground to make monster tracks. Mandy got such a terrible attack from the Gracha guards that you assumed, the next day, that I had attacked her, although it was actually the Grachas who had attacked her.

"However, at that moment, Crazy Max came down and took me prisoner on his spaceship. He tried to shoot at me with his gun, but I shielded off all of the bullets.

"Then, he took out his last weapon, which was a special blasting device and he blasted me inside his Mind Deck and locked me inside. I was now cut away from all that was going on outside the ship.

"However, while I was there, I made a lot of mind images and Percia's being taken away happened to be one of them. I suppose it communicated to your Mind Deck as well."

"And how did you know those scenes in the Mind Deck in such perfect detail?" asked Melissa.

The Stolen Treasure

"Crazy Max has quite a sophisticated deck," Alcarsh explained. "All I had to do was say the date and location of the scenes I wanted to make, and they appeared in the Mind Deck, in perfect detail, exactly as they had happened. I did this because I wanted to find out as much as I could about Percia's past."

"Then why didn't you use his deck to find the location of the treasure?"

"Because I need someone to trust me. I need someone else to see, for themselves, where the treasure is, in order for that person to believe me properly. My transformation can only be reversed if I receive the trust of another and successfully complete a mission, against Crazy Max, with that person."

"How did you come to rescue us?" continued Melissa.

"Crazy Max did let me out of the Mind Deck when he wasn't doing anything he didn't want me to know about, but the first time I was ever let out onto land again was when Crazy Max attacked you. It felt like I had been brought back to life when I was let out of the ship after so long, even in the freezing cold. In that ship, I had been drinking rusty water out of the sink and eating old and stale food from the pantry.

"The only reason that I made it out onto the planet was because Crazy Max had been absentminded enough to think that I was in the Mind Deck at the time. When I set foot in the snow, Crazy Max drew out his shooter and shot me far away.

Then, Alcarsh turned to Captain Ing. "I broke into a frantic rush when I saw Crazy Max leave the planet. When I returned to where The Equator used to be, I discovered that Crazy Max had forgotten his portable rocket and his shooter. I put the rocket on and blasted myself toward The Horizon, and turned Crazy Max's ship away with his own shooter."

Once again, Alcarsh gazed around at all of the members of the trip. The crew finally appeared satisfied, and were nodding their heads, and the passengers were facing Captain Ing, who looked as though he was finally starting to believe Alcarsh's story a little bit, even though he didn't want to.

"Explain this plan of yours," said Lieutenant Gordon.

Alcarsh set the inventions down on the table, except the Mindcoat, which he kept in his hand, letting it hang down as he showed it around.

"One of you will use the Mindcoat to go back to the time when the inventions were stolen, using Mandy's point of view," Alcarsh explained. "When that person returns to the present, he or she will remove the coat and tell us where the treasure is and we will go out to recover it."

"That sounds like an extremely adventurous plan," stated Mr. Gordon. "Are we really going to see Mandy's past when we wear that thing?"

"Whoever is wearing the coat will see her past," explained Alcarsh. "There are risks and dangers though. Mandy might wake up from her stun and catch us, and Crazy Max will probably be there. However, if all goes well, we should be able to find the treasure and bring it back to the Grachas. We should also be able to find out the rest of what Mandy has been doing on this ship, while I was with Crazy Max. Are you willing to try my plan?"

"I think our first priority would be to shut Mandy up somewhere so she can't stop us," said the Captain.

"I agree," said Rick. "Let's lock her in her bedroom."

Captain Ing took Mandy's shoulders, and Alcarsh took her feet. They carried her out of the Bridge, laid her in her sleeping quarter, shut the door, and the Captain cyber-locked it.

When Captain Ing and Alcarsh arrived back in the Bridge, Captain Ing made a decisive expression for a few seconds. Then, he

The Stolen Treasure

looked at everyone else in the ship. "What do you think?" he asked. "Should we believe him?"

"I think that it's at least worth a try," explained Jame. "All right, we'll do it."

"Brilliant," said Alcarsh, finally beginning to smile. "Who would like to wear the coat and go back?"

"I will!" cried Jame.

Jame took the Mindcoat from Alcarsh's outstretched hand and put it on.

"Latimus Prospector Mandy Finks on midnight, March the twelfth," cried Jame with confidence.

"Good luck," beamed Melissa.

26 Alcarsh's Plan

The scene of the ship vanished before Jame's eyes and so did the stars outside the window. Even the floor seemed to disappear and she was standing in complete nothingness until a black floor came into existence under her feet and she found herself in another ship, facing Crazy Max.

The only difference was that Jame felt a few inches taller, her hair was shorter and brown instead of black, her dark skin was now fair and she was wearing the pink uniform and shoes that Mandy had been wearing all through the trip.

She was in the form of Mandy Finks.

"Stab," grinned Crazy Max, "What news do you bring me?"

Uncontrollably, Jame, who was now Mandy, replied, "I spy a treasure chest, my lord. A treasure made of Latimus by the Grachas. It will help you become more powerful."

"Bring it to me," cackled Crazy Max. "Are there any dangers, though?"

"None, whatsoever," Jame felt herself grin, "except maybe certain advanced technology. Last time I took some of my prospected Latimus over to you, I noticed Tonya. In these scanning pictures, I noticed her leave some of her inventions with some small and young-looking kid. If I'm not mistaken, they were the Dome Clothes, an ERL and a Mindcoat. I have watched her since and she has also given this child a treasure map. I will keep all scans on what happens to these inventions but I have also picked up the young girl giving the treasure map to an older girl."

"Those could be obstacles in our plan," snarled Crazy Max, "Take them away. Hide the ERL some place else, but either hide the rest with you or bring them to me. You know the punishment if you

The Stolen Treasure

disobey your lord," laughed Crazy Max, pointing the Colodiggan Gun at Jame.

"Yes, master," Jame stuttered, who was now beginning to regret going back in time with the Mindcoat. She feared all the horrible things that she would probably end up doing uncontrollably and hoped that seeing these events really would help the treasure.

The Mindcoat made Jame stride across the floor and lift a Portable Rocket off of the floor.

Next, she had left the ship and headed toward Earth. Surprisingly enough, Crazy Max's ship was disguised as a meteoroid on the outside. She removed a microphone from her pocket and pressed a button on the bottom.

"This is Latimus Prospector Mandy Finks here," she called, "I have terrible news. Alcarsh has told Crazy Max all about the Grachas' treasure at Atwydolyn."

Jame involuntarily shut the microphone off and shoved it back into her pocket.

When Jame got close to Earth, she pressed a red button, which turned the portable rocket off. For a few seconds, Jame plummeted toward the ground, with nothing to stop her, before a parachute opened and she floated down like an autumn leaf.

It was night when Jame reached Earth, and just ahead was Melissa's house, the very house Jame knew that she was uncontrollably about to rob.

Yet, through her panic, Jame pondered the concept of how Mandy had entered the house and taken the cyberlock off of the cupboard.

However, before Jame's feet even touched the ground, she slowly began to rise again. She was levitating toward the window of Melissa's room.

Jame remembered that it must be the high-heeled shoes on her feet that were making her float, the exact same devices that had made Mandy rise when she was prospecting for Latimus.

When Jame had reached the window, she noticed a small burglar alarm on the wall, so instead of beaming herself into the house, she reached into her pockets, lifted out gloves and pulled them onto her hands. Once again, she dug into her left pocket and this time, pulled out a sharp lock pick and began to chip away at the lock on the window.

It was a long job, but the Mindcoat finally made Jame move to the window and slide it open.

There was a fraction of a second of the burglar alarm sounding as Jame shot it with her zapshot and fried its circuit.

Melissa stirred in her bed and Jame floated underneath the window, to hide herself from Melissa's sight.

After a few seconds, Melissa became quiet again and lay still and Jame entered the room through the open window.

Melissa appeared so gentle and graceful in her sleep that even the thought of stealing from such a pure child made Jame's stomach turn, but Jame started her dirty work all the same.

Jame levitated about a foot off the floor. With her gloved hand, she reached toward the cupboard. Somehow, as though she already knew what the code was, she opened the lock, pulled it open and opened the cupboard doors. Then, Jame started removing all of the contents. She pulled the Mindcoat under her uniform and tied it around her waist. Then, she folded the ERL into the Mindcoat and stuffed that in her uniform as well.

Jame floated out of the house and shut the window behind her, gently and quietly. Then, she levitated so high off the ground that she couldn't be seen and started to find her way to Jame's house.

When Jame arrived at her own house, she followed through with the same procedure, by chipping away at the lock on the window

The Stolen Treasure

and entering. Jame's house didn't happen to have a burglar alarm, so that caused no interference with the theft.

All that the Mindcoat made Jame do was remove the treasure map from its drawer, open the heel of her right shoe and slide it inside.

Then, she left Earth and headed back to Crazy Max. On her way there, she tossed the ERL aside.

I have obeyed your command, my lord," Jame smiled to Crazy Max when she had reached the ship.

"Wonderful," he cackled confidently.

"I have taken the ERL, the treasure map, the Mindcoat and the Dome Clothes."

"Are you sure that is everything?" he asked.

"I'm certain," Jame replied.

"Are you absolutely positive?" growled Crazy Max. "Why don't you make sure, just for good measure?"

"I don't need to make sure."

"Are you considering disobeying my command?" Crazy Max yelled. "You know what happens if you rebel," crazy Max pointed a Colodiggan Gun at Jame's chest.

"What do you want this time?"

"Burn down their houses," laughed Crazy Max. "That way, all devices will be destroyed and I will be clear to take the Latimus treasure and gain power, unless, of course, you deliver the treasure to me."

"I could never burn down someone's house," cried the Jame Mandy. Even this was uncontrolled, through the Mindcoat.

"YOU HEARD ME, DIDN'T YOU?!" bellowed Crazy Max, pointing the gun closer. "I rescued you, didn't I? Listen, you will go back to those same houses tomorrow night, whether you like it or not, and you will burn both houses with your zapshot."

207

"Yes, Crazy Max," replied Jame.

Reluctantly, Jame decided to close her eyes, and whispered, "Latimus Prospector, Mandy Finks, March the twelfth at twenty-one hundred hours."

The next thing Jame knew, she was levitating toward her own house, once again.

Knowing what was about to happen, she tried to move herself away from the house. However, she soon discovered that she couldn't move her body at her will and couldn't speak when she had her eyes open. Therefore, the thought occurred to Jame that speaking with her eyes shut must be the only way she could change the moment.

All the same, she found herself before her own house again in the black of the night. Despite the fact that Jame hated the idea, she found herself drawing out her zapshot and shot, a long continuous shot, that burned at the siding more and more until it produced smoke, then sparks, then finally flames.

When Jame had reached Melissa's house, she drew out her zapshot a second time to shoot, only this time, a shocking miracle occurred. A quick spark flashed from the zapshot and burnt out.

Jame pressed the trigger again, but nothing happened.

"What in the universe?!" cried Jame, pressing the trigger many times.

"I burnt down both houses," Jame explained the next time she reached Crazy Max.

"Excellent, my proud servant," grinned Crazy Max, showing many rotting teeth in his grimy mouth. "You have done well for me. I will take the treasure."

"The great Alcarsh is mighty and fierce, my lord. You are better at capturing prisoners, but all planets have their eyes out for you. You will never be able to take the Latimus in peace. I will take the treasure, while resting with great explorer Captain Ing, where I can't be suspected. He thinks I'm off with my Prospectors right now. That goes to show how little he knows."

"I suppose you're right, my clever thief," grinned Crazy Max. "Head off to your Ing, but don't delay taking the treasure too long. Try to get rid of Alcarsh while you are at it. We can't have him witnessing our scheme."

Jame shut her eyes and concentrated on the day that Alcarsh had entered Captain Ing's ship. Then, Jame was snapped awake by the sound of footsteps heading into the room and, immediately, she saw Alcarsh.

The crew began screaming, just like they had when the incident had really happened, and Jame, as Mandy, dashed down the hallway shrieking, followed by the monster and then the passengers.

Just as before, Jame tripped at the top of the stairs and her shoe fell off. She heard a faint click and a slide as Alcarsh pulled the treasure map out of the shoe.

The Mindcoat made Jame pull herself back onto her feet and remove her other shoe. Then, she strode into the Bridge, with Alcarsh, the passengers and the crew behind.

The zapshot shots reoccurred and, once again, Alcarsh trapped the Commander in the corner. She tried to run away from her trap but it was no use. Alcarsh instantly slashed his paw up Mandy's uniform. Jame let out a great cry of pain as Alcarsh pulled out the Mindcoat.

Captain Ing tried to pull the monster away, but the monster shot him.

"Is he dead?" asked the Ensign.

"No, he's just stunned," replied the Doctor, examining the Captain.

Meanwhile, Alcarsh was searching the ship for the Dome Clothes and found them in the drawer of the side wall, just as he had explained. Everyone else was still looking down at Captain Ing.

When Alcarsh showed the devices that the Commander had stolen, the real Jame cried, "Tonya's inventions."

Alcarsh jumped into his ship and began to pilot it toward Atwydolyn.

After the arguing that had gone on before happened. Then, all the members of the trip stepped back to back. Jame put on her Portable Rocket, left the ship and headed for Atwydolyn.

Alcarsh's ship was not far ahead, as Jame rocketed to Atwydolyn, and she shot at it a few times, but Alcarsh dodged his ship out of the way each time.

When the Jame Mandy had landed on Atwydolyn, she used her shoes to levitate above the ground. The treasure was just ahead and she began to move toward it.

As instantly as the bang from a firecracker, Crazy Max's ship appeared in the sky and beamed the monster into his ship with the beam that Alcarsh had mentioned. Hopefully, now would be the part in which Jame would discover where the treasure was truly hidden.

A great herd of Grachas popped out from behind the treasure, hissing and snapping viciously. They jumped all over the Commander, biting every bit of flesh they could find. Jame could feel blood streaming out of her everywhere. It stained her uniform and, if it weren't for the knowledge of Mandy's recovery in Sickbay, she would have wondered if she was going to die.

However, she managed to snap out her zapshot and stun every single one.

Then, (with a great deal of force) Jame lifted the treasure off the ground and set the chest inside the monster's abandoned ship, and took off.

"Crazy Max will soon have his spoil," she grinned as she manipulated the control board and started piloting the ship to an

The Stolen Treasure

unknown planet.

Eventually, a dull, brown planet arrived in front of Jame's eyes. It didn't appear to be suitable for any life.

However, it was when Jame landed the ship, that she guessed what it must be; Dry Dust.

Again, she lifted the treasure and took it out of the ship. There, she set it on the ground and left it there.

Then, she got out of the ship and lifted a small black ball with a wire attached to it out of her pocket and set it on the floor of Alcarsh's ship. She shot at it with her zapshot and immediately sprinted away from the ship as fast as she could.

"KABLOOOOOOOOM!" The ship exploded, scattering tiny pieces of debris, which nearly reached where Jame was hurrying at top speed.

She used her Portable Rocket to head back to Captain Ing's ship.

Jame shut her eyes and thought of when the crew was leaving Captain Ing's Mind Deck after seeing it for the first time. Jame recalled how Captain Ing had provided light with his fingernails and turned the Mind Deck on with the light provided. She wanted to see, for sure, if the Captain had forgotten to turn the deck off.

Jame found herself in the scene of Captain Ing's planet. Near it, Jame's school and Atwydolyn were still in sight.

Everyone clapped their hands and all three scenes started disappearing, into their heads, to reveal pitch blackness.

"Wow!" cried the voices of everyone in the room, except Captain Ing, who called, "This way."

"That was indeed the most fascinating experience in my life," Rick smiled.

This time, Jame noticed that they left without Captain Ing turning the deck off.

Satisfied, Jame closed both eyes and thought of the night in which their old Lieutenant had been abducted.

The crew's bedroom was silent as Jame, still as the Commander, stretched in the night, tiptoed out of her bed and began to talk into the holoputer connected to the wall. She whispered a quick code of numbers and began to talk to Crazy Max.

"This is your loyal servant, Stab, calling," she whispered. "I am informing you that Linda now knows about Percia Gordon. She has also told her crew and all other members of this ship. You can take her away."

"Good for you for informing me," grinned the holographic image of Crazy Max. "I will come right over."

Several minutes after the screen had gone blank, Crazy Max's ship appeared outside the ship's window and connected.

Slowly and carefully, with all the stealth that she could possibly contain, Jame lifted Linda out of her bed, pressed her gently against the ship's window, pressed a tiny white button on the wall about a millimetre in diameter and beamed her through. Once Linda was inside Crazy Max's ship, a muted bang from a gun sounded.

An eye peeped open beside Jame. It was the Ensign.

"You should come back later," Jame whispered. "You will never be able to get everyone in a ship with so many corridors like this. I will come to you later and make arrangements."

"All right," growled Crazy Max. "I will trust you." He left Captain Ing's ship.

Next, Jame decided to think about when Captain Ing had taken everyone to his planet to arrange for a new Lieutenant.

The next thing Jame knew, she was setting foot on the world on which the Captain had always lived and the first of the Blue Clouds were appearing over the horizon.

Tiffany began to jump around excitedly. "Those must be the

The Stolen Treasure

Blue Clouds!" she cried as everyone else gazed at the sky, waiting for them to spread.

Instead of staying at the planet to watch the show, Jame attached her Portable Rocket to her back and left.

Jame arrived on Crazy Max's ship, and hissed in his ear, "My dearest lord, when our new Lieutenant arrives, take yourself to the North Pole of Uberdan and disguise yourself as the treasure. I will take Captain Ing and his crew and then lead them to you."

"Your plans are always perfect, Stab," smirked Crazy Max. "Very well then."

"I've got to get back to Captain Ing," she whispered. "He is watching the Blue Clouds and he can't notice that I'm gone."

"So long, my thief," grinned Crazy Max and Jame left the ship.

Finally satisfied, Jame shut her eyes, and, this time, she removed the Mindcoat. She found herself as Jame Maguire, once more, standing on the floor of The Horizon.

"What did you see?" asked Mr. Gordon inquisitively.

"I have been watching the Grachas and I saw where the treasure is," smiled Jame. "It is located on the planet, Dry Dust, latitude and longitude 30 degrees North, 60 degrees East according to The Equator's coordinates."

"Wonderful," beamed Captain Ing.

"And neither Alcarsh, nor Crazy Max, set foot on this ship when Linda was abducted," Jame continued. "Crazy Max connected himself to the outside of the ship, and Mandy pressed a button that was so small you could barely see it, and beamed the Lieutenant out of the ship. While we were watching the Blue Clouds, Mandy told Crazy Max to go to Uberdan and look like the treasure, so that he could trick us into being assimilated. Mandy floated to steal the inventions on The Horizon."

"I never knew there was a transporter button in the room!"

213

cried Captain Ing, shocked. "Somebody must have secretly installed it."

"Mandy, I suspect," said Jame. "Also, she came here so she wouldn't be suspected and Crazy Max made his ship look like an asteroid and it's true that Crazy Max wants the treasure so he can digest the Latimus and become yet more powerful."

"What happened to Alcarsh's ship?" asked the Engineer.

"Mandy blew it up with a bomb when she reached Dry Dust and used her Portable Rocket to head back to this ship."

"It's been proven then!" cried the Engineer. "It is time to go to Dry Dust."

Captain Ing took the controls and set a course for the planet.

"Are we safe from Crazy Max now?" asked Lieutenant Gordon.

"Just as long as Crazy Max is within the shooter's Alcarsh's range," he replied. "As we all know, the repulsion light is so much stronger."

"What does that mean?" said the Ensign.

The Ensign's question was immediately answered, for, from quite a long distance this time, another torpedo blast almost hit the ship.

"Crazy Max has regained his path toward our ship," cried Captain Ing. "We must go faster if we want to escape."

This time, the shots were distant and Crazy Max had a greater chance of missing, but Captain Ing piloted his ship into Space Swoop all the same.

"Dry Dust should be coming up soon!" called the Engineer.

In the distance, a brown and lifeless planet was starting to appear.

"Put these on!" cried Alcarsh, holding out the Dome Clothes.

Every person ran up to Alcarsh and started putting on the repulsion suits.

The Stolen Treasure

"I see the treasure!" Captain Ing cried.

"Brilliant!" cried the Engineer, "the Grachas will soon have their money back and will be able to spread it among themselves at last."

"It's time to land the ship," Captain Ing announced.

The ship came to a halt on the dry surface. Then, everyone followed the Captain out of the ship, and onto lifeless ground.

"Where's the treasure?" asked the Ensign.

"This way," called Captain Ing.

Crazy Max seemed to have completely forgotten about shooting Captain Ing's ship. However, out of nowhere, Captain Ing was startled by a grasp on his shoulder. He swirled around and found himself face to face with Mandy.

"Oh no, you don't!" she cried.

Mandy must have flown over the crew and passengers with her rocket and descended in front of the Captain to be unnoticed. Her face wasn't remotely sweet or gentle anymore, but angry and hateful, and her eyes had the look of Percia.

"Get away!" she screamed, "or you will all wish that you had never been born. Did you really think that locking me up would keep me at bay? I keep an extra powerful zapshot with me at all times that Crazy Max gave me, and I blasted the door to smithereens. I now have the power to kill all!"

"You have been my friend for three Earth years," protested Captain Ing. "You would never dream of killing me."

"We will see about that one, won't we," she hissed. "Robots!" she called into the microphone attached to her rocket. She turned to face the Captain again, "And don't even think you can destroy these ones. They upgraded from that one you saw on Atwydolyn. They don't rely on any power source."

A mob of Gracha-hunter lookalikes climbed over the rocks.

"You see?" she hissed. "Crazy Max has been loyal enough to me to supply me with an unbeatable army."

"Nothing is unbeatable for me," said Alcarsh. He held out the shooter and began to move the robots away

"Give me that!" cackled a voice and a hand grabbed the shooter off Alcarsh. It was Crazy Max.

"That just so happens to be mine!" Crazy Max yelled, and slapped Alcarsh in the face.

"Run!" yelled Captain Ing and they took off at full speed.

"Don't just stand there, you cowards," shrieked Mandy. "Fight dirty."

The robots ran and shot at Captain Ing. Captain Ing shot back at them. However, they all dodged the shots coming from Captain Ing's zapshot. They soon surrounded the treasure.

"It looks like we're barred," sighed Captain Ing.

"See if you can get past these," hissed Mandy.

Alcarsh tried to stun one with his zapshot, but the shot only deflected off its hideous surface, leaving the robot unharmed.

With a great spark, one of them shot from the treasure, landed around Alcarsh and coiled its arms around his neck.

Alcarsh tried to pull the robot off himself, but its grip was superior. Even when Captain Ing, and everyone else together, tried to pull the robot away, its strength was stronger than that of every ship member combined. They shot at it several times, but they bounced back all the time.

The seconds ticked by in suspense as Alcarsh was strangled and panic was arising about whether or not he would make it.

Crazy Max was becoming so desperate that he was now shooting the treasure chest, but it still remained intact.

One of the robots appeared to be thinking hard, but finally announced, "I've been scanning the Grachas. The password is 'Row-

The Stolen Treasure

shee-doo.'"

Crazy Max heaved the treasure chest lid once more and much to his delight, it opened, but only to reveal a great fright to Crazy Max.

The ERL kicked in and with a yell, Crazy Max was instantly blasted away and the treasure remained untouched.

The robot that was clinging onto Alcarsh's neck dropped to the ground, as Alcarsh breathed deeply to regain his air.

The robots that had been around the treasure shot around in every direction to look for their master.

"Now is our chance," announced Alcarsh. "The treasure is unguarded."

Captain Ing stood at one end of the treasure chest and Alcarsh stood at the other end. Together, they lifted the enormous chest.

"We can do it," called the Engineer as he, too, joined in helping to carry the treasure toward the ship. The rest of the crew and passengers gathered around to help.

"Get them, you stupid Gracha hunters!" screamed Mandy stamping her feet. The mechanical fiends marched across the ground once more.

"Hurry," Captain Ing breathed. "Run."

However, it was impossible to run, while carrying such a heavy load. They trudged along, while the robots got closer.

"I'll run to the ship," huffed the Captain, "and bring it over here." Captain Ing let go of the treasure, and ran off towards the ship.

"Faster!" yelled the Ensign. "We don't have much time left."

The robots were rocketing themselves along at short distances at a time and were constantly gaining on the crew and passengers, who were slowly tugging the treasure along.

"Put it down," cried Mandy, now consumed with fury. She started reaching into the treasure chest.

"Get your hand out of there or else," yelled the Ensign.

"It's too late," she hissed, pulling out the ERL. "You will no longer have it to repel Crazy Max." She let it go and it smashed on the ground.

"What have you done?!" the Ensign cried.

"I hope Captain Ing reaches the ship soon," grunted Alcarsh, gazing at the Captain, who still had a fair distance left to run.

"The robots are nearly here," cried the Engineer. "Come on, faster!"

"I never knew that the recovery of the treasure would be such an ordeal," grumbled Mr. Gordon. "Just when we have found the Latimus, the worst happens."

The robots had practically reached the treasure now, and the crew and passengers were almost in the range of their arms' reach.

"Captain Ing had better hurry up," yelled the Lieutenant.

The explorers' strength had nearly bottomed out when Captain Ing finally disappeared behind the door of The Horizon.

After a few stressful seconds, the ship moved slightly off the ground and glided toward the rest of his friends.

"The ship's here!" cried the Lieutenant as the tip of a robot's finger touched the heel of his boot.

The crew and passengers broke into a run up the staircase as the robots tried to come in after them and Mandy tried to pull the treasure away.

"In! In!" yelled the Engineer, forcing the chest away from Mandy's arms. "The robots are trying to enter our ship!"

"We've got the treasure in," shouted Alcarsh. "Shut the door, quick."

Captain Ing switched the door tightly closed as Mandy dashed back into the ship. A robot's arm got caught in the door and there was a monstrous cry as it yanked it out.

The Stolen Treasure

"We made it!" cried Captain Ing in triumph. "To Atwydolyn."

"That was close," breathed Lieutenant Gordon in a huge sigh of relief.

"You have won our full confidence now, Alcarsh," grinned the Ensign. "We will trust you from now on. Let's shake hands."

Alcarsh held out his black and hairy hand and shook hands with the Ensign.

"He's not Alcarsh," smiled Captain Ing. "He's Mr. Noin."

"Let's give a hand to everyone!" beamed the Doctor.

In the middle of the applause, a ship appeared outside the window.

"Who is that?" asked the Jame.

"That will be Detective Freefall and the rest of my company," explained Captain Ing. "I think they see the treasure."

"Oh no," cried Jame, "not now; he'll think we're stealing it."

"If he sees Alcarsh, he's probably going to think that he assimilated all of us into helping Crazy Max get the treasure," cried The Engineer. "He won't understand."

Suddenly, a second ship arrived in Captain Ing's sight.

"Who's that?" asked Rick.

"It's Tonya," replied Captain Ing.

"What's she going to say?" Rick.

"I don't know," replied the Captain. "I hope she understands."

"Here come the Latimus Prospectors," called Mandy, as a third ship moved into sight.

"They're following us," explained Captain Ing. "They might understand we're recovering the treasure if we make it to Atwydolyn."

"Well," declared Mandy, "I am going to make it doubly certain that Alcarsh is more than locked up and kept safe. I will make sure he is dead; him and the rest of you. Crazy Max will get the treasure.

Just you wait." She snatched out her zapshot, set it to kill, and pointed it around the room.

Mandy's hand slowly trembled and, of all wonders, she shifted her arm to her side and dropped the zapshot, while the crew, Alcarsh and Captain Ing stood in amazement. The Captain took this opportunity and snatched Mandy's zapshot away from under her.

"You don't want to kill us?" cried the Engineer, in surprise and amazement.

"Yes I do!" she cried. She lunged at Captain Ing to retrieve her zapshot, but stopped just before her hand touched him. Mandy sighed, "I don't believe this. I can't do it. It was all so wrong when I did it before."

"Who did you kill before, Mandy?" Captain Ing asked her, incredulously.

Mandy ignored the question. "I will turn you and Alcarsh in to Detective Freefall, anyway. Thankfully, Freefall doesn't suspect you're helping the monster, and since he would never believe that Alcarsh is your beloved Noin hero, Freefall will only think Alcarsh assimilated you all. You are all doomed, no matter what."

Meanwhile, Captain Ing was gazing at a picture, in the corner of him and his crew. He bent down and lifted it up.

"You can have this picture Jame," Captain Ing smiled. "If it wasn't for your bravery to look through the Mindcoat at all the evil deeds that Mandy has done, we wouldn't have the treasure right now."

"So you admit it?" Jame asked. "You are saying that Mandy was the thief?"

"Now that it has been proven," he replied. "I would have never believed it if it hadn't, but Mandy was my friend." Captain Ing sat down, disappointed.

"Thanks for the picture, Captain Ing. When we get back to

The Stolen Treasure

Earth, we will put it on the mantelpiece in our living room."

"Atwydolyn is coming up," announced Tiffany. "These three ships are still following us."

"I saw three ships come cruising in with Captain Ing with Captain Ing. I saw three ships come cruising in with Captain Ing to Atwydolyn," sang Rick.

"Quiet!" cried the Engineer. "This is serious. They think we're thieves."

"They won't when we return the treasure," smiled Captain Ing. "Down to Atwydolyn."

When the ship had landed, Captain Ing and Alcarsh lifted the treasure out of the ship and carried it to the area where it had originally been.

Meanwhile, the other ships came down, one by one, came Detective Freefall, Samantha and Joseph John from the first, Tonya from the second and Arst, and his fellow Prospectors, from the third.

"I don't believe it," cried the Detective. "It's Alcarsh, the monster who stole the Grachas' treasure from Atwydolyn."

"But this is Atwydolyn," cried Tonya.

Detective Freefall acted as though he hadn't heard her. "And look who has been helping him this time."

"What?!" cried Captain Ing, "I'm your friend. You have always helped me. We have recovered the treasure and brought it back to the Grachas."

"Well, there certainly don't seem to be any Grachas around here," Freefall cried. "I see that Alcarsh has tricked you all into helping him, by setting wild and ridiculous stories into your, newly discovered, easily corruptible minds."

"You are out of your mind," Tonya cried. "The Grachas now have their treasure back. It is safe."

"Alcarsh was trying to help the treasure all the time," explained

Jame. "I saw it through Tonya's Mindcoat."

"We are taking the monster away," declared Detective Freefall. "Come on you two. Help me take him to the ship."

Samantha and Joseph John ran toward the monster and grabbed his arms. When Alcarsh shoved them away, Samantha and Joseph John clung on him with a firm, hard grip and the Detective grasped him by the legs.

"He's not the thief!" yelled Tiffany, running toward Detective Freefall. "He is innocent. We are on Atwydolyn right now. Can't you tell a planet when you see one?"

"So it seems like this culprit has been caught," muttered Arst.

"He is not the culprit!" yelled Tonya.

Every member of the trip, and Tonya, dashed toward Freefall, Samantha and Joseph John and started pulling them away as Freefall pulled Alcarsh in the opposite direction towards his ship. Alcarsh was jerking, snapping and biting, trying to struggle free.

"Don't you see what he's doing?!" cried Joseph John. "He's snapping viciously. He's a monster, a killer."

"At least, we know you're innocent," Melissa reassured the monster-figure, "and that we have helped you. We will always believe that you care about the universe. We are your friends."

Suddenly, the small, grey inhabitants of Atwydolyn hopped out from behind a rock and dashed excitedly toward the treasure.

In amazement, Detective Freefall, Samantha and Joseph John dropped Alcarsh. Their mouths were open, but no speech was coming from them.

"Grachas!" Detective Freefall finally exclaimed. "I don't believe it. This really is Atwydolyn."

The Grachas opened the treasure chest and started spreading the Latimus around to other Grachas, who picked up small boulders and started what was probably arranging them to build new houses.

The Stolen Treasure

However, a yet more shocking event, to Detective Freefall, occurred. The black hair covering Alcarsh started disappearing; his red eyes turned to a dull greyish blue; his whole body started shrinking and his head turned to the shape of a vertically stretched circle.

Finally, a man with grey hair and tattered clothing, was lying on the ground of Atwydolyn. His tired face broke out into a grin as he stretched his body and looked his new, but old, appearance over.

Meanwhile everybody, except Captain Ing and the people on his ship, were standing as still as stone and their faces bore shocked expressions, as though what they were seeing were impossible.

"M-m-mister N-n-noin," Detective Freefall stuttered at last, after a few minutes that contained an hour.

Suddenly, Mandy broke out in tears and, immediately after, everyone found out why. Her face was growing thinner, her eyes turned angry and cold and her rippling hair was turning worn and tattered.

"Percia," Mr. Gordon gasped, his voice in a shocked, astonished whisper.

"Father," she wept.

27 An Acceptance and a Promotion

Several minutes passed on the surface of Atwydolyn that contained nothing but the sound of the wind brushing the alien trees and the terrified weeping of Percia, who was crouching at her father's feet.

"But Noin was eaten up," gasped the Detective. "We thought he was devoured. Mandy was thought to be a genetically modified person."

"Crazy Max transformed me," explained Mr. Noin. "I went searching when Percia and Michael disappeared from our party. Crazy Max encountered me and turned me into a monster and Percia into a lovely-looking woman. The only way we could be changed back was if I had someone to trust me and accomplish a mission."

"But that sounds impossible."

"When you travel to defend those you love, you will find that nothing is impossible."

"Noin went to guard the treasure," stated Captain Ing, "and he took Tonya's inventions to keep them safe. Crazy Max regained his strength when Percia knocked the Latimus nugget out of Michael's hand and sent it flying through the window. Crazy Max ingested the Latimus nugget while it was unprotected and gained power."

"No," sobbed Percia, "don't say any more."

"That must be how Crazy Max has been gaining power all these years," said Mr. Gordon. "Percia here has been taking her prospected Latimus over to him."

"Father," Percia pleaded, "you wouldn't say such things about your own child would you?"

The Ensign turned to make eye contact with the detective. "Mr. Noin didn't attack Percia. It was the Grachas. They were only trying to defend their treasure."

"It was Percia who stole Tonya's inventions," explained the Engineer.

"What?!" said Mr. Gordon.

"Stop," wailed Percia. "That's enough."

"She told Crazy Max about the treasure," explained the Doctor. "That was how Crazy Max found out about it."

At this, Percia dashed up to her father and started to tug at his sleeves. "Father, don't be mad. You couldn't hate your own daughter, could you?"

"Get away! Yechh!" he frowned as he wiped his sleeve on a nearby patch of grass.

"But she spared your life," protested Tiffany. "When she took us all out to Crazy Max on the North Pole of Uberdan, she told you to stay in the ship. Deep down, she still loves you. You just can't admit it."

"Well, she definitely didn't love Michael."

"You don't understand," pressed Percia. "Crazy Max threatened me with his Colodiggan Gun. I had to steal Tonya's inventions and turn in our Lieutenant. If he had shot me and I had been assimilated, it wouldn't have made any difference."

"That is where you are wrong!" countered Mr. Noin. "You could have made the choice of leaving Crazy Max. You didn't have to do more evil, Percia Alexandra Gordon."

"But Crazy Max is my friend," insisted Percia. "He rescued me. If he hadn't come along, I would have been locked in jail for murder."

"If he made you do even more evil, he did not rescue you," countered Captain Ing.

"But you made me your friend," pressed Percia. "You trusted me and looked after me in your spaceship. I served you and your crew."

"You betrayed our Lieutenant," Captain Ing frowned, ashamed of who his best friend had turned out to be, "and, as I understand it, you only came onto my ship so you could hide among us, gain our trust, and then assimilate us all with Crazy Max."

"But how could you become a Commander?" puzzled Mr. Gordon. "You are so young with less experience of space than me, but that's a whole rank higher than I am."

"Crazy Max used telepathy to impart all of his knowledge onto me," replied Percia. "That's how I was able to pilot his ship the night he rescued me. He, himself, told me that everything he'd do for me would be his reward to me for restoring him with the Latimus nugget. Because I had killed my brother, similarly to how he had killed the Star Masters, he announced that he saw me as his equal. He also made me identification and documentation to appear as a real space Commander."

"And what about all your deceit while serving Crazy Max and serving as Commander? Did Crazy Max shoot you with a Colodiggan Gun or were you acting of your own free will?"

Percia sighed and said, "My own free will."

"I suppose that wraps it up then," sighed Detective Freefall. "We will take Percia Gordon away. We will leave her uniform here with the Grachas to shred. I will launch a plea to court for the treasure to be destroyed."

"What?!" yelled Captain Ing, "destroy the treasure? After all we went through to recover it?"

"I'm afraid it will have to be the case," the Detective replied. "If Latimus is that dangerous when it comes to Crazy Max, it will have to be broken down into the materials it was before."

"But what about us?!" cried Arst.

"The Latimus Prospectors will have to stop their work."

The Stolen Treasure

"I am not going to let you do this," cried Captain Ing. "We have to stop him."

"Hold it, everyone," said Tonya. "I'm afraid that this decision might be the right one. Crazy Max can't gain yet more power if he doesn't have Latimus. The treasure will be restored, but with a new material."

"Come on, Percia," grumbled Detective Freefall. "It is time to give you your well-delayed arrest."

Mr. Gordon forced a smiling face. A tear started to trickle out of his eye as the detective stepped towards his daughter. Detective Freefall held out his hand, and Percia removed her Commander uniform with a grudging expression. Once she had handed it to Detective Freefall, he tossed it to the Grachas, who ripped and tore it until it lay in hundreds of tiny shreds.

Detective Freefall pointed at Parcia's Latimus Prospector boots then held out his hand again. Percia removed her boots and Detective Freefall tossed them to the Grachas who bashed the heels and soles with rocks and ripped the boots apart.

Percia looked on and mouthed, "such a shame."

"It is time," stated Samantha as Samantha, Joseph John, and Detective Freefall brought her into their ship.

"Goodbye," called Captain Ing as the ships took off, one after another.

Captain Ing watched, as the ships grew smaller, until they looked like stars in the daytime. Then, they shot off.

Mr. Gordon sat down on a boulder and cried.

Melissa sat next to him. "I'm sorry your daughter is like this," she said.

Mr. Gordon shook his head. "I thought my life was all perfect," he muttered, "but that was many many years ago when I was young and foolish."

"Tell me," Melissa beckoned.

"I was a teenage boy, a high school student," explained Lieutenant Gordon. "My marks were superior. I was on the honour roll. I met Alexandra Hatford at a school dance. It was the most enchanting, magical, romantic dance ever. Alexandra was graceful, gorgeous, tender, everything a guy could hope for. The minute I saw her, I didn't want to leave her; I couldn't take my eyes off her. We started to dance, and I felt like I was, like we were, in heaven. I felt like I was dancing with a princess, an angel, a goddess."

"That's what people often call 'love at first sight,'" Melissa replied. "But you still didn't know her well."

Mr. Gordon laughed a bit. "Looking back on it, it was more obsession than love. When the dance was over, my heart ached. I didn't want it to end. I asked for her holoputer number. I even tried to follow her home. She didn't like me doing that. Didn't get angry, but reassured me that she would be at school, in the cafeteria, the next day and we could see each other then. That one night following the dance, away from my beloved Alexandra, until I saw her again the next day, was the longest night in my life. I was in awe, I couldn't get to sleep, and, when I finally slept, I dreamed about her.

"From then on, I could never stop thinking about Alexandra. We met every day at school, and started dating. We married right after we finished high school. Alexandra Hatford became Alexandra Gordon. My parents didn't approve, and neither did hers. They thought we were too young, that we didn't know what we were doing, but we were determined that we loved each other and wanted to make a life-long commitment."

"But you stayed married," Melissa explained, "and had two children. After your wife's death, your life fell apart, but at least you remained happy to the end. Maybe you will meet someone else to love."

The Stolen Treasure

"Actually, I wasn't happy," Mr. Gordon explained, "at least, not as much as I had hoped. That magical charm that Alexandra carried when we first met wore away, and she seemed like just another woman. Well, I didn't dislike her. We got along, fought sometimes, but I was starting to regret rushing into a married life with her. She gave birth to Michael when we were both twenty years old, and gave birth to Percia sixteen months later. We were married, with two children, making a living off of designing costumes for plays, and later taking my first space education. It was a tough life.

"It soon became apparent that Michael was destined to become a costume designer too. Even when he was a little boy, he had a talent for drawing his surroundings, and making his own Halloween costumes. We promptly got him into art classes, and drama classes to embellish his talent. We hoped he would become a great costume designer, like my wife and I were, but he never lived to see that through. Stabbed to death by his own sister ten days short of his twentieth birthday. And now, that's what my life is, a graveyard, with a wife perished from illness, a murdered son, and a murderer daughter."

"But you helped us save the treasure," Melissa reassured him, "and you saved Mr. Noin from a life as a monster, and now, you have a life ahead as a respectable space man. But I think you can really help yourself by, at least, accepting Percia as your daughter. It may be hard for you, but I think it's the only way. You may hate her. You may be horrified at her, but, believe me, she was a great cook."

Mr. Gordon actually smiled at Melissa's insight.

"You know?" he beamed. "In a strange way, I feel you are right."

"What will you do then?" Melissa asked him.

"I will visit Percia in prison often," Mr. Gordon decided. "I promise. She may be a big part of why I feel so miserable, but if I can see her as my baby that I fathered, and she can see me as the father who helped bring her into the world, I believe I can begin to heal the wound in my heart that has haunted me for years. I think, in the end, it could heal both me and her."

"So you do love her?"

"Melissa," Fred Gordon sighed. "I hate her. I despise her. I will never be able to get over the grief she has caused me. It would have been so much fun to see Michael grow up, become a man, become a costume designer, get married, have his own kids. I miss him every day; him and my wife. But, underneath all of that hatred, oh Melissa, I think I love her." Fred paused, looked thoughtful, and shook his head. "Yes, I do love her."

"Then you are a noble, strong-hearted man," Melissa smiled. "Good for you for choosing to accept Percia, and good luck."

"My wife never would have wanted to see me turn my back on my family," said Mr. Gordon. "Percia is the last piece I have of that enchanting beauty, Alexandra, I danced with many years ago."

At once, Fred and Melissa's attention were drawn away, when, out of the sky, a giant black ship appeared and Crazy Max stuck his head out the window.

"I am going to turn you back into a monster, Noin," he cried. "Just you wait. You will never get out of it this time."

"I have power beyond what you could ever dream of now," Mr. Noin called.

"We will see about that," yelled Crazy Max. He shut his eyes and concentrated his thoughts on Mr. Noin. Then, he drew out a long, metal wand and shot an orange beam toward the handsome Space Explorer.

Mr. Noin clapped his hands and the beam darted off in the opposite direction hitting Crazy Max, turning him into a hideous monster with black hair and red eyes.

The Stolen Treasure

"I'm a shapeshifter anyway," growled Crazy Max as he changed back into himself. "You cannot make me transform. Go back into the forest where you have been hiding all these years, where you belong, or I will shoot all of your friends right here."

"I have learnt my powers," yelled Mr. Noin. "There is nothing you can do to me or to us. Now that I have looked like a monster for five years, I have practiced shielding off transforming beams and someday, I will be a shape shifter too."

All the same, Crazy Max drew out a Colodiggan Gun and shot. The bullet bounced off a shield Mr. Noin generated. Even though Crazy Max quickly sped sideways, the bullet smashed through the window of The Equator and hit him in the shoulder.

Crazy Max jumped back in alarm. The bullet popped out and the wound quickly disappeared, but he was still wearing an expression of hatred and fury.

"Fine!" hollered Crazy Max, the most furious anyone had ever heard him. "I'll kill all of you, just like I killed Gongo, and Rogan, Albin, Sordin and Mark!"

He withdrew a zapshot, set it to kill, and shot. Tiffany whipped her mirror out of her pants pocket. The zapshot beam bounced off the glass and hit Crazy Max. A new window moved down to replace the shattered one as Crazy Max slowly stood back up, suddenly seeming as though he were an old and frail man.

Still cross, he closed his eyes, focussed his thoughts and pointed the transforming tube at Mr. Noin, but all that came out this time were a couple of sparks.

"You have lost me my power!" he yelled and sped The Equator away.

"Good going, Noin, my friend," grinned Captain Ing. "You showed him, and good going Tiffany. It's a good thing you carry your mirror for applying your lipstick with you all the time."

"Welcome back," smiled Melissa, shaking hands with Mr. Noin. "I'm so grateful for all that has happened. My name is Melissa Maguire. We are all from Earth."

"It's a pleasure to meet you, Melissa," Mr. Noin smiled back.

"Oh look!" Captain Ing exclaimed. "What is that?"

"It looks like a parachute," stated Mr. Noin. "I think it's coming down to us."

The parachute was coming closer to the ground and to the members of the trip. They soon noticed that the person landing looked familiar.

"It can't be," Captain Ing puzzled.

The parachute landed and their former Lieutenant, Linda, gazed at everyone. His face was no longer sinister, but friendly, human, and somewhat surprised.

"Linda," said Captain Ing as his old Lieutenant faced him.

"Captain Ing," he smiled as he ran to the Captain. They hugged each other.

"How did you get down?" Captain Ing asked.

"Whatever ship I was on must have released me as it was taking off," he explained.

"I'm so happy to see you," Captain Ing beamed.

"What happened?" asked Linda. "I don't remember anything since I told you what happened in the Mind Deck."

"Crazy Max changed you," Captain Ing explained. "You were made one with him. Our Commander betrayed you. In the night after you told us Percia's story, our Commander transported you out the window onto Crazy Max's ship. Crazy Max shot you with his Colodiggan gun and turned you evil."

"Oh dear!" cried Linda, looking himself over, "but why would Mandy do something like that?"

Captain Ing told Linda the story of the true being of Mandy and

The Stolen Treasure

Alcarsh, the recovery of the treasure and how Crazy Max and Mr. Noin had just duelled, with Crazy Max losing, leaving him powerless.

"But unfortunately, the treasure has to be destroyed," Captain Ing concluded.

"But why?"

"The Latimus is what gives Crazy Max his power."

Linda gazed at everyone who was standing on Atwydolyn. "Thank you all," he beamed. "Thank you for solving the mystery and undoing what Crazy Max has done. If it weren't for all of you, I wouldn't be who I am now."

"Say," beamed Captain Ing. "That gives me an idea. You were so helpful to us when you came out of the Mind Deck. Would you like a promotion?"

"A promotion?" smiled Lieutenant Linda. "That would be wonderful."

Captain Ing had Linda kneel down before him. "In honour of our new Lieutenant Mr. Fred Gordon, I hereby dub you our new Commander. Be a great guardian of space and bring many new wonders."

Commander Linda stood up. "Thank you. It is more than I could ever ask for. Deep down, I think I have always wanted to be a Commander."

Captain Ing turned to Mr. Noin. "You can be our cook then."

"I would be honoured," Mr. Noin grinned in reply.

The rest of the passengers introduced themselves to Mr. Noin in turn and Captain Ing introduced the rest of his crew, pointing to each person he was introducing.

"It couldn't have happened without all of you," beamed Mr. Noin, with a tear of happiness. "That's a great crew you've got yourself there. Come on, Captain Ing. I'm ready to go home."

28 A Friend's Return

On The Horizon, on the way home, everyone welcomed Mr. Noin back like an old friend.

"I would just like to thank you again for the service that you have done me," grinned Mr. Noin. "It was very brave of all of you to trust the monster you had thought was the thief, and carry out my plan. I can tell you that, if I were in your situation, it would have been just as hard for me."

"Thank you too for helping us to recover the treasure," smiled Captain Ing. "We couldn't have recovered the treasure without you. If it weren't for you, I'd still be trusting that sneaky Gordon girl."

"Lieutenant Gordon," smiled Captain Ing, turning to the Lieutenant. "For being such an amazing helper on my ship, I have decided that you can keep the Space Chess." He set the box into the Lieutenant's hands. "You can take it to prison to play with Percia."

"Thank you very much," the Lieutenant smiled, as he took the board.

"So Jame," asked Mr. Noin, "what was it like going back to see Percia's past?"

It was so creepy to face some of the things she has done, but there is one thing that I still couldn't understand.

"And what is that?"

"How did she know the code of Melissa's cyberlock?"

"Ah, very good," said Mr. Noin. "Melissa?" he asked, "would you mind going into your packing bag and bringing us the lock for your cupboard?"

"I wouldn't mind at all. It's just in my sleeping quarter." Melissa left The Lounge and disappeared into the top deck.

"Captain Ing," said Tiffany. "How come Crazy Max didn't

234

The Stolen Treasure

die?"

"Remember what Tonya told us when we first met her. Crazy Max made himself immortal and indestructible," replied the Captain. "However, any quality of life, given enough time, becomes a burden. If the Latimus Prospectors destroy their Latimus, including what is in the Grachas' chest, Crazy Max will spend all eternity a weak and feeble man. If I am not mistaken, Crazy Max has created an eternity of hell, all to himself."

The door opened, and Melissa stepped back in to The Lounge, carrying the lock.

"All you have to do to find out how Percia opened that is to pull the tape off of the back."

Melissa glanced at the strip of tape bearing the name "Melissa Maguire" as Jame stepped up to her side to watch what was going on. Then, Melissa slowly began to pull it away. Over that was what seemed to be a thin layer of sliver paint, which she scraped away with her fingernail. The name showed underneath was a big shock.

Percia Gordon.

"What?" stuttered Melissa, "Percia's lock? But how can that be?"

"It's a long story," replied Mr. Noin. "After Michael was killed, Fred Gordon here took the lock that Percia had always used when she was in school, stuck the password back onto its back and threw it onto the street, and guess who the very person who happened to pick it up was."

"My mom?" muttered Melissa.

"Correct," replied Mr. Noin.

"But why didn't she like ... try to give it back to whoever lost it?"

"She did try," explained Mr. Noin. "When no person or store claimed it, she took it to you."

"Mr. Noin?" asked Melissa, "how do you know all of this?"

"I was following Percia, remember," Mr. Noin replied.

"I hope they don't destroy the treasure," said Rick.

"Oh, you don't, do you?" asked Mr. Noin. "Without the Latimus, Crazy Max can't gain power. It's a dangerous material. We can't have it exist anymore.

"But what will they use instead?" pressed Rick.

"Grachas are like us, humans, in many ways, protective, cautious, and resourceful, but they are also very flexible and very adaptable. The Latimus Prospectors will work on another kind of currency for the Grachas to use."

"You have a wonderful ship, by the way," smiled Mr. Noin, turning from Rick to the Captain. "I can see a brilliant view of the starry sky right from here."

"Stars are wonderful things to watch, aren't they?" grinned Captain Ing.

"And I see you have learned to grow tropical fish," Mr. Noin beamed as he glanced over at Captain Ing's Furlicas.

"Besides space, raising animals has always been another one of my fascinations," the Captain said.

"Thank you very much for the wonderful trip," cried Tiffany. "It was such an adventure. I'm so grateful that I could come along."

"It was nothing," beamed Captain Ing. "You were all a big help."

"Mr. Noin," smiled Melissa, stepping toward him. "It would be wonderful if you stayed on Earth with us for a while."

Mr. Noin bowed his head with a grin across his face. "I could do that. When would you like me to stay?"

"Why don't you come tomorrow, while I'm at class, so you can visit and then, you could stay at my house for a while?"

"I would love that," said Mr. Noin.

29 Tonya's Last Message

Earth came as a heavenly paradise before everybody's eyes as they made their way out of the ship and onto the spaceport of their home planet. There was a thin overcast of clouds, but the air was warm and welcoming all the same.

The cars were already arriving beside the Grand Lodge Spaceport and all of the passengers were excited that they would be seeing their homes again.

"It looks like we arrived just in time," smiled Captain Ing. "The parents are just arriving."

The first person to step out was Melissa's mother. Melissa gave a grateful cry of excitement and ran toward Mrs. Maguire who caught Melissa tightly in her arms.

"So how did the trip go, sweetheart?" grinned Mr. Maguire, stepping out of the car next.

"It was a big adventure," cried Melissa with joy. "We managed to bring the treasure back to the Grachas and we also brought home a surprise."

"What's that?" asked her mother.

Mr. Noin showed himself. "I thought you might want to shake hands with an old celebrity," he beamed.

"Robert," said Katrina Maguire in astonishment. "Robert Noin, is that really you?"

"It is I," he replied.

"But ... but I thought you were eaten," said Mrs. Maguire.

"Oh, it was a burden," he grinned, "but I came back. I'll explain later."

"You know him?" asked Melissa.

Mrs. Maguire smiled and laughed. "Mr. Noin has always been

one of my favourite space heroes. It broke my heart when I heard on space news that a monster had eaten him." She turned back to face Mr. Noin. "That's why I'm so amazed and overjoyed that I'm standing next to you right now."

"And mum," said Melissa, "that cyberlock you gave me; it belonged to Percia Gordon, the villain who stole the treasure. That is how she was able to break into my room."

"Oh, dear," said Mrs. Maguire. "I am so sorry. I guess I'd better take a closer look at what I pick up from now on. I promise to buy you a new lock."

"Are you all ready to go back home?" called Tiffany's mother.

"Yes mum," Tiffany replied.

"We will see each other again soon," smiled Rick as he shook hands with Melissa; Tiffany smiled as she shook hands with Jame.

"I think I'm about ready to see my own planet Earth once more," smiled Mr. Noin.

As the Maguires drove away, Melissa gazed behind her at the spaceport. Melissa and Jame spent the next few minutes talking about their adventures in space with Mrs. Maguire.

"That's wonderful," beamed Katrina, her blue eyes sparkling like Melissa's. "Jame, I am so glad to see you, and we're so glad you all had a great time and accomplished so much."

***

At school the next day, Mrs. Kent had an announcement. "I would like to show you all an honoured and, shall we say, unexpected guest."

Mr. Noin presented himself at the front of the room as the class remained speechless.

"I *am* Mr. Noin," he explained in happy tones. "It was all a

The Stolen Treasure

misunderstanding. I was transformed by Crazy Max, not eaten by a monster."

There was still silence, as though the class were wondering if this could be true.

"Come on," smiled the teacher. "Let's give him a big hand."

One boy in the corner of the room began clapping nervously. After a few seconds, a few others joined him. More students around the room joined the applause too. The applause spread until everyone was clapping. Soon, the children even began standing up, and, in the end, the classroom was alight with children standing, clapping, and cheering, welcoming Mr. Noin back.

"And now, I have something to show you," Mr. Noin explained, smiling to the class. "Captain Ing gave these to me. He made some videos of the trip." Mr. Noin lifted a set of chips and slipped one into a slot in the wall.

A hologram flashed out of the class projector and Atwydolyn appeared. It was the very scene where the passengers had stood, when Captain Ing had brought them to check on the treasure. The students smiled and some laughed a little. At that point, many of the students wished that they had been there.

Then, the scene changed to show the Latimus Prospectors, busy chipping their way at the rock face, while everyone below stood watching in amazement and wonder. There were Captain Ing's Companions and even the recovery of the treasure in which Captain Ing and his troop narrowly escaped the robots.

"What an adventure," said the boy who started the applause. "Everything you did was amazing."

After school had ended for the day, Tiffany, Rick and Mr. Noin came to Melissa's house to celebrate. Mrs. Maguire set their picnic cloth on the backyard lawn and they began to have a picnic. It was late May and the sun was dazzling and many birds were singing.

"Home sweet home," grinned Mr. Noin as he gazed at the view. "I feel so free, now that the truth has been revealed. Being on my home planet feels even better than gazing at Atwydolyn."

"It was great that you could spend some time with us," smiled Melissa, munching on an egg sandwich. "Thank you for coming."

"It was nothing," he grinned. "This is one of the moments on Earth I treasure best. I love picnics under the trees, with the sandwiches and fruit juices. What I enjoy the most, even now that I'm a Space Explorer, is being with friends and family."

There was nothing but joy as they all finished eating in the gorgeous sunshine with the wind sweeping at the leaves in the trees.

When they had finished their picnic, and made their way back into the house, the holoputer beeped.

"Who is it?" asked Rick.

"I'll answer it," smiled Mr. Noin.

When he answered, much to everyone's surprise, the holoputer projected an image of Tonya. She was on Atwydolyn, standing beside the treasure chest.

"How is it going?" asked Tonya. "It's great to see all of you together, including Mr. Noin."

"We are doing great," smiled Rick. "How is the treasure doing? Do we see it right there?"

"It's empty," replied Tonya sadly. "Detective Freefall and even the Prospectors, themselves, have destroyed the Latimus that was inside it. Don't worry. We have negotiated with the Grachas, and have donated them gold coins from Earth. In addition, the Latimus Prospectors will switch to prospecting gold instead of Latimus, which the Grachas will use from now on. As for me, not all is sad anymore."

At that moment, Tonya's hologram was accompanied by Mr. Gordon's.

The Stolen Treasure

"Things are getting better," Mr. Gordon smiled. "I am getting to know Tonya, and I think I can feel a relationship growing."

"Mr. Gordon," smiled Mrs. Maguire. "That is wonderful. But don't get your hopes up too high."

"Oh, we aren't," explained Tonya. "It isn't anything new really. I had a niggling feeling all along that Fred was right for me. We are seeing each other from time to time, walking together, talking together, even starting to find each other quite agreeable. I can't say for sure yet that there will be a wedding or even that we will become partners, but at least we are both happy."

"Well, it's good to see that you're finding happiness once again, Lieutenant Gordon," beamed Mr. Noin.

"And I think things are going better for Percia too," Mr. Gordon continued. "She has confessed everything to the police, including Michael's murder and all the thefts and deceit on the space trip. She's in jail now awaiting trial. Tonya and I visited her briefly today. I think she's starting to feel some true remorse for all she's done. She even says she's going to plead guilty. She told me, today, in the saddest, most thoughtful, sincere voice I have ever heard from her, 'Dad, I'm really really sorry I killed Michael.'"

"I just hope she means it," stated Mr. Noin.

"I just told her that what is in the past is over and cannot be undone, but that the choice will be hers, from now on, of where to go. If she does mean it, it will be her, and her alone, who will be able to prove that. I told her I kept the space chess, and she's keen to play it with me the next time I see her."

"I am just visiting the house of Melissa and Jame, two of my favourite heroines," grinned Mr. Noin.

"All people who attended that trip are heroes," grinned Tonya. "I'm glad you're staying Mr. Noin."

"I'm going to be returning to Captain Ing soon," Mr. Noin

explained. "I think he would like me back with him."

Tonya smiled in understanding. "That's good. All of you, how does it feel to be back on Earth after spending all that time in space?"

"It feels great," beamed Rick. "But it will take some getting used to."

"All right, then," said Tonya. "I won't keep you anymore. Goodbye."

"Bye," they all called and the projection of Tonya and Lieutenant Gordon disappeared.

"It's about time I headed back to the spaceport," explained Mr. Noin.

They bundled back into the car to drop Mr. Noin off.

***

The Horizon had returned, and some very interesting people were standing outside. One looked somewhat like Mr. Noin, only a lot older.

"Is that really you, Robert?" asked the woman who appeared to be getting old. "Could that possibly be you?"

"It's me," he replied, his face breaking out in a grin. "Mum, dad. It's really your son. I got changed."

"So I have heard," grinned the man, who was obviously his father.

"And we were trying to catch this killer monster all this time," sighed his mother. "We would have never guessed that it was you all this time. Robert, we are so sorry we sent Space Explorers after you to imprison you."

"It's all right," replied Mr. Noin. "All I can say is, I can't express how happy I am to be myself again. Crazy Max is defeated forever. There will not be enough Latimus to restore him to his

The Stolen Treasure

former strength, and the treasure has been destroyed. Tonya was just speaking to us, and she has announced that the Grachas have agreed to use gold.

"I have to go now," Mr. Noin finished, "but I promise that I'll be back to see all of you soon. I will holoputer you; you and my incredible passengers," he beamed, turning back to them all. "Goodbye."

"Goodbye," they all smiled, as they waved at Mr. Noin, who was stepping up to Captain Ing, whose face was barely visible within the door of his spaceship.

Everyone watched in amazement, as the ship took off. All the passengers and Mr. Noin's family gazed in awe.

"There goes one of the greatest space heroes of all time," smiled Tiffany.

When Melissa and her family returned home, Tiffany and Rick left for their houses.

"We're home at last," smiled Jame to Melissa, as they headed for the living room. Jame was carrying the picture that Captain Ing had given them. "Come on, Melissa. Let's put our picture on the mantelpiece."

Melissa gazed up at the mantelpiece. "I can't quite reach," she replied. "You can put it up."

"I will lift you," Jame smiled. "That way, we can put it up together, just like we helped the Grachas together and saved Mr. Noin together."

"Really?" grinned Melissa. "Jame, that's a wonderful idea!"

Jame handed the picture to Melissa, who took hold of it. Then, Jame held her hands around Melissa and lifted her a short distance off the floor. Melissa set Captain Ing's picture on the mantelpiece.

Then, Melissa and Jame sat on the couch and gazed at the picture in awe.

"Mr. Noin called us heroines," beamed Melissa. "It's one of the biggest compliments anyone could ever receive."

"Indeed it is," replied Jame.

Melissa looked into Jame's eyes. There was no hurt, abused, lost child there anymore. All Melissa could see was happiness, kindness and love, a girl who had been saved, a young woman with wondrous potential and a fruitful destiny. At this sight, Melissa knew what an extraordinary deed she had done, and it touched Melissa inside.

"I'm glad to have you as my friend and my new sister," Melissa replied.

"Where do you think Captain Ing is now?" asked Jame.

"He's probably enjoying his time in space, meditating in the clouds or in the stars."

"I'll bet he's in space, celebrating with Mr. Noin," smiled Jame.

"I'm sure he is," smiled Melissa.

Melissa and Jame gazed peacefully, through the sunny window, at the trees and the grass, then at the sky, which contained the planets, stars and the universe beyond.

Afterword

I wrote "The Stolen Treasure" in 2004 for a grade 10 creative writing assignment. My sister, Angela, has always been a fan of the TV series Star Trek, Deep Space Nine, and Voyager. This inspired me to create my own science fiction story.

The Stolen Treasure presents human children from this planet, Earth, who have a sense of adventure (as most kids do) to travel beyond this planet, and the reader has the opportunity to see this childhood dream become reality. The Stolen Treasure also presents human difficulties from this planet, such as struggling for friendship (as is shown in Jame's life) and struggling with loss (as is shown in Mr. Gordon's).

The reader will see instances of violence, such as the ship being chased, as is often seen in science fiction, but these scenes are more incidental to the story, rather than an instigator for action in the story. The murder in the Black Bear Inn is based on a murder mystery that our High School librarian set up every year around Halloween in the library. She set up a mannequin called "Max Jordan" who represented a murder victim's dead body, and we, the students, examined suspects to figure out who killed "Max Jordan." In my grade eight year, I wrote a short story about how Max's sister, Morganna, had killed Max in the "Blue Boar Inn" because she was jealous that Max's mother had given Max her all-time-favourite ring on her deathbed. Detective Threlfall was the detective investigating the case.

Manufactured by Amazon.ca
Bolton, ON